Detox Hotel

Detox Hotel

Jonah Frick

Copyright © 2021 Jonah Frick
All rights reserved
ISBN: 978-0-578-85175-4

The characters and events portrayed in this book are fictitious. Any similarity to real persons, living or dead, is coincidental and not intended by the author.

No part of this book may be reproduced, or stored in a retrieval system, or transmitted in any form or by any means, electronic, mechanical, photocopying, recording, or otherwise, without express written permission of the publisher.

Editor — Kristi Phillips
Cover Designer — Amy Hunter

CHAPTER 1
PRELUDE TO AN ADDICT
(FIRST DAY OF THE REST OF YOUR LIFE)

JUNE 21, 1973 (FIRST DAY OF SUMMER)

When Randolph Grey was a child, his mother taught him to believe that people who use drugs and lived on the street were mentally ill, lazy, or pure evil. She told him addiction was the devil's disease and not to waste a precious day of his life on it. If he ever kept a tally, today would have marked 3,650 days of not listening to a word of his mother's advice.

For Randolph, it was just another Wednesday afternoon. Sitting on the corner of Jefferson Avenue and Detroit's Main Street, he lit up a rolled cigarette brimming with cigarette-butt tobacco he'd found scattered on the sidewalk. He looked across the busy streets, through the moving onslaught of rush-hour traffic and past the jogger wearing a sky-blue track suit, at a face he hadn't seen in a while—the face of a man who was pushing a grocery cart.

"You making any money out there today?" Cliff, a veteran panhandler with a grizzled beard, freckled skin tone, and a gap-toothed grin, yelled from across the street.

Randolph reached into his pockets for any loose change. He mustered up maybe two dollars in quarters, which wasn't even enough to buy a quarter of a gram of heroin. The muscle aches, sniffling, and itching began. Withdrawal "It's a dry day out here. No money to be made," he shouted back.

Cliff hit the brakes on his stolen shopping cart converted into a mobile home. "Always money to be made out on these streets," he replied.

The cart was full of useless items, like a broken radio with speaker wires entangled over the antenna like little circuit vines. A tan teddy bear with an empty eye socket and dismembered leg sat upright in the child seat. The front wheel started to wobble, and Cliff heard the familiar rattle of aluminum. *That's a five-cent score right there*, he thought. He'd hobbled over to fetch the empty can and add it to his collection when he heard footsteps shuffling across the concrete.

"Who's there?" he shouted.

No one answered.

Randolph sat on the curb cross-legged, sun beaming into his eyes as he witnessed across the street a hooded figure rise from behind the Stop sign and make a dash in the opposite direction with Cliff's grocery cart.

"Hey, get back here! That's my cart. Damn you! It's mine!" Cliff started sprinting but was soon out of breath. His tired bones couldn't keep up with the little heathen who'd run off with his livelihood.

Randolph felt bad. He knew Cliff hoarded all his possessions in the small metallic box on wheels. There had been no time to warn him, so all Randolph could do was watch. He took one last drag of his smoke before pitching it down. The cigarette butt landed on top of a mounded sand hill of ants nesting over the sidewalk's cracks. Randolph imagined hellfire raining down on several marching ants whose villages were scorched to ashes. He was the creator of their demise. Randolph loved all creatures, but the idea of setting in motion those tiny insects' apocalypse gave him a brief and cynical sense of satisfaction.

The satisfaction didn't last long. His friend Cliff had disappeared, probably still chasing down the hoodlum and the lost cart. There was no one to talk to now. Randolph's muscles started to ache again, and his head hammered against his skull like the hunchback of his withdrawal tolling the bells of addiction. His last taste of heroin had been a few hours ago. All the change Randolph had earned wouldn't even buy him a burger, but the day was still young. His stomach growled the more he thought about that flame-broiled sandwich he couldn't afford. But then again, brown powder in a spoon sounded even more delicious.

Randolph tried to distract himself. He looked up and saw a plane. The faint drone of the jet's engine streaming across the sky made his head hum with static. For a moment, he wondered how many of the passengers on that plane had ever had a grocery cart full of garbage stolen from them by a mysterious thug on the streets of Detroit. He bet that not many could share such a domestic war story.

The distraction was soon over. Work was letting out and people were marching by like the ants Randolph had cigarette-bombed on top of Ant-Burger Hill. One particular man hustling along was the typical businessman in proper attire. He had on a dotted blue tie that he kept loosening from his collar but then retightening afterward. He didn't seem content.

Randolph pegged him as a man of wealth.

"Spare any change? Anything helps," Randolph said to the man.

The tailor-suited, white-collared jerk turned and shouted, "Get a job!" The asshole tossed a mere penny, which ended up stuck between two jagged cracks in the sidewalk next to the blazed village of ants.

"Thank you, kind sir." Randolph shrugged his shoulders and hung his head low. Shame overwhelmed him. Life hadn't always been empty wallets and stealing sleeping bags under the bridge. Five years earlier, he'd been a productive assembly-line worker at a Ford Motor Company plant until he'd fallen twenty feet off the loading dock and almost broken his back. He'd had money, a girlfriend, and a home, but his injury had caught him in the spiderweb of pharmaceuticals. Now, the scripts had expired and he was just a relic of a man weathered by chronic morphine abuse and poverty.

Randolph gritted his teeth, pulled out his red-plated Swiss Army knife with the rusty blade and scratched Abe Lincoln's face off the copper coin. "Fuck the elite!" Randolph put the penny in his pocket as a reminder that some people with money are the root of all evil.

The businessman was one of hundreds Randolph encountered on a daily basis. They all came from different walks of life, but they all had a few things in common: they were predictable men who loved money, hated the poor, and cared only for themselves. However, that day, June 21, 1973, Randolph encountered the most unpredictable businessman he would ever meet. A man who would change his life forever.

"Where's your sign or coffee bin today, Randolph? You haven't given up yet, have you?" A shadow of a man eclipsed the radiant sun from Randolph's eyes. The man stood about six feet tall and was cloaked in a long dark leather jacket even though it was the first day of summer. Randolph found that quite odd. But then again, resting his dirty bare feet on hot, melting concrete was a bit peculiar as well.

The tall old man stroked his white beard and winced, his wrinkled eyes focused on the poor soul below him on the curb. The old stranger looked like he came from money, so Randolph knew he had to try to play it cool. Money might be the root of all evil, but it was a necessary evil for him right then if he wanted to score.

"I left them at home. But I have my hands and a pocket today, sir," Randolph answered.

"Oh yeah? Where's home, Randolph?"

"Over …" Randolph went to point in the direction of the nearest bridge but withdrew his hand. "How do you know my name?"

"Answer my question about where is home and I'll tell you," the old man said.

"Home is where the heart is and wherever my spirit takes me."

"That's what I thought, Randolph. I know your name because I'm here to help you. You look hungry, sunburned, and in need of maybe a shower and some new clothes. I can't offer you any money, but I can help you get on your feet if you follow me." The stranger pointed to his Volkswagen parked on the other side of Detroit's busy main strip. "I have a car waiting across the street." He extended his hand down to Randolph.

"What's the catch?" Randolph asked. He remembered the time his mother bought him a new blue bicycle for his birthday. The next day, she made him chop wood for four hours straight. Ma had told him he had to earn that bike. Daddy hadn't been around to deliver the message that nothing in life is free.

The tall man noticed when the derelict spoke that his teeth were mustard-yellow, sharp, and long overdue for a meeting with a toothbrush. "There's no catch. Just a warm meal, some fresh clothes, and a hot shower. I could probably throw in some deodorant and toothpaste if you like. Looks like you could probably use it."

Randolph took the stranger's hand and stood up. Then he dusted patches of sidewalk dirt and debris off his torn denim jeans. "What the hell? What do I have to lose?"

Together, they walked across the street to the Volkswagen. The old man opened the back door. "My name is Lance Burrows and I'm glad you decided to join me, Randolph. Today is the first day of the rest of your life."

Chapter 2
The Overdose

6:00 p.m., Monday, September 21, 2020 (First day of fall)

A junkie sat alone in an empty room in an abandoned crack house on the east side of Detroit. It was home for now. Or, as his friends called it, The Hood Pack Mansion. Upstairs, Trevor Dugan hid in the darkness, next to a dirty mattress wounded with broken springs poking through the sides like dragon claws ready to violently embrace someone's backside. The bed made him uncomfortable. A few nights before, he swore he saw bedbugs scurrying out of one of the holes, unless he'd been hallucinating. No, he was pretty convinced they were there. He needed to find another place to cook up his magic recipe where he wouldn't get eaten alive.

Trevor staggered his way into the bathroom and hopped on the john. The bathroom's conditions weren't much more pleasant, but at least it appeared termite-free. After all, his girlfriend, Mary, had extensively swept out roaches, cobwebs, and dust when jacked up on meth the previous Sunday night. Trevor reached into a sink covered in rusted enamel chips and turned on the faucet. Brown rust water slowly forced its way out. He pulled out his spoon and gathered a few droplets of water that leaked like blood being slowly squeezed out of the intestines of eroded pipes.

When he reached inside the tiny bag for the main ingredient, he felt nothing. All that remained was brown powder residue. He'd forgotten that he'd spiked the last of the poison hours before. Trevor's breathing amped up, shallow and dry. His pores were bathing him in sweat.

"Where's Mary? She should be back by now." She'd been gone for almost four hours. She was supposed to go to the plasma center to donate, cop some dope, and return home. Was his girlfriend getting high without him? The former protocol had been to wait for each other before indulging in their poison. But lately, the selfishness of addiction was rearing its ugly head. Heroin was a commodity, and sharing only meant less in a world where more meant everything.

He took a heated breath and looked up at the letter art that decorated the whitewashed wall: *Mary and Trevor Forever.* He gritted his teeth and screamed out "Argh!" driving his fist through the cracked drywall. The young-love graffiti art split into veins and crumbled to the floor.

He left the bathroom and started pacing. The creaky floorboards whimpered under his worn feet. He remembered that his friend Jake, who also dwelled in this shithole, had hidden a 9 mm pistol somewhere in the house's wreckage. *Jake never has to know it's gone, and if he does find out, then we can deal with that later,* the voice of addiction whispered inside the young junkie's mind. This would be Trevor's ticket to getting more medicine. Maybe he could use it to rob the dope man, Anton, and get high for years. Or, he could trade the gun for a small bag of heroin. Either way, the sky was the limit, but he needed to find the gun first.

Trevor made laps around the condemned house. First, he ransacked the sea of garbage bags stuffed with clothes from the Goodwill and the Salvation Army. Nothing. However, the secondhand inventory did remind him that he hadn't changed outfits in three days. But that could come later. First things first.

He returned to the tarnished queen-size mattress and flipped it over. A fountain of bedbugs splashed down to the sawdust floor below. Trevor dry heaved as he felt a new kind of sharp pain in his stomach. "Disgusting," he muttered. He double-checked the bathroom and raided the medicine cabinet above the sink like a SWAT team storming through in pursuit of a drug lord's stash. The cabinet was empty except for a couple of expired, dusty prescription bottles of Xanax and Vicodin left behind. He shook both bottles and, to his surprise, found one lonely two-milligram Xanax tablet.

"You poor guy. Did you not get consumed like the others? I'll help you out," he whispered to the inanimate narcotic before swallowing it whole. Trevor had some blurred lines between imagination and reality. Heroin was a hell of a drug. A Xanax would have to do for now.

He ran downstairs, stepping over shattered glass, to the main living room. The floor was almost extinct beneath rubble from former ceilings. He frantically lifted up a black leather couch that was torn, peeking his head underneath and finding nothing. He ripped through all the cushions to no avail. He hopscotched over collapsed tiles and debris to the dilapidated kitchen, furiously emptying all the cupboards. Nothing.

Trevor took a moment to think and lit up a cigarette to calm his nerves. He stepped backward and almost tripped over a shredded copy of the *Detroit Free Press*. A black metal handle was tucked away under one of the ripped pages. The gun. He carefully grabbed the handle and lifted the chrome weapon over his head, marveling at its splendor and acknowledging the power it possessed.

"Of course I would almost trip over you, my sweet friend," he said.

A sudden rush of adrenaline trickled down his spine. Without pause, he texted Anton's phone: *I have something for you. Can we meet up?*

No immediate response. But then Anton replied: *Half a cookie is one dollar. Get it while it's fresh off the oven.*

Trevor: *I have something better than money. Just wait, where can we meet?*

Anton: *Better than money? This better be good. Meet me at Grand Circus Park.*

Trevor texted back *ok* and quickly deleted their entire text conversation. He reminded himself to buy a new SIM card later. Texting drug deals even when speaking in code, like a *half cookie* for *heroin* or *energy drink* for *meth*, was dangerous. When Trevor was a boy, his dad had worked for the DEA. So Trevor had secretly watched him bury himself in induction coil, listening to thousands of intercepted conversations between drug dealers and snitches using those same phrases. He wouldn't allow himself to end up prison food like those idiots.

Trevor finished his cigarette then cleared his head long enough to begin his journey. Outside, the air was cool, and the slight chill was welcome after such a long humid summer. The summer of 2020, when everything and nothing had happened. Everyone wanted to forget the past six months or so, especially Trevor. It wasn't just that he wanted to forget that he was living in complete abandon and eating out of dumpsters. But the fact that he accepted this as his new norm scared the living shit out of him. He felt like he was living two lives: sober Trevor, who couldn't stand to be inside his own skin, and high Trevor, who didn't give a fuck. The more he could bury sober Trevor, the less he gave a shit about anything else.

Trevor jumped on the 261 bus heading downtown. It was four blocks and two stops until Grand Circus Park, but the driver wouldn't let him on without a mask. A sweet, elderly lady in a pink blouse gave Trevor an extra mask she kept in her purse. "Thank you ma'am," he said, nodding and smiling. Trevor was a professional at nodding and smiling. All the seats were occupied by masked passengers, some with fully covered faces and others wearing their mask like a chin diaper. *Sheeple,* Trevor thought.

The slightly overweight driver with a long red ZZ Top beard missed Trevor's stop. Trevor argued for a minute with the driver to let him off half a block away. ZZ Top relented eventually, tired of Trevor's obnoxious presence.

After his grand departure, he headed to the park and eagerly texted Anton: *Hey I'm at Grand Circus. Meet me on the east side of the fountain.* Trevor didn't get a response right away.

The park was five acres of immaculate emerald grass that bred several concession stands, a dog park, and various monuments of historical Detroit figures. Waiting for Anton, Trevor sat on the lawn next to a colossal water fountain that shimmered specks of crystal diamonds against the crease of sunlight in his eyes. Grand Circus Park truly was a circus as traffic steadily circulated all around it. The rustic oak benches were congested with parents attached to their phones, like zombies checking social media newsfeeds and scrolling through Facebook comment wars on controversial political posts. All the while, their children played, innocent and wild, on seesaws, a couple of slick yellow slides, and a rusted merry-go-round that squawked with every rotation. Every now and then, the parents would look up and holler at their little ones to "stay close" or "don't hit your brother." Trevor had no intention of ever becoming like them: parents or family.

Trevor's ringtone of A-ha's "Take on Me" gently echoed throughout the park. A few of the park patrons shot their eyes in his direction. He saw their stares and felt his head start to cave like they knew he didn't belong in the park. They knew he was waiting on a drug deal. Maybe some of these parents were undercover task force agents closing in on his petty deal. He looked down at the caller ID: *Anton*.

He picked up the phone. "Why are you calling? I thought we agreed to stick to texts."

"Hey, White boy. Get into the car!" Anton yelled.

"What car? Where?"

A black Cadillac's engine growled a short distance away. Anton's ride was stationed in a no-parking zone on the outskirts of the park. Trevor advanced closer, trembling, excited, and afraid. He hated these intense Detroit drug deals. He loved heroin though. When he slowly walked up to the back door, he caught a glimpse of an unknown Black man in the driver's seat. The man's lower face hid behind a red bandana with two teardrop tattoos under his left eye. He looked straight ahead, refusing to acknowledge Trevor's presence. Anton sat in the front passenger seat and unlocked the back door by pushing a button. "Get in man!" he shouted. Heavy, musky cologne lingered in the car. Trevor's nostrils flared.

"So, what do you have for me, Trev, that's better than money?" Then Anton turned to the driver. "Because we like money, don't we, Dez?"

The strange driver now had a name: Dez. He nodded but said nothing. His eyes glared Trevor down through the rearview mirror.

Trevor's palms sweated. He just wanted what he came for, and he would be out the back door of the car and on his way to euphoria. But instead, he had to play these stupid mind games with the drug dealers. The games consisted of him lying, and they wouldn't believe a word he said. Next, he would lie some more but make that lie more credible. In the end, the dealer just wanted the drug addict's money. However, Trevor had spent so much money with Anton that he hoped this time Anton would settle for Jake's gun. Trevor patted the small pistol in his pants pocket to remind himself that it was still there. Something was off about all of this. He knew Anton, but who was this Dez? If they made a move, he had the advantage in the back seat, but he'd forgotten to check the chamber for bullets. For all he knew, he could be clutching a useless weapon.

"What's it going to be, White boy? I'm tired of ya'll wasting my time, and you already owe me for the last bag."

Trevor had forgotten about the debt from last time. *Shit!* he thought. "I heard you guys were low on guns," Trevor lied. Anton Cole was one of the most well-known local street dealers with ties to some of the biggest gangbangers and low-level mobsters on the east side of Detroit. The last thing he would be low on was guns, and Trevor knew this. He swallowed nervous air. "I have a Glock for you. I'll take what I can get."

Anton turned back toward Trevor. "Let me see that rusty thing." The Glock was metallic black, but the rust was shaving off its color. The dealer studied the ins and outs of the weapon, gripping the handle, opening up the chamber, and discovering no bullets. "Well, at least I know you wasn't going to kill me with this. Hey, Dez, you ever hear about these dope fiend White boys trying to stick up their dealers for product?" Anton's voice was firm and patronizing.

"Hmmm" Dez grunted, almost speaking.

The hair on Trevor's arm stood at attention. His pulse raised to Guinness Book of World Records, off-the-chart numbers.

"Is it hot? The serial numbers are scratched off." Anton's voice returned to a cooler tone.

"I don't know. Most likely." Then, his nose tingling, Trevor sneezed. "Achoo!"

"You getting that itch, huh?" Anton snickered a little. He knew the sickness better than the ill did. He'd seen it with his own mother and every one of his customers since he'd started dealing at the age of thirteen.

"Yeah, man. I'm getting sick. Can you hook me up or not? I'm sure if you don't want it, then I can find someone who will."

"I'm going to look out for you, Trevor. But we have to make a stop first," Anton said.

"A stop where?" Trevor's question trembled with anxiety.

Neither man in the front answered. The car drove for what seemed miles, zigzagging and speeding through the main strips with no concern about getting pulled over. They were invincible. Trevor looked out the window and realized they were driving into the Cass Corridor neighborhood. He purposely avoided this area for many reasons. For one, he wouldn't be recognized by anyone. Trevor lived on the east side, and the people there had become familiar with him, offering safe passage.

The Cadillac slowed down and turned in next to a closed liquor store with boarded-up windows, another casualty of COVID-19. The alleyway was narrow and thin like an endless syringe injecting Trevor into uncertain doom. Dez drove slower than five miles per hour. Trevor tried to play it cool, but his heavy breathing gave him away. He turned around to say goodbye to the main road they'd just left behind. The left and right windows showed little hope—just a wire fence and trash-covered cobblestone pathways. Ahead of them, the alley dead-ended at the back entrance to another brick building. Anton and Dez were smart. There were no witnesses. No one would miss him.

Dez punched the brakes and looked at Anton.

Anton turned around to face Trevor with the rusty pistol pointed between Trevor's eyes. "This gun right here is a piece of shit. I have it pointed at your head, but that doesn't mean anything because it's empty, right?"

"Uh hum," Trevor nodded. He gasped, but his lungs refused to swallow air.

"Now let me show you something." Anton opened the glove compartment and exchanged the tarnished gun for a shiny chrome Beretta, rust-free. "Now this is a Beretta 92. Fully loaded, six chambers." He pointed the new weapon in the same direction: at Trevor's unibrow. "Now does this mean something to you?" Anton squinted his eye, scoping Trevor's reaction.

"Yes, sir."

"Okay, so here's what I'm going to do." Anton lowered his gun and placed it back in the glovebox. "Dez thought I should shoot you, but I'm a nicer guy than Dez, so you're lucky. Also, you've brought me a lot of business in the past, and I'm willing to overlook a lot of the dumb shit you pull, like this stunt right here. I'm going to keep your gun, throw you a little boy. But next time I see you, I want straight cash or bring me a real pistol, rust-free, with bullets." Anton dug under his seat cushion and threw Trevor a small bag of heroin. "Now I need you to get out now."

Trevor was confused. "Wait. Right here? I don't even know where we are."

Anton motioned his head to the right. "Get the hell out now before I change my mind about Dez's suggestion."

Trevor jumped out without asking any more questions.

The walk home seemed infinite. His tired feet stalked across the cracked pavement eroded by decades of traffic storms and violent winters. The corridor was a concrete prison sealed up with dead buildings and gravestone skyscrapers. A herd of masked strangers following orders shuffled past the young addict, projecting judgment and sharp stares of disgust. After all, Trevor had forgotten his borrowed mask on the bus after arguing with the driver. He always seemed to forget his mask somewhere, but he had a much deadlier disease than COVID-19 to worry about: addiction.

His tunnel vision didn't capture images of the people. They were mere shadows on the sideline. As he sweated profusely, his temperature rose despite the cool breeze. He wiped his brow and reached into his flannel front pocket for his set of plastic dollar-store earbuds. Gently, he placed them in both ears and tuned in to his favorite podcast: *Jungian Hour*. The previous night's episode was titled "The Shadow and Pizza-gate."

"Hi, Mark Taylor here, and with me, Kristi Ross on Jungian Hour. Today we are going to talk about the archetypes hidden in conspiracy theories."

The left ear bud hissed static. Audio was drowning out, but the right earbud was flawless. Trevor flicked his left earlobe as if that would improve the sound's quality.

Mark: *Let's rewind to the 2016 presidential campaign. The whole thing was a mess, conspiracy theory eruption. And don't get me wrong, Kristi and myself are firm seekers of the truth. But something wasn't right about these outrageous allegations.*

Kristi: *Frankly, Mark, Pizza-gate was an abomination of conspiracy theories that put restaurants out of business, threatened employee lives, and even led a self-proclaimed "anti-hero" to Comet Ping Pong Pizza, where he unloaded an AR-15 rifle, taking down the restaurant's walls, a desk, and a door. Luckily, no one was injured or killed.*

Trevor trudged along past a sad gallery of closed businesses. The last casualty on the block was Uncle Jester's Pizzeria, buried under hammered boards, shielded from the light of day. Dripping red spray paint, a tagged, padlocked steel door that blocked the main entrance read, *Fuck you Covid.*

Mark: *For those unfamiliar—which, if you are listening, I would be disappointed if you are—but right-wingers and even left-wingers believed these pizza restaurants were covert breeding grounds for pedophilia, sex trafficking, human sacrifice, Satanism, and even cannibalism. And Hillary and Bill Clinton were the ringleaders behind it all.*

"The formula was too elaborate and cliché ... the cover-up was a cover-up for something bigger." Trevor whispered like he was joining in as a special guest on the podcast.

He imagined his introduction as a guest. *Welcome expert conspiracy theorist and heroin addict Trevor Dugan on the show. What are your thoughts, Trevor?* If he only had the chance he would shake the cult icons' hands, take a seat on a plush cushioned chair next to the DJ's microphone, and shout out loud to the world: "The conspiracy was created by QAnon to trick the gullible and amateur theorists into buying their branded agenda. Pedophiles do exist among the elite, but in this particular case these children weren't molested. They were being experimented on with alien technology."

Trevor's vivid imagination of aliens had transformed into an obsession after his father left. He convinced himself that his dad knew about their technology and was forced into hiding. So when Trevor passed an abandoned gas station with a disc-shaped aluminum roof that bore resemblance to a UFO and a marquee that priced unleaded gas at $3.99 a gallon, he knew the station had to have been closed for a while—or at least since the extraterrestrials had commandeered the property.

In the distance he saw the sign for the Hamtramck bus station like a glimmer of lights sparkling amidst the darkness of the city.

Mark: *The darkness in the Jungian archetype thirsts for taboo scapegoats. The narrow-minded host of a shadow will believe whatever he or she is fed through media, YouTube, and even podcasts like ours, Kristi.*

Kristi: *We are no exception.*

Trevor finally made it to the bus station door and was stopped by a security guard before he could enter. He had no mask. He was no exception.

"Come on, I really need to use the bathroom!" Trevor pleaded. He held his crotch and started shuffling his feet around. It was a little move Anton and other dealers in Detroit called "the junkie junkie shakes."

The security guard, who had a marine buzz cut and cleft chin, could empathize with a man having to drain his lizard. He reached into his back pocket and retrieved a mask for Trevor.

"Thank you," Trevor said, pausing the podcast on his phone. Then he placed the earbuds back in his flannel pocket. He was sure he was close to exceeding his prepaid data limit by now.

Inside, the station was at half capacity. A little girl in a red jacket was role-playing gymnastics in front of an old man with a light-brown crew neck sweater that identified him as *World's Best Grandpa* in chalk-white letters. Trevor caught their eyes and awkwardly smiled. Then he turned around too fast and accidentally bumped shoulders with some college-aged punk with sandy-blond hair who was sporting a Michigan State Spartans football jersey. The jersey reminded Trevor of his perfect brother, Ryan, who had gone to MSU, dropped out, and still ended up stupid rich.

"Watch where you're going." The punk's holler even sounded like Trevor's brother. Trevor tried to ignore the asshole and the memory of his brother's yell, but he couldn't drown out either noise.

Trevor tapped himself on the head, brushed off his shoulder, and found the public restroom right behind two middle school kids who were wearing Minecraft hoodies, giggling, and kicking a Pepsi vending machine. *All these children, all those experiments*, he thought. Then he thought about the secrets behind the Pizza-gate scandal again. He remembered all the anonymous blogs on the God Size Productions conspiracy website that claimed that after the experimentations, all the kids mysteriously disappeared like a pencil under a magician's top hat. He remembered eavesdropping on one of his dad's late night business calls from work and hearing his father explicitly whisper that someone or something was "abracadabra gone." Trevor couldn't fathom the collusion his father had been wrapped up in, but he knew it had something to do with those lost kids. And like a younger version of the *X-Files'* Fox Mulder, Trevor was determined to discover the truth that was still out there.

Trevor's current truth was that the back of his throat had gone desert dry after his long trek. A lonely half bottle of Dasani water rested on the bathroom counter. There was no one else in there to watch him snag it up. Dying of thirst, he picked up the bottle and cradled his precious new water. In mid-embrace, he glanced in the mirror, staring at a Gollum-like human fiendishly chugging the water. Then he stopped himself because he had to save a little bit for his heroin recipe.

Trevor was in no denial about how ragged he appeared to the world. He was clothed in a torn burgundy flannel shirt. Dark lines formed a gray circle around his sunken eyes. He sported a candy-red St. Louis Cardinals baseball cap that sat backward on his head. He had no idea how he'd acquired it. He'd never been to St. Louis. The bill was sweat-stained and awkwardly creased down the middle. The once-white C was now discolored—a figment of gray. Dappled and disheveled brown hair snuck out under the cap's brim to take refuge over the top of his eyebrows and ears. He wore that hat everywhere, and under the grimy sweatband was where he hid the valuable heroin. His thirsty veins reminded him to seek isolated sanctuary.

The first empty stall was covered with feces and overfilled with urine-stained cigarette butts and flies. The next stall wasn't much of an improvement, with only curses written on the walls and empty toilet paper rolls littering the ground. Trevor anxiously stripped off his belt as he prepared for his favorite ritual. Spoon, check. Lighter, check. Water, check. Needle, check. Heroin, check.

Sometimes, the ritual before the dance was more euphoric than the act of getting high. The sense of anticipation, a nervous discord mixed with excitement. He lit the flame, ready to melt down the brown powder. He vigilantly pulled out the same needle he'd been using for days and even shared with others. God only knew how many different types of hepatitis were layered in its reservoir. He mixed the powder with the water from the Dasani bottle, filling the used needle with thirty cc's of brown poison.

The rest was history. The needle entered the vein and Trevor immediately felt the darkness surround himself. His eyes rolled back, ghost-white, and he was abracadabra gone.

CHAPTER 3
THE SHADOW

11:00 P.M., MONDAY, SEPTEMBER 22, 2020

Trevor woke up alone except for the shadow beside him. Always the shadow. That daunting contour had stalked him throughout his childhood, adolescence, and adult life. He remembered the time he shot a pebble at his brother's treehouse with a slingshot. The small rock inadvertently demolished a swarming beehive. A vengeful colony returned the attack, stabbing the seven-year-old Trevor into an allergic coma. The shadow was there, staring over the paralyzed boy with sweet amusement. A shot of an Epi-Pen salvaged his young life much like a Narcan kit would resurrect him after one of his several overdoses some fifteen years later. With each overdose, intentional or accidental, the shadow was there, mocking and antagonizing Trevor's pathetic existence.

Then there was the time at the age of ten when he almost drowned in Lake Michigan. With reckless abandon and disregard for his father's orders, Trevor had swum out past the buoys. He was always a bad listener. The wind had made a drastic change in direction. The markers were being red-flagged to warn everyone in the water to come to shore. He was too far out to see the markers when something pulled him under. Fear surfaced, Trevor sunk. The shadow was right next to him, choking, pressing down on his lungs. A shattered light broke through the waves, but all Trevor could see were floating specks, pieces of the shadow. His neck tensed up, and the shadow's fingers pushed inward against his esophagus, throttling him. He tried to push his way forward but collided with an invisible force like he was trapped behind a glass wall. There was another world on the other side of that glass. An abandoned house or hotel sat on top of a hill full of dead grass, and there was a narrow, winding road. Trevor could even see a little car driving toward it with its headlights on. He smashed his fists into the invisible wall, trying to crack himself into that world, into that freedom, but to no avail. Instead, he was now just stuck between the shadow and the shield protecting this other world from his. When he finally pressed his hands up one last time against the barrier in defeat and closed his eyes, sharp beams of sunlight opened them right back up. Chest compressions and artificial ventilation from a blonde paramedic named Amber who smelled like thick tanning lotion jerked him back into consciousness. Water was ejected from his lungs and newfound oxygen was embraced. Air: a small necessity he would never take for granted again. His savior, Amber, clutched her chest, grateful he didn't die on her watch. Trevor dreamed about Amber for the next couple of months, reliving her wet, wild, gold hair hanging down, caressing his face as she breathed life back into his dead body.

Considering this to be another vivid flashback that accompanied his countless close calls with death via overdose, it only made sense that the shadow made another cameo. This close encounter felt like a warm blanket inside a mother's womb. Trevor visualized being in his safe place in Grandpa George's backyard, sitting on the rocking swing and watching pine cones gracefully fall like wooden raindrops from the sky. Such a beautiful view at Grandpa George's, sitting on the back porch in the fall, drinking apple cider. Above the sky, beyond the clouds, loomed the vast, shadowy figure encompassing the horizon. The monstrous silhouette held an illumination in its cavernous belly—an illumination that served as a looking glass, reflecting glimpses of his own funeral. The mirrored images included his parents shaking their heads in disbelief. His brother, Ryan, pointing his finger and laughing while they stood over his casket in some cemetery he assumed was near his old home. Mary and Jake were in the back of the graveyard shooting up as an ode to their fallen comrade. *Fuck, I really hope God is a forgiving dude because I really messed this life up*, Trevor thought. As he prepared his remorseful plea to God to let him into the pearly gates of Heaven, he was met by a great rip current and pulled below to what seemed to be Lake Michigan. And then he opened his eyes to realize he wasn't drowning after all and no blonde, oil-sprayed lifeguard was there to save him.

Water thrown from a mop bucket drenched his dirty, tattered clothes. Clear water (without rust) was the closest thing to a shower Trevor had had in days. He attempted to see what was happening, but his vision was distorted; it was like looking through an aquatic lens. He tried to stand up before noticing his hands were tied with rope to an old wooden dining room chair and his mouth gagged with a cloth that smelled like it had been used to clean out gutters. A mysterious figure with the bucket had vanished after slamming a metal door shut without any explanation.

Trevor assessed his surroundings. The room was empty with the exception of the dining room chair and a clanging cast iron radiator next to a boarded-up window that concealed the light of day and dark of night. He assumed the room he was locked in was a part of an abandoned house. He also felt elevated, as if he was in the upstairs of the house. The floors were constructed with pale wood resembling the scales of dead fish. A ceiling light, centered above, flickered on and off like a dying strobe. At least there was electricity, a small upgrade from The Hood Pack Mansion. Flowered Victorian-style wallpaper was peeling off, revealing the rotting drywall hidden underneath. There were several holes in the wall, as if someone had tried to bust through it. Galvanized steel had been installed behind the flimsy Sheetrock to deter escape. In the corner of the wooden floor, a blue Narcotics Anonymous book sat alienated among the rest of the room's décor. *Is this what a twelve-step meeting looks like these days?* Trevor wondered. In the center of the decaying wallpaper hung a painting of a fruit bowl, illustrating plum-purple grapes, a shiny yellow banana, a crimson apple, and a sunlit orange. The still-life painting reminded him of simpler times spent at his dear grandmother's house. But these weren't simpler times.

Maybe I'm actually dead and this is just part of the afterlife before I wait to meet God, Trevor thought. *Yeah, God is going to come into this room any second, untie me, and send me upstairs to Heaven. We'll have a nice laugh about how He played a funny little trick on me.* Another possibility was that Trevor was in fact in hell—cursed to spend the rest of eternity tied up, gagged, and bound to a dining room chair in the middle of an empty room alone. The worst-case scenario floating through his hard-knocked cranium suggested that he'd been kidnapped by the DEA, CIA, or FBI after overdosing. They wanted him to hand over Anton, and this was their interrogation room.

There was another possibility he was afraid of, far more detrimental than the government staking out a local drug dealer. Trevor recalled the rumors of his old man having access to covert operations through his employer, Department of Homeland Security. So when the agency was under scrutiny by the FBI, Trevor's dad had been deemed a loose string, a threat to their investigation. So his dad had left. Perhaps now his past had come to haunt Trevor.

Trevor's chest inflated like a blowtorched hot air balloon. He was trying to catch his breath when he heard a faint squeak. Small cracks in the baseboard provided entry for an unexpected visitor. The little mouse resembled not an FBI agent but the rat the FBI would waterboard Trevor into. The rodent had a sharp, pointed nose like a pencil tip, with beady, tiny eyes clothed in warm, gray skin. Its tail flailed about like a clock hand gone haywire. Trevor decided to name his pet mouse Jimbo because it looked like a Jimbo.

"Jimbo, come here," Trevor said, his voice muffled through the dirty rag. He prayed the mouse would hear his cries. He even tried telepathic communication, summoning the rodent over to gnaw on the rope until he could break free. "You can eat the rope, little one."

Jimbo paid him no mind. He just scurried about the creaking floor, prowling for loose crumbs or maybe a nice sandwich. A scent of grilled cheese lingered in the air. Trevor missed those melty globs of mayo and American cheese slathered on buttered bread that Grandma Doris used to fix up for him. Meanwhile, he'd paw through her purse, searching for loose change so he could go get a fix.

The smell grew closer. Heavy footsteps thudded on the other side of the cracked wall. Slowly, the door creaked open. Trevor had been awake for only five minutes, but it felt like forever. A beast of a man wearing a white tank top with red blemishes splattered on the straps and a snug, oak-brown burlap sack serving as a mask swaggered his way through the door. A huge letter X was marked on the front of the mask with 215907 printed in small font right below it. The burlap veil draped over his entire head. There were two small holes cut out to the left and right side of the

X to allow vision. A thin opening was slit under the X to allow speaking. *Man, this guy really took the mask requirement to a whole new level,* Trevor mused. The man proceeded forward, looming above small Trevor. Faded amateur tattoos that resembled grade school prison art decorated his bulging arms. Trevor couldn't distinguish the deformed dragon head from the cliché Chinese symbols trailing like a snake up the man's arms and onto his neck. Although the masked stranger wasn't quite as ripped as the Incredible Hulk, he could easily pass as a solid Thor. But this man was no superhero. Trevor could sense he identified more as the supervillain type, what with the kidnapping and all.

The unidentified villain removed the gag from Trevor's mouth.

"Holy shit, what the fuck is going on? Who the fuck are you?" Trevor gasped. His lips felt like dust after having been pressed back so long.

Immediately, the man shoved the rag back into Trevor's mouth. Trevor screamed under his gag. "If you want a ransom, no one gives a shit about me, so let me go!"

The bulky man couldn't make out a word of his mumbling. "If I take it out again, you need to promise not to scream, okay?" Evil Thor said through his burlap veil. "I swear to God, if you get out of line, I'll shove this thing right to the back of your throat! Got it?"

Trevor nodded his sweat-soaked head.

The man removed the gag. Trevor took a deep breath. He felt alive. The air felt so fresh. "Are you the FBI," he finally asked with a lower tone. "Because I know nothing."

The strange man flung the mangled rag into Trevor's eyes like a schoolyard bully taunting his prey. "No, I'm not the FBI."

"Then what do you want from me?"

"I saved your life. You overdosed in a disgusting bathroom. You should be thanking me."

"Okay, thank you. But who are you and why am I tied up to this chair in whatever this place is?" Trevor's eyes scanned the room and his voice elevated.

"Ah, ah, ah, our deal?" The man waved the dirty cloth in front of Trevor.

Trevor took another long breath. "Okay, I think I know why I'm here. But I have to tell you, I haven't seen my father in years and I don't know anything about his investigations with the FBI and Homeland Security." Trevor stiffened his shoulders. "And even if I did, I wouldn't tell you."

The stranger laughed. "What makes you think I give a shit about your dad? He was a coward."

"My father may have been a lot of things, but he was no coward. He was on the brink of exposing the truth before—"

"Before he disappeared?"

"How do you know so much about him?" Trevor's face blanched.

"I could tell you a lot of things about me and about everything I know, but we aren't here because of me. We're here because of you. Right now I want you to eat this sandwich. We need to get your energy up. You're going to need it for later." The stranger reached into his back pocket and pulled out something wrapped in a brown paper towel. When he uncovered it, Trevor saw a fresh grilled cheese sandwich being held out to him.

"How do I know you didn't poison that?" Trevor muttered.

"You don't know if I poisoned it or not, but it's up to you if you're hungry enough to eat it. I'm sure you're starving." The man held the sandwich up to Trevor's nose, waving it back and forth, enticing his prisoner to take a bite before he set it on the floor next to him.

Trevor was hungry, but his stomach felt like a litter of Jimbo mice were clawing his organs out from the inside. This wasn't entirely unordinary for the initial stage of withdrawal. He jerked his head back and forth, rubbing his chin across his shoulder to remove the invisible bedbugs that must have attached themselves to his clothes from back home.

"How am I supposed to eat it with my hands tied behind the chair? I need them in order to eat," Trevor said.

Burlap sack man leaned forward. "Ha! No you don't. All you need is that little mouth of yours, and I can slowly feed it to you like the good little boy you are." His words drooled mockery.

"I'm too sick to eat anyway. I know this may go against your whole kidnap plot here, but the truth is, in a few minutes I'm about to get super sick. And I need you to let me out so I can go get my medicine, or this going to get very bad for both of us." Trevor's expression shifted from sternness to desperation.

The man chuckled softly to himself before smacking Trevor abruptly across the side of his face. Trevor collapsed onto the floor, taking the chair with him. He hadn't been hit that hard since he was jumped for stealing that Mongoose bike from the wrong eighteen-year-old on Woodward Avenue five months earlier.

The mystery man quickly flung the door shut behind him, leaving both his prisoner and the cheese sandwich lying on the floor. The grilled cheese slowly melted as Trevor's hunger began to increase. Jimbo sat next to his side, but not to help him escape—only to enjoy the fallen remains of the sandwich. Trevor clenched his abdomen and decided there was only one release right now. He slowly closed his eyes and prayed to Heaven above to grant him a few hours of sleep. There must have been a God because the room and sandwich began to slowly slip away.

Trevor slept, but the shadow was still there, half of its form clinging to the wall. The other half remained suspended in midair, delighted to see the mouse eat Trevor's dinner.

Chapter 4
Sweet Innocent Mary

6:00 p.m., Tuesday, September 22, 2020

"I'm sorry, Ms. Hopkins. Your temperature is 100.4 degrees. We can't let you donate. At this time, we advise you to go to your local ER to get tested for COVID." A middle-aged, haggard-looking phlebotomist with an employee badge that read *Angel* swept the digital thermometer across Mary Hopkins's forehead for the third time.

Mary desperately tried to push back a cough behind her disposable mask, but it came out anyway. "I don't have this coronavirus thingy. I was just tested the other day. Look, it's just really hot outside and I'm stressed. That's all." She spoke with a mild Southern drawl that she'd inherited from the first eighteen years of her life growing up in Lowell, Arkansas.

"It's fifty degrees outside, darling." The phlebotomist, Angel, rolled her eyes and tapped her long fake nails on the marble counter with impatience.

"Well, it feels a lot warmer, ma'am. Please just let me donate. I really need this money. I, I, I'm behind on my rent," Mary lied. She had no rent to pay.

Angel inhaled deeply, looked over both of her shoulders, and exhaled, annoyed. She'd heard this line a million times a day from addicts just like Mary who treaded into her plasma center, dope sick and coughing, needing to donate plasma to get their next fix. "Look darling, I understand your struggle, and I see it all the time. But I can't let you in here. I could lose my job and get this place closed down."

Mary gritted her teeth. She could feel her heart palpitate. Her palms were clammy and she felt nauseous. All the symptoms were aligning, a precursor to one of her episodes. Mary had the face of a gaunt angel, presenting sweet and innocent on a good day. But rejection and lack of her "medicine" created a furious demon inside. This Southern angel was about to unleash her wrath onto the plasma center's Angel.

"This is bullshit." Mary stomped her way out the door. No head bashing today. She wanted to rip that bitch's nails off the tops of her fingers. But a conscience still floated around inside her somewhere and gently reminded her, *It's not her fault. Blame it on the dope, Mary. Always the dope.*

The cool air outside was a slight reprieve from the inferno Mary breathed inside herself. She ripped off her constricting, insubstantial mask and stuck it inside her purse. The handbag crossed over to the other side of her neck. She kept it strapped close against her tombstone-gray hooded sweatshirt with the word *Wolverines* stenciled in gold. Black, torn leggings with a trail of purple bleach stains shaped like puppy paws splattered along her backside.

A semi handsome man (if it hadn't been for his tiny Hitler mustache) passed her by and blatantly studied her top to bottom. *Eyes off, Nazi boy. I'm not a prostitute,* she angrily thought. Mary may have been poor, but she was no whore. She did, however, have a tendency to unintentionally captivate the hearts of the seediest men in town. There was something about her, as if she possessed a magnetic energy. She had shoulder-length, curly blonde hair that reminded people of an electric ball of light. Her eyes were a peculiar shade of hazel but turned blue at certain angles. Although she appeared rough and wore a few subtle scars like badges of experience across the side of her angular cheekbones, she was still a lady of vital illumination.

Mary always referred to herself as a damaged goddess rather than damaged goods. But all of her friends and associates had nicknamed her Sweet Innocent Mary because she was from down South and reminded city folk of kindness and hospitality with a slight topping of scorned-woman fury. Her life down South had left her so scattered, she'd run to Michigan, of all places. So this damaged goddess spent a lot of her time when she wasn't getting high trying to achieve a means to her end, to survive and escape her past. The desperate routine of hustle had become redundant and exhausting. First stop was the plasma center. They paid forty dollars a donation, but Mary wasn't always able to donate. Running a fever caused a pandemic panic everywhere now. If she were down South, they probably wouldn't have given two shits, Mary imagined. The Yankees up north seemed a little more uptight about rules and regulations.

So if the plasma center wasn't an option, Mary would go to a retail store like Lowe's to steal a wide variety of power tools and miscellaneous items and return them to the store. The clerks weren't allowed to give customers cash back without a receipt, but she could still receive a gift card. Mary was a self-proclaimed professional at finding loopholes. High-maintenance dope dealers like Anton wouldn't always take the gift cards in exchange for their product, but Mary always had a way of finding one who would.

Mary strutted down the sidewalk off Clifford Street, oblivious to her surroundings. She searched on her phone's Google app for the nearest Lowe's to see if it was open. Unfortunately, the website reported the store was closed due to employees being exposed to coronavirus. *God dang corona-flu is messing everything up*, she thought. She peeled her eyes back from the phone long enough to catch sight of a tall, lanky man wearing a Lions jersey and pressing an attractive woman, his girlfriend presumably, up against a brick building, softly pecking wet kisses across her slender neck and rosy, blushed cheeks. Mary darted her eyes forward. *Focus on the mission*, she scolded herself. But she couldn't help but turn back and stare. Jealousy rented space in her mind. She remembered when Trevor used to gently caress her neck like the tall man was doing to his girlfriend. But the playful cuddles, pillow talk, and random quickies in public bathroom stalls had been non-existent for some time. The sex was still there, but the passion had dissipated. She longed for that affection again, but the drugs claimed that territory, just as they claimed everything else. Her jealousy was a small first step toward rage, which was usually followed by self-pity. *But not today, Satan.* She would be in Trevor's arms soon enough, and they could have all the heroin sex they wanted. Euphoric morphine orgasms in the back seats of stolen cars. American-made, of course.

"Sweet innocent Mary, is that you?" a voice cried out.

Mary looked in all directions for the coarse voice that had called out to her. Then she heard it again. "Down here, sweetie." Blind Bobby gently tapped her heel with his walking stick.

Blind Bobby, as the local eastside had nicknamed him, was sitting on the sidewalk at her feet. He always wore a smile. Despite the fact that he lived on the streets half the time and the other half in a shelter, Bobby always cracked open a grin for those who graced his presence. And when in his presence long enough, they would learn the poor man spent all his Social Security money on booze and crack at the beginning of the month.

"Bobby, whatchya doing down there? You startled me." She put her hand on her chest and gasped before realizing it was Bobby. "I thought you was some creeper, and I almost gave you the boot." She sighed in relief.

Mary briefly caught her reflection in Bobby's gray plastic sunglass lenses, which concealed the white holes where pupils once dilated. She took another moment to forget herself and explore all of Bobby's features. He wore a thick, soiled green jacket. His skin was faded dark and creased like vellum. Mary always liked to feel his hair if he would let her. It was coarse-textured, coal black, and gunmetal gray. She imagined that thirty years before, back when he was a soldier in Iraq, he'd been a handsome man. But then hazard caught up with him.

Diabetes and cataracts had robbed Blind Bobby of his vision but not his determination to hustle up a few bucks. "You need to pay the toll, Mary, to cross this here bridge."

There was an awkward silence before they both burst out laughing. They knew there wasn't a dime to spare between them. And if there was, they surely wouldn't share with each other. However, Mary enjoyed the company of Bobby, and he was entertained by her presence. Bobby, a blind Iraq veteran, was a vagrant on the street, but he offered the young, naïve, lost soul words of wisdom, solace, and advice. "We need to survive out here, Mary."

Mary loitered over him like a shadow before sitting down and joining him on the sidewalk. She lit two menthol cigarettes at once and passed one to her homeless companion. "How did you know it was me?"

The blind vagrant laughed. "I smelled you coming."

"Oh, gee thanks! I know it's only been a day or two since I showered, but damn, Bobby, be easy on me," she half chuckled. The other half of her tone echoed the pain of truth in his statement.

"Youngblood. I can smell anything coming a mile away. But I know your scent in particular because I know you and your off-brand perfume." She smelled like strawberries, Bobby's favorite fruit.

Mary laughed authentically this time. "Yeah it's off-brand Chanel. I forgot the name of it. Five-finger discount at Walmart though. I almost got caught this time. The security chased me out of there faster than a one-legged man at a butt-kicking contest." She giggled but her laugh wasn't reciprocated.

"Five-finger discount?" He pretended to not understand.

Mary nudged his kneecap playfully. "Come on, you know what I mean." Her smile slowly dissolved.

Mary watched a sea of legs march past them on the sidewalk. She started thinking about how the system had failed Blind Bobby by not providing appropriate services upon his discharge from the military. But what was her excuse? She came from a prominent, loving family down in Arkansas. Of course, her dad was an addict and died from an overdose five years before. She moved up North to leave her past behind and discovered the hell that was in Michigan. But did that give her the right to storm these awful streets and take whatever she wanted, like a petty bottle of perfume?

"Cheer up, youngblood." Bobby could sense her shameful energy. Mary had a tendency to wear her emotions on her sleeve, and Bobby had a superpower instinct to read people when they were hurting. A perk to being blind, he supposed.

"It's hard, Bobby, to cheer up when I get all dope sick. I got turned away from the plasma center to donate because my temperature is too high. They think I got that damn COVID virus, but it's because I'm not well. And to top it off, my mom won't answer any of my calls." She stared down at the ground and kicked some loose pebbles. "I mean, I can't really blame her after me just leaving like I did after Pa died, but I felt like I had no choice."

Bobby lifted his head and looked toward the radiant sun as if he could see it. He could, however, see small glimpses of light cracking through the dark corridor of his mind. "Weren't you going to be a social worker or psychologist at some point? I remember you telling me something of that nature."

Mary took a moment to remember that failed dream. "Yes. After my pa passed, I decided to leave the South. I moved up here to start college and even graduated with my bachelor's degree in psychology at the University of Michigan. And then I met my boyfriend, Trevor." She paused, hung her head low, focusing on the pebbles. Kicking them, those damn, useless pebbles. Residue from the cheap roads—rocks whose sole purpose was getting caught in your shoes. "Fucking pebbles," she muttered under her breath.

"And that's when it all went downhill, huh? He talked you into something?"

"Ha! You could say that. At the time, it seemed so convincing. The life I was trying to live was all a lie. At least he made it seem that way. But I fell for it. I couldn't resist him and all his red flags. He was slicker than snot on a doorknob. It was all fun in the beginning. Now look at me, trying to hustle up enough money to score some dope." Her eyes returned to the scattered gray pebbles.

"Is it still fun?" he asked.

"I just want it to go back to the way it was before." She avoided eye contact.

Although blind, Bobby saw right through her. "Well, did you have a choice in the matter, sweet Mary?"

The question caught her off guard. She lit up another cigarette and took a deep drag. Of course she'd had a choice, but life was so much more tolerable when she blamed others and played the victim. She began to speak but caught herself, attempting to conjure up one of the thousand excuses that she used to rationalize her predicament. But there was no point. She knew she couldn't fool Blind Bobby.

He sensed her shame and heard her kicking the small stones next to him. "You know, life can sometimes be like that gravel rock you're knocking around."

"How so?" She perked up, interested in hearing one of his wise allegories.

"Mary, you think you have it hard. Think about those loose stones being kicked around in every which direction. Completely powerless over where they land. They could end up off the sidewalk and run over by a city bus. Or end up falling down into the sewer, living out the rest of their days in the gutter, wet and dirty."

"And?" She lifted her arms over her head. "These rocks aren't alive."

"Exactly! The lesson here is the rocks have no choice. But that doesn't mean they don't have a consciousness." Bobby believed this because he knew this. Being blind came with certain gifts, like awareness of life beyond the human world. The rocks, trees, plants, water all breathed the same air humans did, and they spoke to each other. Most people couldn't hear them communicate. Or if they could, they wouldn't have been able to fathom their language. But Bobby heard them, and he understood. However, not everything they spoke about Earth and its inhabitants was favorable. It was often destructive. "Those little humans are destroying themselves, but we shall always remain," they said. Oh, some days he wished he could give back the clairvoyant curse to whoever had bestowed it upon him.

"So the rocks are alive?" Mary rolled her eyes, dismissing this nonsense as one of the vagrant's wild delusions.

"You best believe they are, youngblood." His voice hardened. "And they mock us and the excuses we come up with as we destroy Mother Earth. Now, you have two choices in this life, Mary. You can lay down, play dead, and let life kick you around, let your boyfriend talk you into stupid shit and continue to get high. Before you know it, you may end up dead. And when you die, you'll be just like those rocks, stuck between the physical and spiritual worlds with no voice. Just consciousness."

Mary didn't want to die. She was afraid of death and knew there was no castle or ranch house in the sky waiting for her. Just stillness. Cold, black, empty.

Bobby's Spidey sense picked up on her façade of indifference. "Or, young lady," he continued, "you can pick yourself up and get into treatment. Leave that life behind you and go live your dreams of becoming a social worker or whatever it is you want to accomplish."

Mary scoffed and raised her brows. "And you're one to be talking, Blind Bobby. You drink a fifth or so a day and whatever else it is you do.

Smoke crack and shit?" She got up and dusted her leggings off. "Time for me to go now."

"Wait, Mary" he pleaded.

She momentarily paused. *Who is he to lecture me and preach about me being just like rocks and trees?* She thought. "What?"

"I chose to be the pebble. I'm sixty years old, fought overseas for our country, got shot in the back, and lived. I chose to drink after I came home and blamed it on the trauma of the war. I was you, except the war was my Trevor. It was the government's fault for sending a Black man overseas to the front lines to take a bullet and watch all his friends die. So when I came back, I drank like a fish and ate like a pig and ended up with diabetes that robbed me of my eyesight. So here I am, my darling, hoping to reach you so you don't make the same mistakes I did. I may be physically blind, but you, Mary, are spiritually blind. There's a spiritual war going on inside you, and it's time to take action." The pores in the old man's forehead beaded with sweat, trickling down over his brows.

Mary's fury relented. She sighed. "I'm just worried about Trevor. I don't know where he is, and we were supposed to meet up later. He's been so distant lately and paranoid. Like, I swear he checks the abandoned dump we live in for bugs. And not just bedbugs, but ya' know, the kind the FBI or CIA plant for surveillance." She crouched back down and sat next to Bobby once again.

"Don't you worry about Trevor, sweetheart. I happen to know he's doing just fine. He checked into the old Detox Hotel." A crooked smile crept over Bobby's face.

"Detox Hotel?"

Bobby nodded. "Yeah, that's what they used to call it back in the seventies. I was just a boy, but my pa went there. He never came back out the same. Cured his addiction, though. They must have reopened, because that's where I can see Trevor now." Bobby removed his sunglasses, exposing his pale, unseeing eyes, transfixed and immovable.

Mary recoiled. "I don't understand. How did he get there?"

Blind Bobby just started laughing. "He took himself there, and only he can get himself out." Bobby's oracle insight knew no limits, and he couldn't control it. But sometimes the clairvoyance extended so far beyond credibility that all the poor blind man could do was laugh. There were other things he saw in that hotel with Trevor. Unmentionable things that would terrify the scared young woman. He would keep those to himself, but he had to let her know that her man was there and not ditching her. Now, the question of whether Trevor was whole or in pieces was another story. "He checked into his new forever home." Bobby started laughing hysterically again and humming like a crazed bird.

Mary knew it was time to leave. The old man kept repeating, "He checked into his new forever home" over and over again. Suddenly, a vibration in her purse prompted her to eagerly check who could be calling at such a perfect time. The number belonging to a dealer named Shamrock appeared on her screen. *Thank God!*

"Hello?"

"Hey, it's me, Shamrock. What do you have for me?" His voice was deep and husky.

Mary's brain scrambled like an egg on drugs or however the decades-old "Say No to Drugs" commercial warned the previous generation of the dangers of substance abuse. She couldn't formulate an idea or articulate a message worth a drug dealer's attention. Then she almost forgot to remember that her EBT food stamps had $16.32 left on the balance. "The plasma center turned me away but I got almost twenty bucks on my bridge card." Her breath couldn't keep up with her words.

"What the hell am I supposed to do with that?" He sounded more than slightly disappointed.

She had no other possessions. All the money had run dry. Moisture formed on the edge of her eyelid. She couldn't tell if it was a tear or sweat from her withdrawal. But she knew at this moment that all the safety nets that had kept her from reducing herself to a morally deficient level of human nature had given way. But the strung-out goddess knew she had one resource that many dealers, friends of Trevor, and associates had craved and blatantly sought out. She'd never once given them the time of day out of respect for Trevor and herself, but the times were changing.

"I have something you been wanting for a while. Meet me at my mansion off Woodward and it's all yours." The attempted seduction in her voice came out flat and brittle behind her accent. Shamrock didn't care. He was going to claim what she was offering anyway.

8:00 p.m.

Mary caught the next bus home. The deed was done. The evening sun was closing to a rest as she sat up in her bed in The Hood Pack Mansion. She wondered where her boyfriend was. Was this Detox Hotel real? Or was the blind man just plumb crazy, more of his marbles falling into the gutter with the rocks and pebbles? She never would have guessed that Trevor's new forever home would have him tied and bound in an abandoned building miles from the "home" he shared with Mary. Shamefully, she dragged her leggings back on and pulled her extra-large Michigan Wolverines hoodie on over her black, lacy bra, which was missing part of a strap. Shamrock, an older Irish brute who resembled a thuggish version of Paul Bunyan and sported blue overalls and a gold chain hanging over his sunburned neck, threw a miniscule bag of heroin at her. It landed on the dirty, queen-size mattress. "There you go, sweet innocent Mary."

He left as quickly as he'd come, which ended up in her favor. She couldn't even stand the full two minutes he'd breathed leftover beef jerky on top of her, pressing his slimy, oily skin against her. Her vessel stayed dry, but Shamrock achieved his goal, and that's all that mattered. *Good riddance!* she thought. Disgusted, Mary wiped the growing tears from her eyes, smearing her makeup and rubbing the residue on the side of her leggings. She then took a good, hard look at her curly blonde hair in the cracked mirror hanging above her mattress. "I really need a fucking new perm, or maybe I should just straighten it out. It looks like crap." She posed and primped her hair in different angles. *Maybe, Mary,* the disease of addiction scolded her in her head, *you should just shut up and go get the bag over there so we can get fucking high. But first brush your teeth.*

The room felt cold and dry. Mary waited for a few for Trevor to show up, but he never did. She hadn't seen him since morning, but she was off on a mission of her own. Maybe he was home earlier, got tired of waiting around, and took off himself. Mary obsessively began to text him. *Hey where are you?* She almost texted, *Blind Bobby told me you are at The Detox Hotel, where is that?* But she knew how crazy that sounded. Mary was hooked to Trevor like the aqua-haired Cabbage Patch doll she'd toted around everyplace she went as a toddler. When she first met Trevor, she'd just wanted to shelter, hold, cuddle, and save him. But there was no saving Trevor. "If you can't beat them, then join them," as her father used to say. Another lesson she'd learned in psychology 101: codependency.

There was still no response from Trevor. *I ended up scoring*, she texted. Again, no response. The intervals between her texts seemed like hours to her, but they were mere seconds.

"Okay. I'm going to wait just a little longer. I can do this, I can wait for him," she said out loud, trying to convince herself of the lie. Then that voice in her head scolded her again. *You know damn well he's getting high without you, Mary, so why don't we do the same?*

"No I'm not going to listen to you today," she answered the voice. The sweating was increasing. She wouldn't be able to hold out much longer.

A daydream swept over her. She started to imagine a luxurious hotel where addicts could check in and enjoy full-body massages, serene horse rides on a ranch, and those spiritual awakenings she'd learned about in psychology class. You'd be accepted with Medicaid—and even if you had no insurance. Maybe Blind Bobby was onto something. Sure, these resorts existed, but she knew damn well Trevor wasn't at one of them. But the idea of such a place being within her grasp had a certain appeal, and she temporarily forgot how sick she was.

The daydream was over in three minutes. Trevor still hadn't returned. She told herself he was probably hiding out somewhere with his own bag, not sharing with anyone. Impatiently, Mary was reaching for the needle and spoon inside her purse when she heard footsteps coming up the stairs. She glanced up and covered her stash. When she realized it was only her friend Jake, she gave a sigh of disappointment. She'd hoped he'd be Trevor but was also relieved he wasn't Shamrock or someone worse.

"There's some dude here looking for Trevor." Jake seemed out of breath after running up the stairs. A friendly but big dog with striped fur had followed him up the steps.

"I haven't seen Trevor. Tell the guy to go away." Mary ignored Jake and began to dig back into her bag.

"He said his name is Ryan and he's Trevor's brother."

Chapter 5
The Withdrawal

7:00 a.m., Tuesday, September 22, 2020

After Jimbo's feast, Trevor motionlessly observed the remains of the grilled cheese sandwich melt further into the floor. He had a massive, throbbing headache and felt like he wanted to vomit. But his stomach didn't have the energy to release the bile. So was he just going to sit there and die? *No, heroin withdrawal doesn't kill you. It just makes you feel like you're going to die*, he reminded himself. So his stomach expanded and the belly's ejecta rose back up.

Crouched over, Trevor felt helpless as he noticed his body shift into the fetal position. His lips quivered as he tasted the lukewarm liquid waste's return. Gross barf draped over most of his face and hair. The stench was unbearable. At this point, death would have been a release. And who was this callous, masked madman holding him hostage? FBI? CIA? One of his dad's ex-partners from the Department of Homeland Security sent to tie up any loose ends from the operation, including all family and friends? The guy seemed to know a lot about Trevor's father, Bill, and almost expected Trevor's responses before he even had time to react.

Would his poor mother, Grace, be safe in that house all alone in Marlin, Michigan? Marlin was the last town Trevor had lived in with his family, ninety miles west of Detroit. And Ryan lived right outside Marlin in his expensive home with his picture-perfect family. Would they be in danger too? Trevor despised his brother, but even he couldn't wish death upon him for the crimes and secrets of their father. Or perhaps the madman had a child who'd been abducted back when Bill worked for the Department of Homeland Security and, instead of protecting the madman's kin, Bill had turned a blind eye to the fate of another lost child being experimented on in the camps. Trevor's Spidey sense detected subtle hints about the man's origins, like the cheap tattoos and the ripped physique that screamed ex-military or ex-convict.

Trevor heard the villain's footsteps again. The floorboards moaned under the thick, heavy soles of his feet. Combat boots, perhaps? Trevor hadn't gotten a clear view of his footwear. Violently, the door flew open, followed by a gust a wind. "What did you do to yourself?" The stranger looked at Trevor in disgust.

Trevor cowered. "It's called being dope sick," he said. The man flipped the chair right side up, grabbed a damp washcloth, and wiped Trevor's face and hair. "I'm sure you wouldn't know anything about that," Trevor said weakly.

"You have no idea." His voice produced such a familiar tone.

"Do I know you? Did you used to work with my dad? You can tell me. I'm no threat. I understand why you may want to do this."

"You have no idea," the man repeated. And there it was again. The familiar voice, like it had been haunting Trevor forever but he was clueless of its origin.

"Do you have any more chairs to tie me to? Or you can just let me go. I promise I won't tell anyone. I don't even know what you look like." Trevor's face lit up.

"Yeah, but you know what I sound like, don't you?"

A flush returned to Trevor's face. "Can you just tell me where I am at the very least, dude?" The only thing worse than being dope sick for Trevor was having no idea where he was, which happened to him a lot.

The masked captor grabbed the mahogany, splintered chair covered in bile and whirled his captive around full circle. "You're a junkie addicted to heroin and conspiracy. You refuse to seek help for your illness. And you shoot up insane amounts of dope per day, alienate everyone in your family, steal and suck the life out of everyone you cross paths with. Trevor, my friend, this place is your rehab, and you're going to detox. Now shut up. I'll be right back." The strange man stomped out of the room once again.

Trevor sat unmoving in the vomit-covered chair, sucking down the man's bitter words, which held much truth.

"Wow, look at you, little bro." A distinct voice bellowed from the back corner of the room. Trevor turned around to see an apparent illusion of his brother staggering about.

"You aren't real, brother. You're just another hallucination of my withdrawal," Trevor mumbled under his breath.

"Oh I'm real, Trevor. I may not be physically present, but I'm always here in spirit." Ryan meticulously examined his brother's current predicament. Around the perimeter of the room, he nonchalantly paced back and forth, whistling and humming to himself. He appeared to be taking enjoyment from witnessing his brother's pain. "Oh, what a mess you got yourself into this time. If only Dad were here to see you now."

"To hell with you and Dad. He's why I'm here right now, I'm sure." Saliva protruded from Trevor's dry lips. He questioned why he was having a conversation with one of his random hallucinations. The usual withdrawal trips were mild and not as real.

Ryan didn't move a muscle. He stood there tall and iconic, like a wax statue of a famous narcissist. Six foot, two inches and one hundred and eighty-five pounds, sandy-blond hair parted to one side and gelled to perfection, and a football player's physique. But something wasn't right about him, other than the fact he was an obvious hallucination from Trevor's breaking sanity or withdrawal.

Ryan's left blue eye kept twitching, and he repeated, "If only Dad were here to see you now, if only Dad were here to see you now, if only Dad were here to see you now, if only Dad were here to see you now ..."

The metal door to the room began to tremble. The floor rattled. A static-white light traveled from under the doorway in a perfect arc and hovered over Ryan. That was when everything froze.

A realization set in that what Trevor was witnessing was beyond just a visual hallucination. He'd spent countless hours between heroin runs researching involuntary microchipping and the effects its technology could have on the human mind and body. Another terrifying likelihood spun his paranoid mind in circles like a manic hamster in the wheel of over-analyzation: he was now being experimented on like all those missing children. He was the next Pizza-gate façade cover-up. But he vowed to die before being injected with the FBI's poison.

A strident bang reverberated through Trevor's eardrums. He looked up and saw his brother again, but Ryan was now holding his chest. Blood seeped through his hands as he tried to cover a gaping hole gushing a cascade of gore from underneath his jacket. "You shot me, brother." Ryan's horrid surprise washed out his face. Trevor wheezed. His brother dummy-dived into a pond of his own blood.

Another flash of light flickered over Ryan's dying corpse, and he vanished for good.

"Trevor?" Yet another soft, familiar voice whispered behind him.

Trevor swiftly turned his head around. There she was in all her beauty, staring wildly and lifelessly at Trevor. If only she were real and not the microchip's digital mirage. He gripped at the double-knotted twine that constricted his movement. He rocked back and forth, wincing and gritting his teeth. "I know you aren't real," he begged, "but be my saving grace and get me out of here."

Mary was sobbing, and her grim expression suggested disenchantment. Then the energy shifted and Trevor sensed she felt abandoned.

"You left me?" She looked at him, lips quivering, sobbing, "Why? Where did you go? You were supposed to wait."

"I'm sorry, baby, but if I'd waited, then you might be right here in this situation with me." He tripped over his words, trying to justify having abandoned her.

"Yeah, I'm sure that's why you ditched me!" Mary was growing sick of his lies.

"Look at where I am right now, Mary! I'm bound to a chair in some crazy man's house, and he's implanting visions and projections of my memories into my head as I'm dying over here from withdrawal. Trust me, you're in a much better position than I am."

"Looks like karma came around after all, Trevor. But I needed to get well too, and the lengths I had to go to … Well, they aren't good, Trevor." She sniffled and turned away from him.

"What are you talking about?" he asked.

"I had to sleep with Shamrock," she replied, looking down at the filthy floor.

"You slept with Shamrock?" His eyes narrowed in on her. He already knew why she had to sleep with the dealer. For a moment all he could imagine was the drug dealer's huge unit pulsating inside Mary as she screamed in agony and pleasure.

She lifted her face up toward him again with a lopsided grin. "He had his way with me, Trevor! It was deep and good!" Mary's voice transitioned from normal Mary to a possessed jezebel taunting her boyfriend.

Trevor looked past her betrayal. She could be forgiven under one condition. "Do you have any left?" he asked. However, she was just a holographic image. *What is she going to do?* he asked himself. *Shoot you up with some digital heroin?* The desperation and insanity of Trevor's words were overshadowed by his horrendous cravings and blistering urge to feel better. He didn't even care about getting high anymore. He just wanted the hurt to go away.

Mary's image was extinguished.

"Don't leave me, please." Trevor voice reached out into the thin air. He felt so alone, so cold in this dusty, murky room.

The hurt never goes away, he reminded himself.

The man swung the door open, bursting through with a pile of fresh, neatly stacked laundry. He tossed over a pair of loose Old Navy jeans—size 30 waist, 34 length—a plain, white cotton Hanes t-shirt, checkered generic boxer briefs, and low-cut white socks with the price tag still hanging. $5.99.

The man removed a rusty but sharp blade from his belt clip. He sliced a small incision into the palm of Trevor's hand as a gentle reminder of who was in charge. Trevor gulped dead air and leaned over to search for his friend Jimbo, but the mouse had disappeared. The stranger advanced forward with the blade. But Trevor's throat didn't get slit. Instead, the rope tying his hands and legs was cut apart.

"Stand up!" the man demanded.

Trevor complied.

"Take off your clothes," the man continued.

"What?" Trevor had almost forgotten the weird sexual perversion stage of government cover-ups. God, he just wanted it to be over with as quickly and painlessly as possible.

"How else are you going to change your clothes?" The man shrugged.

"With you in here?"

"Well, you need to get cleaned and washed up first. You're disgusting right now!" The mystery man held the small blade out in front of him. He slowly walked backward out of the room and into the hallway.

Trevor almost had a chance to push the asshole down, steal his knife, and make a run for it. But he was too busy thinking about how awkward a rapey snuff film with his masked captor would make him feel. Fortunately, his Spidey sense picked up the idea that potential kidnap porn was probably not in the cards.

"Okay, so can you just reassure me you're not going to do any rapey—" But before Trevor could finish his sentence, the man dragged in a black hose connected to a motor pump. He squeezed the nozzle's trigger and began power washing Trevor through his soiled attire.

"Give me a second," Trevor said, taking off his discolored jeans, stained shirt, and filthy socks. The man threw a bar of Ivory soap and a dry facecloth his direction. Trevor retrieved the soap and began scrubbing, trying to maintain his balance against the acute pressure of the water. This was probably the first proper bath he'd had in almost a week.

Mr. X, as Trevor had decided now to call him, concluded the decontamination. But Trevor knew that the purification process hadn't even begun. Mr. X pitched him a towel and ordered, "Now you can get dressed!"

Trevor quickly threw on the new undies and changed into the crisp white cotton shirt and dryer-warm, ironed blue jeans. He then put on the socks. Fresh-linen heaven. But Mr. X wasn't done playing nice. Next he tossed Trevor a Newport 100 cigarette.

"Are you going to let me go?" Trevor always had a way of getting ahead of himself.

"Not a chance." Mr. X hovered over Trevor with a stern expression drawn on his face.

"Well, why are you being so nice then?"

"Sit down!" Mr. X instructed.

"You just released me from that chair, and now you want me sit back on it? It's filthy."

Mr. X tossed Trevor the washrag. "Clean this shit up, then."

Trevor froze. The man then pulled out a 9 mm pistol from his back pocket and aimed the weapon at Trevor's petrified face. Trevor almost didn't adhere, but the pressure of cold steel pressed against his forehead subdued him into compliance. He grudgingly accepted the rag and within seconds, the chair was spotless.

"Look, this is how it's going to go," the man growled. "You're going to listen to me and do as I say. I don't want to kill you, but I will if I have to. If you try to escape, I'll kill you. I'll leave you in the room free to roam, but you can't leave. If you give me any crap, I'll gag you and tie you down so tight your hands and feet will bleed out until you die. Do you understand me?"

Trevor couldn't see Mr. X's face under the mask, but he imagined it was cold and stoic, like an emotionless mother who pitched unwanted babies down a trash chute without blinking an eye.

Trevor nodded in agreement. "Will you just talk to me, explain to me why I'm here? Did you implant those images of my girlfriend and my brother in my mind?"

"I'm not at liberty to tell you anything other than if you cooperate, you walk out of this alive." Mr. X grabbed a white plastic bucket with no lid from under the power hose. He placed it in the center of the room and headed for the door. Then he stopped himself and turned. "Also, those images weren't planted in your head. Those were your memories of before and after. By the way, you're responsible for cleaning up your own shit and piss. You're welcome for the bucket."

Thanks, asshole! Trevor thought. He sat there dumbfounded. "Well look, mister. You saved my life, or so it sounds like, and I'm grateful for that. I have no idea what your plan is, but I believe if you want to keep me alive, you need to help me." Trevor gently kicked the bucket and gave a quick gander at the loose dirt swimming in the bottom. "I won't try to leave if you can score me some dope. I'm going to get so sick all over the place, and I could die."

Mr. X placed his hands on his hips and laughed. "You aren't going to die. You're just going to feel like you want to die. But you already knew that." Mr. X took a step toward the helpless young man. Trevor flinched back, almost dropping the cigarette that hung from his chapped lips. The stranger drew out a blue Bic lighter—the same kind Trevor always used for his dirty little spoons. He lit Trevor's smoke and, as he walked out of the room, said, "Don't burn the house down."

Chapter 6
The Relapse

8:00 p.m., Saturday, September 19, 2020

Ryan Dugan sped down Interstate 69 after a discouraging meeting in Lansing with his bankruptcy lawyer. The appointment hadn't gone well, and Ryan was tackling severe financial distress. His profit margins since the pandemic had tanked. Business had picked up slightly in July after more restrictions had been lifted from the governor's executive order. But the numbers of confirmed COVID cases were rising, and people were becoming more afraid to go out to eat. Or, they just didn't want to wear a mask. And if they didn't, his employees were mandated to refuse them service. By September, expenses had inflated, revenue was down, and Ryan was forced to lay off ten employees from all three of his Ry's Burger Joint locations. His attorney, Frank, who had squinty Clint Eastwood eyes and a silver-gray Fu Manchu mustache, explained to him that he had no choice but to file for bankruptcy. So at the tender age of twenty-six, when most young men would be just graduating college or getting their feet wet, Ryan Dugan had already dropped out of college, built a business from the ground up, got married, had kids, and now was filing for bankruptcy.

Ryan accelerated from seventy-five to ninety miles per hour, cutting through traffic and honking at slow semi-truck drivers who were trying to pass other semi-trucks but driving at a slower speed than the other truck drivers. He made a point to flip the bird to an oblivious jackass trucker, hoping the guy would realize how inconvenient his driving was to Ryan in that moment.

Moments earlier, he'd ended a lengthy phone call with his sponsor. He'd had the same sponsor since the beginning of his AA meeting attendance. Tomorrow was going be his one-year sober anniversary date.

Ryan scanned through different stations on Pandora, seeking the ideal song to validate the empty pit he felt in his stomach. Johnny Cash's version of "Hurt" won the radio station lottery. RSL, or radio station lottery, was a game Ryan had played with his brother and dad when no one could decide on a song or station to play in the car. One of the three would pick a number between one and ten. Picking number five, Ryan dialed five different stations until it landed on the Man in Black covering Nine Inch Nails.

Outside, the sun fell behind the horizon, painting the sky shades of red and pink. Threads of light merged into swaying clouds, reminding Ryan that darkness might be coming but shreds of light still remained. After he'd had an insightful conversation with his sponsor, Jim, and internalized the majestic beauty of the sunset, Ryan's mood had sweetened, and he changed the depressing Johnny Cash song to a classic rock station blaring Queen's upbeat "Fat Bottomed Girls." The lyrics and tempo aroused thoughts of his gorgeous wife, Jessica, and his sudden desire to go home and dive into her arms.

Brian Ray's bluesy guitar riffs and Freddie Mercury's flamboyant voice were suddenly interrupted when the face of Ryan's mother, Grace, appeared on the Bluetooth radio screen. Something had to be wrong. Grace never called unless it was necessary.

"Hey, Grace. Is everything okay?" Ryan never addressed Grace as "Mom."

"It's your father, Ryan. He passed away." Grace cut right to the point.

Ryan almost didn't respond. Finally he said, "No one has seen him in seven years. How did you find out?"

Grace sounded like she was sobbing. "I got a call from Homeland Security. The details are sketchy, but it doesn't look good."

Ryan turned off onto the next exit and parked on the shoulder. He gripped the phone, firmly pressed it against his perspiring forehead, and continuously hit himself until he split the screen. He took a long, deep breath before replying. "I'm sorry, Mom." He abruptly hung up.

This was the first time he'd called her "Mom" since he was in high school. But he knew how much Grace loved his dad even after the selfish prick had just up and left the family seven years earlier. He needed her to be his mom right now and not just Grace.

Ryan didn't want to think about himself, but his brainwaves were stepping over each other, clawing to find an exit from his overcrowded mind. The first thought that leaked out was stopping at the next liquor store to purchase a nice bottle of Popov vodka to drown out all the dead-dad noise—or maybe he should be a good recovering alcoholic, call his sponsor back, and get honest about his desire to drink. But that damn voice in his head that the AA members referred to as the disease of alcoholism made itself heard:

You shouldn't call your sponsor back, Ryan.

You shouldn't go make love to your wife, Ryan.

You should go get inebriated, Ryan.

"What if I just went to a bar and didn't drink? I could just hang out for a while," he said to himself. But he knew how stupid that sounded. *Yeah, let's go hang out at the whorehouse to listen to a piano player.* When he was tempted to make stupid decisions in his recovery, he frequently thought about this analogy that he'd learned from his sponsor. But Ryan had now lost the ability to reason within logic. He was going to go mingle at the most socially deformed hole, a bar, on the west side of Michigan—the one place he could think of that was the perfect, disposable refuge for hiding from himself.

Ernie's Dive proudly lived up to its inconspicuous name. Owned by a drunk, rich redneck called Ernie, it was a hotspot for hunters, fishermen, truck drivers (the ones who drive real slowly in the passing lane), and elderly Social Security recipients who bitched about minorities collecting welfare while living on taxpayers' dollars themselves. Ryan figured he'd drink to that ignorant notion right along with them.

Having dressed for his rendezvous with his good-for-nothing attorney, Ryan was overdressed for a piss-hole bar. But he was the type of man who wore dress socks to bed. He'd donned navy-blue pants that had been ironed creaseless and were held up by a Bulliant leather belt. The left sleeve of his button-down blue-and-white striped shirt was rolled up to his elbow, revealing the cliché barbed wire tattoo wrapping around his toned forearm. He made a discreet entrance through the bar's dim light, noticing only a few of the locals present who were chain-smoking Marlboro Reds.

Two older men, faces flushed and vision blurred, pointed ugly glares Ryan's way. He pulled up a skeleton-thin stool next to the bar. An old neon beer sign gave a strobe-lit view of the bartender's ass crack as he bent over to fetch glasses from his minifridge. Shabby décor, like pennies, were pasted in columns and rows on the back wall. Out-of-season red-and-green Christmas lights hung from the ceiling's utility hooks. A mounted fake bass's dead eyes peered at Ryan like it was judging his every move. Ryan saw the exit, and he could easily walk right out that door. A faint voice of reason inside Ryan's scattered mind was shouting at him. *Leave, call your sponsor, and confess your craving to relapse.*

But he was already at the bar and had driven all that way. He considered his options. Why not stick around a just a little bit and go find a jam to rock out to on the jukebox? Give those old geezers another reason to judge and stare. Ryan took a dollar out of his wallet and went up to the jukebox. The selection was mostly country, like Garth Brooks, Randy Travis, and a whole discography of Elvis. But there it was, like a shiny diamond in the otherwise rough patch of hillbilly western swing music: a song that took him back to his childhood and growing up in the early 2000s. The song was from a decade before his time, but "Down in a Hole" by Alice in Chains was the soundtrack to his adolescence. The emotional pain of his youth he converted to toxic masculinity was able to vent itself through Layne Staley's dark, harmonic words. The song also reminded him of his younger brother, Trevor. They used to stay up all night, listen to the song on repeat on their CD player, and sing out loud until the sun rose.

Ryan placed his butt back down on the bar stool and got lost in nostalgia for the good old days. Regaining focus, he looked down and saw a vodka spritzer with a flimsy red straw sitting in front of him on the bar. "How did this get here? I didn't order it. Or did I?" he asked the bartender.

The dull bartender, wearing overalls and a Make America Great Again lid to conceal his receding hairline, looked up from polishing empty glasses. "You sure did, bub. You even gave me a nice tip." MAGA man cracked a crooked smile, revealing caverns of rampant tooth decay, and proudly held up his newly earned, crisp twenty-dollar bill.

"Well, I guess I did." Ryan wrinkled his nose. There was something about vodka's nail polish remover aroma that seduced him. He began to push the tiny red straw around the ice cubes in a circular motion. The ice scraped up against the glass, and Ryan stared down at it almost in a trance.

He thought for a minute about everything this last year of sobriety had given him. He was still bankrupt, still having problems in his marriage, and nothing was truly fixed.

"Fuck it." Ryan snatched the tiny red straw out of the glass and tossed it across the bar, landing it in a nearby wastebasket. He took a big gulp and finished the mixed drink with one swallow. "Bartender, I need another."

Ryan almost closed the bar down that night. But instead of passing out like a college girl who'd drunk too many White Claws at a frat party, he continued his grandiose self-pity party in his car. Before sneaking out of the bar, he'd snatched a fifth of Bacardi while the bartender (who he discovered went by Mearl) was distracted turning the channel on his TV back to Fox News. The rest of the night, Ryan sat in his car with the radio blasting Alice in Chains and other post-grunge/new-metal hit songs while upsurging his drunken stupor. After finishing off the Bacardi, he was too intoxicated to find the keys to his 2018 cherry-red, two-door Dodge Charger. Otherwise, he could have planted himself in the middle of a tree or telephone pole.

10:00 a.m. Sunday, September 20, 2020

Ryan was fast asleep in a deep REM cycle when his nap was interrupted by a sharp, piercing tap on the driver-side window. His ears felt like a sword was impaling his swollen skull through his eardrums. A stubby, disheveled police officer with a shiny yellow badge kept knuckle-drumming the

Charger's window. Ryan didn't immediately respond. He thought maybe he was still dreaming or, if not, the cop would just magically disappear.

The short cop reminded Ryan of the D.A.R.E. officer who'd visited his third-grade class to scare the children away from drugs. He remembered the officer's name was Deputy Gus. So this new version of Deputy Gus let out an impatient sigh and signaled once again for Ryan to roll down the window. The window lever seemed to be caught. After struggling for a bit, Ryan was able to fling his door open.

"Looks like you had a fun night," the cop said sarcastically. "May I ask what you're doing here?" The officer studied the scene. His face expressed amusement that Ryan couldn't see under his black cloth mask.

"I don't know. I just didn't drive home, it looks like. So that's good. Right, officer?" Ryan shifted his eyes away from the cop.

Gus rubbed the back of his neck. "Yeah, if what you're telling me is the truth. I'm not going to write anything up. But I suggest you wait a couple hours, get some coffee, and walk it off before you head home. Luckily, you're in the passenger seat. Because if you were in the driver's side, I could technically arrest you for a DUI."

Ryan silently mocked the officer in his head but nodded. "Okay, officer." The cop left him alone.

But Ryan didn't follow directions well. After about ten minutes, he found his car keys and erratically drove home. When he arrived, he squealed his tires and almost ran into the garage door. He exited the Charger and staggered his way up to the house. There was a note on the front door from his wife, Jessica: *We went to my mom's house, call me if you're sober. The kids and I can't do this again.*

"Wait, how did they know?" Ryan mumbled.

The note was yet another wake-up call. Jessica, Lukas, and Lucy had endured so much for over two years before Ryan finally decided to get sober. He knew they'd watched his business go under and stood by his side. But he knew Jessica wouldn't watch him drink himself into oblivion again. Feeling like an idiot, Ryan punched himself in the head and screamed out to no one. He caught his breath and completed a silent meditation of counting backward from ten. *10, 9, 8, 7, 6, 5, 4, 3, 2, 1.* He'd learned the technique in an anger management group he'd attended the year before after being seconds away from throwing a lamp at his wife in a drunken rage. After one more deep breath he jumped in the shower, made some coffee, and called his sponsor, Jim.

"I messed up again, Jim. My dad died, and I didn't know what to do. I should have called you, but instead …"

Jim was silent for a minute. Then he said, "You did what alcoholics normally do in times of tragedy: they drink. But you're in recovery now, so the responsibility is on you to get your ass to a meeting now!" Jim followed a strict line of sponsorship helping alcoholics find recovery. He could love you and kick your ass at the same time.

7:00 p.m., Sunday, September 20, 2020

"God grant me the serenity to accept the things I cannot change, the courage to change the things I can, and the wisdom to know the difference." Ryan Dugan recited the serenity prayer to himself outside the old haunted drunk-priest suicide church that held his favorite Sunday-night AA speaker meeting. Keeping his head low, he ambled his way inside.

Five years earlier, the ordained priest at St. Philips Catholic church climbed up to the roof of the building to the top steeple and swan dived into the concrete parking lot below. His blood alcohol content was .39. Afterward, the church closed down and was converted into a town hall for Alcoholics Anonymous meetings. The clergy voted to donate the building to the AA fellowship and considered it to be God's will to do so.

The transition from church to recovery hall was almost complete before the pandemic, but progress was still being made. The original mocha-tan carpet had been stripped and the floor laminated with polished hardwood. Instead of pews, rows of aluminum folding chairs lined up six feet apart on Xs marked with duct tape. The only remnants left behind of a Catholic church were the high, arched windows with stained glass depictions of St. Philip, Mother Mary, and Jesus himself.

Ryan attempted not to disturb others as he grasped a folding chair off the side of the wall while his new tennis shoes squeaked across the polished floor. The earsplitting commotion turned a few heads as people examined who dared show up so late. But you're never late for a meeting. At least, that's what his sponsor always told him. He was already apprehensive about showing up; the last thing he wanted was unnecessary attention.

Promptly, he took his seat and was just in time for the clean-time countdown celebration. Ryan cringed when Charles M. went to pick up his one-year sober medallion. Charles was a slim, nineteen-year-old kid who'd just gotten off probation. He was sleeved up with body art from his neck down to his wrist. Ryan thought he looked like a skinny version of Fred Durst from Limp Bizkit, as he always wore a backward red starter cap and baggy blue jeans. But the worst part about Charlie "Durst" was that he always bragged during the pre-meeting smoke session outside the church about how he smoked weed daily now that he was off probation. And today he was picking up his "sober" medallion. Ryan's sponsor called that move "marijuana maintenance" and highly advised against. Charlie Durst was technically sober only from alcohol but not living in recovery. Ryan realized he was projecting a little of his own shit from his relapse the previous night onto poor Charlie Durst. *But seriously,* he thought, *fuck Charlie Durst.*

The clean-time countdown had only one more anniversary to celebrate after Charlie's, as no one else stood up to claim sobriety dates. A tan woman with gold, feathered hair who appeared to Ryan to be in her early fifties was asked to approach the podium. Claire M. was celebrating twenty-five years of sobriety. She was also the main speaker for the meeting.

The chairperson gave Claire her twenty-five-year chip and an awkward, sideways hug before stepping off the podium and saying, "Let's give it up for Claire M. and twenty-five years in recovery."

The crowd exploded into an opus of applause.

Claire clammed her hands together and shook them in victory toward the crowd. "I didn't do this. We did this, my friends. Thank you so much."

Oh God. Is she about to give an acceptance speech for the sober Academy fucking Awards? A voice spoke up in Ryan's mind. He tried to ignore the voice. He wanted to listen to Claire.

Eventually, the noise ceased and Claire cleared her throat. "My name is Claire and I'm an alcoholic."

"Hi, Claire," the crowd replied.

"I used to be so selfish when I drank. It was all about me. How could I get my next drink? I didn't think about my husband and children. I let my job for the union go to waste. It's hard to work for a union when you show up to all the meetings smelling like wine and bad decisions." Scattered laughter echoed in the first rows of the room. "My husband died when I had twenty years sober. Five years ago to this very day. I hurt so badly and all I wanted to do was drink. I came very close, as I remember picking up the bottle of Boone's Farm from the local liquor store. But then I went home and looked in the mirror, and that very moment, my sponsor called me. I debated whether or not I should answer. Thank God I answered. We talked for hours, and I began to feel some specks of hope. Afterward, I poured the entire bottle of wine down my toilet and flushed that poison away." The crowd began to clap and cheer in synchronicity. Ryan joined the applause with a slow clap.

Claire scanned the audience, giving almost each member direct eye contact. "And the way he died was terrible. He was killed by a drunk driver."

Soft murmurs dispersed among the crowd. Ryan's ears perked up.

"The harsh realization of knowing that could have been me who killed my own husband at one point in my life. I used to drink and drive like it was nobody's business. Thankfully, I never hurt myself or anyone else. By the grace of God, I never got arrested or caught. But if I had, I would probably still be in prison." Claire gave a deep sigh. "A lot of people asked how I managed to get through his death without picking up a drink. Well, I'll tell you, it wasn't easy. If it wasn't for my sponsor, the women in this program, and most importantly my higher power who carried me through it, I don't think I'd be standing here today in front of you all."

Ryan lost focus for a minute during the redundant gratitude speech he had heard recycled over a hundred times at the AA tables. He started thinking about when he'd attended this same church as a high school senior with Grace, Dad, and Trevor. The priest had also referred to this higher power that Claire gave credit to for seeing her through addiction. But Ryan wondered if the father had been calling attention to the same God. Maybe Claire's higher power was a doorknob that he once heard an alcoholic identify as his higher power. Ryan had no clue how anyone could worship a doorknob, but the guy said it was helping him stay sober. Ryan knew it probably wasn't the doorknob. But whoever this power greater than himself was, could it help Ryan recover from his drinking if he just surrendered, like the priest and Claire suggested?

Claire went on and Ryan regained focus. "I will say, keeping an attitude of gratitude and helping others who were struggling tremendously helped me more than I probably helped them. There was this one newcomer who had just asked me to sponsor her. I told her to call me for thirty days, every day, or text. If I didn't answer, leave a message. Religiously, she called me every day like clockwork. However, after about three weeks, she stopped calling, and I didn't hear from her for a while. I thought to myself, *Maybe she isn't ready for recovery.* But that explanation just didn't settle too well with me." Claire paced back and forth behind the podium like a motivational speaker getting riled up by her own words.

Ryan leaned in closer to better listen. "So I decided to reach out and call her. Unfortunately, her phone was shut off. Maybe she forgot to pay the bill. Who knows? A few more weeks had passed by, and it was about two in the morning when I got a phone call from a random number. It woke me up out of sound sleep, and I wasn't exactly in the best mood. If you know me, that isn't all that unusual. My sleep is very important to me. I mean, I'm old for crying out loud."

The crowd squeaked out a few more laughs, but it didn't distract Ryan's fixed attention. He was completely tuned in. But then the speaker had lost track of her speech, and Ryan lost his attention once again to study all the anonymous faces concealed under masks in the auditorium. The faces came from all walks of life. Some came straight off the streets, like the homeless folk who used to stand outside one of the burger joints he owned and beg for change from the guests as they came and went. He remembered how they reeked of cheap wine and stale cigarettes, but he didn't smell that in here. Other masked faces were businessmen, lawyers, wives, husbands, doctors, social workers, bus drivers, and even bartenders. Ryan himself was a business owner who'd hit his rock bottom.

"I lost where I was at. It happens with old age, you know," Claire said. She chuckled with a cracked, hoarse voice attributed to decades of chain-smoking Virginia Slims. She stood before them all like a reborn giant. Her leather-tinted skin glistened in the glow of the ceiling light above her, which shone like the halo of an angel delivering a message from God to Ryan's lost soul. Claire was probably about thirty-plus years older than Ryan, but this didn't discourage his odd attraction to this woman. She had spiritual wisdom that appealed to him. And God, he would love to slide his hands over every inch of her bronze flesh.

The angelic woman went on to say, "Oh yes, it was my sponsee, and she was in trouble. She called me in a frenzy, told me she was in a bad place in Detroit and if she didn't get out, she might not make it out alive. Now, what I'm about to tell you, I don't recommend. But I didn't call the police." Claire paused and closed her eyes, searching for the best way to deliver the rest of her speech. "I decided to grab my semi-automatic rifle, and I wrote down her location. I got my ass in my old 1995 station wagon and drove to the hood of Detroit to pick this woman up. I remember pulling up outside this scary-looking crack house. I saw a couple shady characters circling around my vehicle. The rifle nestled in my lap just in case. Thank God, no violence broke out." She opened her arms wide and bent her neck back to give praise to her higher power. "No one had to die that night. But I was ready to shoot a motherfucker that would try to get in the way of me helping my lost 'sister.'"

A thunderous applause erupted, but Claire shot her index finger up to silence the crowd. Her story wasn't over yet. "My sponsee was hysterical and crying. There were needle marks all over her arms. It was obvious she'd been using. I took her in and dropped her off at rehab the next morning. This woman is here in the front row with me now. She has been sober five years, and I'm sorry I just told part of your story, Sarah. Oops, and I just shared your name." Claire laughed softly, pretending to be embarrassed for busting her sponsee out. But she wasn't really embarrassed at all. Claire signaled for Sarah to stand up and accept a round of applause. "That's all I have to share," Claire said, signaling the end of her speech.

All the recovering drunks got up to give Claire a standing ovation. She sat down as the chairperson stepped back up to the podium. "Would anyone else like to come up here and share before we end the meeting?"

Ryan's sponsor turned around in his seat and gave him those fixed eyes. A gentle nudge in the right direction. Reluctantly, Ryan got up and dragged himself up to the podium.

"Hi, my name is Ryan and I'm an alcoholic."

"Hi, Ryan," the group said in unison.

Ryan's hands trembled excessively. He didn't really like talking in front of large groups. There were probably over thirty people at this particular AA meeting. He clutched his "One Day at a Time" medallion in his left pocket for good luck and courage. He closed his eyes and mumbled a little prayer as he stood there. "You got this. God grant me the serenity," he slightly coughed before continuing louder, "to accept the things I cannot change, courage to change the things I can, and the wisdom to know the difference."

The audience chanted the prayer with him before a pin-drop silence fell over the room. "So, um, today, I would have had one year sober." A couple of alcoholics started a slow clap. Ryan lifted his hand up like a bookmark to cease their applause. "No, don't clap, because last night I got news that my father passed away. I didn't really like my father. He left my mom, brother, and myself over seven years ago. He gave us some bullshit reason, and my younger brother bought up every last lie. Well, my mom called me last night, and he's gone. And even though I hated my dad for leaving us, the pain was still there. I allowed it to be my excuse to go get wasted. I'm here today, with one day sober. Thank you all." Ryan stepped back down. He felt slightly less ashamed with a sense of relief.

Once again, the flock of alcoholics got up to applaud. Claire walked up to Ryan, sliding the back of an aging, wrinkled hand across his face. To his surprise, she tugged him close for a warm, embracing hug. Apparently, alcoholics in Marlin had no concept of the social distancing guidelines. Or at least Claire, who kept her mask next to a pack of Virginia Slims in her brown Coach purse, wasn't worried about any diseases except alcoholism.

The next anti-masker, his sponsor, Jim, walked up, shook his hand, and whispered, "Welcome home."

There was a sudden vibration coming from Ryan's phone. He opened it up to find his mother, Grace, calling him. He excused himself to walk outside.

"Hey. What's up, Mom? I'm in a meeting," he said.

"Oh, I'm sorry, honey, to bother you. I just wanted to let you know that the funeral is being held at Tompkins Funeral home behind the Congregational Church on Friday. Visitation is at two o'clock, followed by the service at three thirty."

"Okay. Thanks, Mom. I'll make sure to be there for you." He had no real desire to attend, but he knew it would mean the world to his mother. He wasn't going to go for himself or because he needed closure with his father. Ryan had already decided he would just go to support Grace.

"Thank you, honey. Oh, and one more thing. I know you haven't spoken to your brother in over a couple years. I have no idea how to get hold of him. But if there's any way you can let him know and get him to come, it would mean the world to me. I know our family has been divided, but maybe Bill's death, if any good can come of it, could be an opportunity to bring us together."

Ryan paused before he answered. He thought, *There's no way in hell I would get him. That punk hates me, and the feeling is mutual.* He then recalled last time he talked to his brother. Trevor had called him begging for some money, lying about needing the cash to pay rent when Ryan knew he didn't pay any rent. In a momentary lapse of judgement, Ryan had agreed. He made sure to get the address to send the check to 618 Saxton Avenue in Detroit. For some odd reason, Ryan was excellent at remembering numbers, addresses, dates, but he couldn't recall what he had for breakfast. But the glazing on the donut was that he could never forget the condescending message he'd written on the memo of the check: *failure funds.*

I'm sorry, Trevor. You aren't a failure, he thought now, reflecting on Claire's story. She'd helped that young woman get sober, which benefited her own recovery. "I'm going to make it right," Ryan whispered out loud to Trevor, wherever he was. "Big brother is going to find you."

"Yeah, Mom. I'll go look for him. I can't promise anything, but I'll do my best."

Chapter 7
Surrender

12:00 p.m., Tuesday, September 22, 2020

Trevor had been in solitary confinement for over twelve hours, and he'd lost all sense of time passing. The heat was unbearable. The stench of his excrement in the plastic bucket added an extra layer of vile that reminded him of Johnny Carzo locking him in porta potty at the state fairgrounds in 2010. And the tainted, skid-marked sock left on the floor reminded him of the time he'd used fallen leaves to wipe off excreted residue after a stoned camping trip back in 2017. He remembered smoking two cigarettes after that dump. Now, he was pacing back and forth, wishing he'd saved the cigarette Mr. X had given him. His soul shivered and craved anything that could make him feel different: nicotine, dope, orgasm. Even an escape plan could get his adrenaline going enough to help with the withdrawal.

Trevor wasn't sure if the heat kept increasing or if it was just his withdrawal symptoms. Actually, he knew the answer to the question. It was late September. The leaves were falling, but he felt like he was sitting inside a furnace in the middle of July. Hot flashes and cold sweats accompanied the heat. He gnawed his thumbs until blood oozed from under his fingernails.

In the corner of the room, a glimmer of sharp copper reflected against the ceiling light, causing Trevor to wince. He sauntered over, picked up the penny that lay tails down, and flipped it over to find Abe Lincoln's head scratched off as if a sharp blade had harbored a resentment against the former president. Trevor was bored and wanted to play with his new toy penny. "Tails," he called. He always called tails. So he flipped his new penny. *Tails it is!* This had to be a sign, a symbol of hope that he would find a way out. Trevor used the coin to carve his signature mark into the walls. *TJD was here.*

Scanning the entire room for a means to escape, mapping out every possible angle, studying every open crevice, he came up short. Even Jimbo had deserted him. The windows were boarded solid shut. He considered trying to rip them off but didn't want to make too much noise. Banging and trying to knock down the door would only attract his captor's attention, and he didn't want the burlap nut sack to come back.

"I'm going to fuck that old man up when he comes back." He tried to convince himself of this notion. The man may have been old, but he was a beast compared to Trevor's feeble stature.

"I would be careful trash talking old men. Even this old guy could probably still get the best of you, son."

Trevor could have recognized that gentle, condescending voice from miles away. "Dad?" He turned to see his father stalking from behind. Trevor scoped Bill up and down, knowing he was only another illusion but still riveted to see his face after all these years. Bill shot him a frightened, forced smile. Trevor knew it was his father, but the image's demeanor and appearance were different. His hairline was receding downward into an ever-growing patch of sparse hair on the back of his neck. Spiral, looped chest hair sprouted from under his V-neck collar. Instead of his usual khaki slacks and button-up shirts, he wore a ragged, gray shirt with small blots of dark-red matter splattered in all directions, as if a blood-filled pen had exploded in the dryer. But in this case, the pen was a knife that had pierced his heart. His matching gray sweatpants, and even the white drawstring, continued the heart's bloody trail down to his solid black boots.

"Yeah, it's me, son. I have to let you know this isn't a nightmare, but I am dead, Trevor. They were coming for me, and they were going to make me talk, so I had to go before they had a chance to dissect the truth from me. And trust me, Trevor, they have their ways."

Trevor shuddered. "What do you mean you're dead?"

Bill reached into his sweatpants pocket and pulled out one of his famous, signature Cuban cigars. The end was damp, but a struck match lit it up. Bill's cigars had always left a burned chocolate aroma lingering in the air that made Trevor nauseous. He couldn't smell that now. The cigar and his dad weren't real. He kept forgetting that.

"These cigars taste way better than those pussy menthol cigarettes I used to find hidden in your underwear drawer." Bill tapped ash off his cigar.

"What happened, Dad?" Trevor's question shook with discomfort.

"I told you they were coming for me, so I had to go. They would have either tortured me to expose the truth or thrown me in a box to keep my mouth shut. I did the job for them. I wasn't going to let them win." Bill chomped some more on his cigar, which was burned down to a stub. Brown shreds of tobacco were caught between his teeth.

Trevor glowered and stepped away from his dad. "What about the guy you know who didn't work for the government and who was going to help you disappear? How did they find out?" Trevor remembered the day his dad packed up his bags to head out to "meet a guy" for protection. And Trevor had been able to tell by his tone that this "guy" wasn't formal and didn't work for any government division. No, he was the kind of guy who operated in the basement of a pawn shop. A customer would have to ask to purchase the "vintage ceramic dolls in the back" in order to see him.

"They have their ways," his dad said blandly.

"So you killed yourself like a coward? Come on, Dad, there had to be another way."

Bill spit the rest of the cigar out of his mouth, shaking his head. "No, Trevor. A coward runs away from a good home to go live on the streets in Detroit. Didn't I teach you anything all those years?"

Trevor gnashed his teeth under a closed mouth. "You left Mom, Ryan, and myself. All you left behind was a letter. You said you had to join some off-the-books witness protection program and needed to go alone because if you took us with you, it would put us in even more danger. Your reasoning didn't fit your own narrative, Dad. Common sense would tell you that leaving us exposed and behind would cause more harm than good."

"In my line of work, I was trained to at all costs protect the ones I love first, and sometimes that means having to lie. I realize that lie took a toll on you, your mom, and Ryan."

"No, Ryan seems to be managing pretty well with his suburban mansion and thriving business." Trevor started circling the room, running his fingernails against the wall.

"Money doesn't buy you happiness, Trevor. Ryan has his own demons."

Trevor scoffed. "I believed you, Dad. I still follow the bread crumbs online, the Rubik's Cube, and the letter you left behind. I was searching for answers, debunking Pizza-gate, and looking for any clues of what happened to those children you mentioned. I went crazy, overanalyzing, trying to figure out where you were. And then I stumbled on heroin. It was the only thing to quiet my mind long enough to let it catch back up with itself."

"Damn it, son!" Bill yelled, the veins on his neck tightening close to combustion. "Stop following the trail. It will lead you nowhere but dead. And don't blame me for disappearing, sparing you the truth that would have driven you to your own grave quicker than heroin. We all have choices. I made my choice and I have to live with it. So live with yours."

"I own it, Dad. Trust me. So now what? Why are you here?"

Bill crouched and let out a barky cough. "I need to warn you about the damn hippie."

"What damn hippie?" Trevor chuckled. He couldn't count how many times his dad had yelled at the TV or out the car window at all the "damn hippies."

"His name was Randolph Grey. He was your biological grandfather. I kept his existence private from everyone. He was one of the first experiments, and I had a terrible hand to play in it. You'll understand once this is all over. But his spirit is here, and he's going to lie to you, try to tempt you to a path of darkness. Don't listen to him. That's all I can say for now. I have to go."

"Wait." Trevor stopped scratching his nails on the wall. "How will I know it's him? And how do I escape from here?"

Bill stood up, walked up to Trevor, and leaned in close to his son. "He's everywhere in this place, and the only way out is through you, son. I love you, son."

A pocket of tears welled in Trevor's eyes. He had no response.

"Look right above the still-life painting," his father whispered in his ear. So Trevor looked up. There it was: a small camera almost invisible to the naked eye unless a ghost pointed it out for you. "He's watching you, Trevor. Be careful. He knows your every move before you make it."

"Randolph?"

"No. The other one you must watch out for."

"The other one?" Trevor withdrew in confusion.

"You'll find out soon enough."

Trevor wiped the tears from his eyes. "Hey, Dad. I may never understand, but that doesn't mean I'm going to stop seeking the truth. Sorry your only way out was death, Dad. I truly hope it was worth it."

"Don't worry, son. I'm glad I had a chance to say goodbye to you even not in physical form because it looks like we both needed a chance to vent." Bill's image faded away.

Just then Jimbo, the little mouse, crawled out of the torn hole in the small vent cover in the wall next to the radiator. Trevor now realized that he needed to cover the surveillance camera without being seen. The fruit bowl painting hung below the camera. He discovered a slender metallic nail above the tiny globe camera-thing. Maybe another fruity painting or portrait of the mysterious hippie Randolph had once hung there. Like his mouse friend Jimbo, Trevor gently tiptoed over to the wall. In concise and careful form, Trevor removed the painting below the camera and placed it over the nail above, shrouding the captor's vision with the darkness of the painting.

Trevor had a basketball player's height and was built like a wiry runner. Growing up, he was a chubby kid, but thanks to the side effects of meth and heroin, he'd been able to shed a few pounds. He pulled his sleeves back, gritted his teeth, then grabbed the hole in the vent's cover and ripped off its frame. He took a deep breath and dove headfirst into the open hole. He slithered through until the sides of the vent caught him by the waist. Finally, he was able to squirm through.

The passageway was dark and smelled of vintage drywall and potent Pink Panther insulation. Trevor wriggled his shoulders, torso, hips, legs, and feet through the claustrophobic tunnel like a worm escaping a hook. Up ahead, about twenty feet, there was another small vent. He inched forward to get a better view. On the other side of this second vent's frame appeared to be some sort of janitor's closet. All he could see was a straw-yellow mop with shredded coarse strings and a Wet Floor sign shrouded in dust, debris, and cobwebs. Unfortunately, this vent was much smaller, with corroded nuts and bolts keeping it tightly secured in its frame. But adrenaline-fueled Trevor was able to knock it out with one firm punch. Following the metallic clang of the fallen vent, he took the plunge with his last ounce of energy. But the force wasn't enough to get his bony behind through. So Trevor pulled himself back into the passageway in search of a new exit.

Cornered off in the main lobby of the hotel, Mr. X was relaxing behind a reception desk. He took a swift drag on his Newport cigarette as he surveyed all the video cameras in the building. His scary X mask rested on a fawn-colored reception desk in the lobby of the vacant hotel. Stacked against the wall overhead, a dozen black-and-white TVs were connected to random security cameras stationed throughout the hotel, allowing him to examine each hallway, room, stairway, entrance, and exit—and even the broken elevator.

He leaned back on his cushioned seat, propped his feet up on the counter, and yawned. He admired the ones who'd sent him there for picking such a remote, discreet location. They'd given him a chance at salvation, just as he was offering salvation to Trevor. But the little bastard didn't realize the pain the man in the burlap sack was saving him from. Trevor looked at the man like a villain, a kidnapper, ignorant to the transformation and metamorphosis that would soon hold ceremony. If Trevor only knew the significant history of this hotel, the generations of addiction, insanity, death, and recovery—and the shadow hiding in the walls.

After being awake for hours—or maybe it was days—organizing this master plan, Mr. X felt his energy depleted, and he caught himself nodding off. His lit cigarette nearly burned the skin off his hand. The security camera to room 202 had gone black. Trevor was trying to escape. Mr. X twisted the cigarette on the counter to put it out and grabbed his Beretta 92, storming out of the office.

As Trevor army-crawled through the very snug passageway to his freedom, he could feel the sickness returning. Sweat began to stream down his forehead and sting his eyelids. He recalled some of the side effects from withdrawal, like mania, delusional thinking, and occasionally hearing voices when coming off some bad heroin. But those weren't the kind of voices he was hearing inside the walls of this cursed place. He had tried to shake and slap his head to revive himself, but to no avail. Soft, disembodied whispers echoing the name "Lance" floated to him from all directions. "Lance, let us out. We need to get a fix. There's something inside here trying to kill us." The echoes grew louder and became deafening. As Trevor edged closer, he heard more soft whispers: "Help us, Trevor, we're stuck. You put us here, Trevor. Let us out!" But these voices weren't harsh or bold; they were the fragile whispers of children. He couldn't shake them either. They wouldn't stop coming from everywhere. Another familiar voice beckoned behind him. Dripping with moisture from his pores, he turned his head around to see white, piercing eyes with black dilated pupils glaring at him. "Trevor, it's me, Sherman! Looks like we all found our new forever home."

Trevor was on the brink of a nervous breakdown. The daunting eyes of this Sherman must have lit a fire under Trevor's ass because he squirmed his way out the next small vent in his path. Below him was a hallway. The carpet was dark maroon, and there were several rooms. Each room was numbered, and in the middle of the hallway an antique ice machine collected more dust with termites scurrying underneath. Trevor was confused. The room he'd been locked in didn't resemble a hotel room, with not even a mint or a Bible to welcome his stay. *There was an NA textbook, and that was weird*, he thought. And he knew motels and low-rated hotels very well. Hell, he'd spent most of his addiction in and out of two-star motels in Detroit. But this hotel was of a different nature. It was empty and had an energy that seemed supernatural.

I've been here before, haven't I? Trevor thought. Something was oddly familiar, and it wasn't the smell of musty old linen and the moldy ceilings above him. He felt a sense of déjà vu, but he couldn't recall when or where he'd seen this place before.

Trevor dropped to the floor below. He advanced toward the end of the hallway. In the center was a broken elevator, and to its right, an emergency stairway. He flung the stairway door open and dashed to the bottom, finding one last door standing between him and freedom. But his only exit appeared to be stuck. He kicked and pushed, but all his efforts weren't budging the door at all. Suddenly, he heard those painstaking footsteps coming for him again. Only this time they were approaching at a much faster pace. Trevor gripped a little tighter and managed to budge the door open a smidgen. *The door was locked, you idiot,* he berated himself. He was in such a manic hurry that he hadn't even seen the dead bolt. Trevor couldn't help but laugh at himself when he wanted to cry as he realized he was heading outside for the first time in what seemed like weeks. But it had been mere hours.

The sun jarred his eyes, which had been accustomed to the dark. He slowly stepped out onto an abandoned deck camouflaged by algae and waste. Next to it was an empty pool brimming with dead leaves and a stagnant collection of trash. He trekked his way around, catching wet garbage that stuck to the soles of his shoes. His pulse rate was increasing. Mr. X had to be closing in. Trevor slapped his head to recoup motivation. He then bolted ahead and aggressively climbed the gate guarding the pool.

Beyond the gate he came across a trail of caterpillar-eaten leaves that led to a random garden that rested comfortably under the droopy branches of a shaggy, autumnal tree. He was baffled by how alive this garden appeared in the middle of September. A cluster of dwindling cosmos reared their purple heads alongside a band of saffron-hued primroses that covered the garden's front entrance. Rose bushes, assorted lilacs, rows of broccoli, cabbage, cauliflower, kohlrabi, and Brussels sprouts grew from renewed soil. This seemed very odd to Trevor. He couldn't imagine anyone coming by to tend a garden, and he didn't peg Mr. X as a horticulturalist. Even stranger were the crucifixes that were planted in the dirt next to the lilacs. They were made of carved sticks and had name tags tied to them with strings.

Trevor stood in amazement, distracted by the garden's beauty. By the time he realized he needed to keep his escape moving, it was too late. From out of nowhere, Trevor felt a sharp thud with blunt force to the back of his head from the strike of a garden hoe. "I surrender," Trevor muttered as he tripped over fallen twigs into a tangled thicket of roses and thorns.

Mr. X stood above him grasping the wooden garden hoe over his shoulder. "I know you surrender, Trevor, but why did you have to go and demolish my rose bush? You know how long that took to blossom? Ugh, I have a lot to teach you, son."

The villain gardener drove the hoe down into the soil next to Trevor's unconscious head.

Chapter 8
Jake the Snake and Bulko

2:00 a.m., Tuesday, September 22, 2020

Jake Johnson always held a special place in his heart for God and dogs. In fact, the two words were interchangeable when spelled backward. For Jake, they embodied unconditional love, and he needed some of that divine grace in his life right about now. Specifically, he needed God to help him find the lost dog he'd sold for crack and heroin.

He kept staring out the window of his foster-brother's truck, hoping he would see some sign of Bulko, his dog, roaming free, but he knew Bulko was being held captive. His foster-brother Jay R. had been trying to talk to Jake for the past few minutes, but Jake tuned him out the way a musician tunes out a guitar to a certain high pitch, drowning out all other noise. Jake was focused on a dog that he'd let down and how he planned to get him back. Small talk was of no importance.

The two brothers were leaving metro Detroit, traveling down Cadillac Street on a near-impossible mission. Jake rolled the passenger-side window down on his brother's Chevy pickup truck. He stuck his head out and felt a gust of the cool night air massage his face. The wet streets smelled crisp. There had been a light rain two hours earlier. Smog and the beaming ringlets of light smoldered in his cataract-impaired vision. He'd been meaning to see an optometrist to get an eye exam. Jake Johnson had been meaning to do a lot of things as of late.

"Man, put your head back inside, fool. You're like a damn dog with his tongue and head out the window." His brother Jay R. shook his head.

Jay R. was beginning to wonder if he should be embarrassed or worried about his little brother.

Jake brought his head back inside and rolled the window up. "That's because dogs are smart, bro, and they can sense everything when they stick their head out of windows."

"Oh yeah, and what did you sense out there?" Jay R. snickered.

Jake's eyes got bigger, fighting to expand out of their lids and staring right into his brother's soul. "I could sense God and His calling for me tonight. But I'm nervous, so I prayed." He looked away and back out the window.

"Jake the Snake is nervous? My young foster-brother from Detroit, who ripped the head off a garter snake in our parents' backyard and took the brutal ass-whooping of a lifetime is scared? But God has your back, cuzzo."

Jake had grown up in various foster homes during his adolescence. One of the homes was near the Cass Corridor area in Detroit, where he'd lived with Jay R. and four other African American foster-brothers. The husband and wife who'd fostered them were interested only in the checks the state would send them for having the boys in their home. But the only care Jake and Jay R. received was being told how black and ugly they were before their foster-daddy would beat them into submission. Although their foster-dad found the decapitated snake's head in the kitchen sink, Jake didn't deserve being flung down a flight of stairs and having a glass vase shattered over his head, leaving six stitches behind his ear and three under his eye.

"Yeah. Imagine that." Jake lit up his fifth menthol cigarette in the past hour as he thought about the look on his stupid foster-dad's face when he found the damn snake head next to all those dishes.

Jake was clothed in a black-and-white striped Adidas jacket and matching jogging pants. He always kept his hood up and down over his eyes. After a handful of his foster-dads had forced Jake to look them in their eyes as they violently abused him, he was no longer a fan of eye contact. But tonight, Jake needed to keep his eyes peeled.

Jay R. turned down Jay-Z and Eminem's "Renegade" on the Pandora hip-hop channel to a low hum. "So let me get this story straight," he said. "You found this blue nose, full-bred pit bull roaming the streets near

Woodward and Alexander. There was no collar, no way to identify the dog, so you decide to make him your sidekick. Then you think it's a good idea to take him back to that flophouse you be staying at with your White friends, Trevor and his crackhead girlfriend. What's her name again?"

"Mary, and she's more than just a crackhead. I mean, she is a crackhead, but much more than that." Jake leaned away from his brother. "You shouldn't be so judgmental, brother. Let he who is without—"

Jay R. snatched his brother's cigarette from his mouth. "Sin cast the first stone," he finished for him. "Yeah, I know the passage. And what's with all this reborn holier-than-thou shit you're trying to pull?"

"I'm not trying to pull anything. This is the new me. I tell you what, bro. I'm going to leave these streets behind. I got approved for treatment at the Felix Center. I go in for detox on Wednesday morning, and God as my witness, I'm never going to use heroin again." He grabbed a spare cigarette from behind his ear and lit it up.

"Okay, Mr. Recovery." Jay R.'s words dribbled sarcasm. "But from now until Wednesday, what are you going to do?"

"Well, I have to stay well. I can't detox until I go into the center, so I'm finna to maintain until I can go in."

"Ahem." Jay R. cleared his throat. "But I thought God had your back. And who's going to watch your dog if and when you do go into treatment? Don't ask me because I can't, bro."

Jake offered no response but instead said a silent prayer for God to watch over him that night. He prayed that his brother Jay R. and other non-believers would soon witness his faith come to light. "Forgive them, Father, for they know not what they say," he whispered to his savior, who he believed heard his words loud and triumphant.

Jay R. had noticed his brother was shutting down and acting stranger by the day. He missed the old Jake Johnson—the one he'd known before heroin had consumed him, before he got tied up with the junkie Bonnie and Clyde couple. He was just their third wheel.

Jake was an attractive man. He could have had any girl he wanted. Sure, Jake had had his fair share of random hookups on the streets, but he was leaving all that behind for Jesus. And he wasn't interested and didn't care what others thought of him. He kept to himself, staying close to his two best friends and his heroin.

Jake had mentioned God to Jay R. in the past, but this was the most intense religious preoccupation Jay R. had ever seen. Maybe it was just a honeymoon phase of wanting to get clean rather than an implementation of action. Jay R. wondered whether Jake was even telling him the truth about getting into a detox center on Wednesday or if his newfound relationship with Christ was just another smoke screen his addiction used as a weapon against his empathetic listeners.

Jay R. had digressed in his thoughts. "So back to what I was saying," he continued. "You're staying with Mary and her boyfriend, and no one there has any food or means to take care of a dog. After selling this dog that you found and traded for dope, now you decide you want to steal him back?"

"Yeah, God willing. That pretty much sums it up."

"Dog Protective Services would remove that dog from your custody and arrest you for being a dumbass." Jay R. laughed and lightly pushed on Jake's shoulder.

Jake didn't find anything funny about the situation. "Dog Protective Services can't arrest anyone."

Jay R. surveyed his brother up and down to see how serious he considered his last statement. *Doesn't he realize there isn't such a thing as Dog Protective Services?* he wondered. His brother's anxiety was clearly clouding his judgment. Jay R. sparked another flame, but not for another cigarette. He slowed the truck down to a subtle creep and lit up a brown Swisher Sweets blunt of Detroit's premium homegrown marijuana and passed it to Jake to calm his nerves.

"I mean, I messed up, Jay R. I had no money, and I sold Bulko to Anton's brother Andre. It was hard to turn down a gram of H for this mutt that I just found on the streets. But Bulko wasn't just any mutt. He means more than that to me." Jake hung his head in shame. "God put that dog in my life and tested me, and now I have to make things right. Andre is going to train that dog to fight and kill, and if Bulko doesn't fight, Andre will kill him. I need to stop that from happening."

Jay R. just looked at him, shaking his head. "Do you have any common sense? Now that your dope is gone is when you decide the dog is going to be harmed and you want him back? Are you a special kind of stupid? What is your master plan? Or God's plan?"

Jake shrugged and looked out the window. "I don't know, man. I'm not just going to go in there and ask for my dog back. That's why we're doing this in the middle of the night. I'm going to jump over the fence, find him, and free him. Then we're out of there."

"Wow, that easy, huh?" Jay R. rolled his eyes. "Alright, Jake. This is your funeral. I'll drop you off and park a few houses down. But the first sign of trouble or gunfire, and I'm out." Jay R. snatched his blunt back. Jake was taking too much time babysitting the expensive, hydroponic cannabis. "I probably shouldn't have even smoked with your ass. Because now you're going to be all clumsy and paranoid, and I don't think God would approve."

"No. Weed helps me focus, and God put it on Earth for a reason," Jake replied smugly. That was a lie. Weed made him crave dope, and he had no idea why God put weed on this planet.

"Hey, man. Take this and don't blow your own head off." Jay R. popped open the middle console, revealing a shiny, chrome Colt Mustang pistol that he tossed to Jake.

"What's this for?" Jake flinched but was able to safely catch the gun in his lap.

Jay R.'s Silverado came to a halt. "Protection. God isn't the only one who has your back tonight. Now get out of my ride and go handle your business."

Jake was dropped off on the corner of Sheldon Avenue and Market Street, on the south side of the city. The road was narrow, and all the houses seemed to be bound together, separated by only a matter of feet. Andre's house was pitch dark and quiet, and the driveway seemed void of any parked vehicles. However, the blue house next door, whose windows were covered with animal-print plastic sheets, seemed to be in complete chaos. A shouting match between tenants; noisy, uncontrollable barking dogs; and the sound of a glass shattering from the back porch caused someone to turn on a light on Andre's back porch. "Great," Jake muttered to himself.

Like a scared kid hiding from the recess bully, Jake jumped behind a tan trash bin overflowing with soiled diapers, plastic water bottles, and empty pizza boxes, praying no one saw him. Little by little, he peeked his head around the corner of the bin to take a closer look at Andre's house.

The dogs in Andre's backyard were now exchanging vicious barks with the neighbor's dogs.

Lowering his butt to the sidewalk, Jake had accepted the fact that he might have to wait awhile. Shaking, he lit up one last cigarette and tightly clutched the silver pistol in his right pocket. He imagined himself, shielded by a mere plastic trash bin, having a Western-style shootout with one of the neighbors. He wondered if Jay R. was still parked down the street waiting for him. A thick mist hovering over the moist street rose up in shadow-gray waves and shrouded the flickering streetlight above. Jake saw it as another sign from God, but it wasn't enough to diminish his fear.

Jay R.'s truck wasn't in sight. Then, at the worst possible time, Jake felt his cell vibrate inside his left pocket.

Jay R. had texted, *What are you waiting for, what's going on?*

I'm going in soon. Just wait please, Jake messaged back.

For a moment, there was no response. In the distance, Jake saw his brother's headlights flash on. The engine growled for a moment before shifting into drive, and Jay R. was gone. Jake couldn't believe his brother had left him. *Lord forgive him*, he thought, *for he knows not what he does.*

Seconds merged into minutes. The minutes felt like hours as Jake hunched behind the trash bin. Finally, the noise simmered down from both houses. He steadily crept with bent knees around the back of Andre's two-story brick home. Yellow caution signs, Beware of Dogs and Trespassers Will Be Shot on Sight, were posted all around the front yard, including on the tall, brown wooden fence that surrounded the backyard. He figured this was where Bulko was being held captive.

He scanned the premises, searching for a ledge or tree branch that he could use to propel himself over. A long hedge rested against the side of the house, but there was nothing sturdy enough to hold his weight. He gave himself a long running start and glided forward at magnificent speed. Reaching above, his hands gripped the spiked top of the fence. Sharp wooden slivers pierced through his flesh and felt like little daggers dancing under his skin.

Jake gasped. He managed to pull himself over the top and landed awkwardly on his kneecaps. Several dogs (mostly pit bulls and Rottweilers) furiously growled and yelped at the incoming intruder. A motion light switched on. Jake went to reach for his Colt Mustang but discovered that it must have fallen out of his pocket. Jake's face flushed and his whole body tingled as he rummaged through the grass. He searched until he felt the cold steel under his sweaty palms.

All the cages were occupied by either muscular, prize-fighting trophies or wounded and damaged pits. The fighting dogs barked with aggression as the weak and beaten whined in defeat. But there was no blue nose Bulko in sight. Then, from out of nowhere, a wet tongue slathered up the side of his face. Distinct silver and white streaks of fur brushed up against the top of his torn-up jeans. He knew the dog was Bulko when the animal started running in frantic circles around him.

"Come on, boy. Let's get you out of here," Jake whispered.

Noises had now emerged from the back porch. Jake could hear at least two men talking.

"Who the hell is out here? Andre! Someone is trying to break in!"

"Look! I see someone over there!" the other voice shouted.

Jake picked up Bulko, who must have weighed almost as much as him, and hopped on top of a cage. With all his strength, Jake tossed Bulko over the fence. The pup let out a short whimper but seemed to be intact on the other side. Jake braced himself to make his glide over to join him. But just then there was a loud banging noise. Before Jake had time to react, he felt the pressure of searing hot metal ripping through his right calf. In complete shock, he returned fire but was sure he didn't hit anything other than a window. He almost gave up. There was no way he was going to make the jump over the fence. But he remembered his prayer from earlier and asked for God's strength one more time.

Jake picked himself up, brushed off his shoulders and pulled out his gun once again. He yelled to Bulko, "Move baby!" Then he fired two rounds into the wooden fence. The impact from the blast had been enough to expand cracks in the wood. In a rush of adrenaline, he limped over to the two holes in the fence and kicked the weakened wood with his good leg. And one last kick created a gap big enough for him to escape through.

"Oh God, you're okay," Jake sighed with relief. He grabbed Bulko's face and pressed their noses together. Wet slobbers were exchanged. Jake embraced the dog with an everlasting hug. He didn't want to let him go. Addiction and selfishness had separated them, but Jake vowed to become a better human. He wanted to be the kind of person Bulko viewed him as. Bulko held no grudges. His love was unconditional, and Jake wanted to return that same kind of love.

Bulko hadn't caught any of the crossfire. So Jake grabbed his new best friend's collar and led him across the yard with a Keyser Söze limp, triggering more dogs to bark. Out of nowhere, Jay R. pulled up in his Silverado and motioned for Jake to get inside. Two of Andre's friends caught Jake jumping in the vehicle and fired a round into the truck's back fender.

"Man, you're crazy," Jay R. said as he peeled off, leaving the violent doghouse in the dust.

"I thought you left me, bro," Jake said.

"I did, but I came back because I knew they would probably kill you. And who else would smoke blunts with me and clean my truck out for me?"

"Thanks, man. And that was one time I cleaned your truck because I was trying to be nice. Don't take advantage of it." Jake laughed and brushed his cheek up to Bulko's partial mouth. Jake was stunned when he noticed the dog had lost a portion of his lip. He assumed it was another casualty of exploiting innocent dogs in a sport for money and blood. There was also a gash above Bulko's right ear that was soaked in wet blood. "Poor guy. I love you, Bulko. We're going to patch you up, buddy boy."

Bulko wagged his tail like an inverted pendulum in hyper speed. He raised his head and licked Jake's face. His tongue felt like a warm, damp velvet glove caressing Jake's skin.

"That's disgusting, man," Jay R laughed. He happened to look down and discovered blood seeping out of Jake's pant leg. "What the hell? You got shot?"

"Yeah, man, I'm fine. We can bandage both our wounds back at your place."

"Oh, yeah. Well maybe you should go to the ER first and get that checked out. You could bleed out."

"No hospitals. There's no time for that now. I have to take care of Bulko."

"And when did you become a doctor?" Jay R. asked.

Jake shrugged. "I watched a lot of movies and took a nursing course at a vocation rehab facility I went to as a youth." He'd spent the majority of his childhood in and out of foster homes, juvenile detention centers, and vocational treatment centers for troubled teens. Through all of his ventures, he'd managed to take a nursing course where he'd learned to bandage gunshot wounds.

5:30 p.m., Tuesday, September 22, 2020

Jake nestled comfortably on his foster-brother's couch playing *Call of Duty* on the Xbox One, baked to maximum capacity. He was beyond the standard brain-dead "I got the munchies" level of being high. No, Jake Johnson had entered the realm of a loud, boasting voice of God condemning him for his sin, then soft whispers that sounded like his friend Trevor. They were telling him to join Trevor at the hotel: "his new forever home."

Jake had an irrational suspicion that his brother Jay R. had laced the weed with fentanyl and was trying to kill him. That way, Jay R. could relish in the small batch of heroin Jake was waiting on to be delivered to him. But Jay R. didn't even use heroin. He sold it. This was why Jake knew he shouldn't have smoked. But after the maddening events of the previous night and the battle wound to his leg, he felt he'd earned it. Before he'd slept for over twelve hours on Jay R.'s couch, he'd doctored himself up by disinfecting and applying a tourniquet over the entry wound. Luckily, he was able to remove most of the bullet from inside the tissue.

Bulko was resting in his lap with fresh gauze and a bandage over his severed right ear. Jake made sure to apply enough antibiotic ointment to reduce the likelihood of infection. The two wounded soldiers were recovering and bonding when an old acquaintance knocked on the door. The loud thud startled Bulko, causing the hyperactive mutt to go haywire. Jake jumped up and peeked out the crooked blinds. There was a cherry-red Dodge Charger in the driveway. THUD! THUD! The knocks became louder and resembled the aggressive touch of police officers before they raid a home.

His dog's ears pointed up and he continued to jump around like he was in the middle of a canine mosh pit.

"Who's here?" Jake yelled through the door.

"I'm looking for Jake Johnson."

Jake almost recognized the voice. He grabbed his brother's pistol, which had been left out on the end table in the middle of the living room. He cocked the loaded rounds, aimed at the door as his target, and slowly twisted the knob with his free hand. When the door was opened, he saw standing on the front porch someone he hadn't seen in forever.

Ryan Dugan stood there with a blank expression on his face. He'd brought his own .38-caliber pistol but left it in the glove compartment of the Charger. At this point, he regretted not keeping it on his person.

"Well hello, Jake." Ryan's fear turned into a smile. He remembered when his brother met Jake when they both attended Marlin High School. And he knew Jake Johnson wasn't going to kill him because if he were, he'd already have done so. "Is this part of the welcoming committee or what?"

Jake relieved his finger from the trigger and put the gun in his pocket.

"Give me my gun back, dude!" Jake could hear Jay R. shout from inside. Jake took the gun out and tossed it back to his foster-brother as he approached the door. Jay R. peeked his head around Jake, trying to get a better view of the visitor. "Who's here? Is that Dion?" he asked. Dion was the runner sent to deliver the batch.

"No, it's not, Jay. Hold up a second!" Jake walked out the door and carefully shut it behind him. Bulko kept barking on the other side. "Quiet Bulko!" he yelled.

Jake didn't want his foster-brother to see some random Caucasian he didn't know on his front porch. "What do you want, Ryan? I almost killed you, man. What are you doing here?"

"I'm looking for Trevor," he replied.

"Well, he isn't here. We don't live here anymore. And how did you find this place, anyway?"

"I sent a check here a while back to Trevor at this address." Ryan stepped back and took a long gander at Trevor's old home.

"Well, he isn't here, and I have to go back inside. I'm waiting on someone actually important, so have a good night." Jake turned to go back in.

"Wait, Jake. This is really important. I need to find him. If you help me find him, I can give you a hundred dollars."

"Hmmm … Make it two hundred." Jake's response was impulsive, almost beyond his control. Money equals drugs. Tunnel vision. *God will forgive,* he thought. He had to stay well until Wednesday.

"Only if you take me to him."

Jake looked at him with a ridiculous grimace. He turned back around to peek at Jay R.'s house. Was he really about to leave with Trevor's worst enemy to go find his friend? However, Dion was bringing back only half a gram, which didn't quite equate to the one and a half grams he could buy with Ryan's money.

Jake shrugged in agreement. "Alright, but you're driving! Oh and one more thing: my dog gets to come." He opened the front door to let his blue nose pit outside. "Go drain your whistle, buddy."

Bulko found an oak tree to relieve himself on. Then the injured mutt waddled his way over to Ryan. He kicked up some dirt and sniffed the strange man. "It's okay, Bulko," Jake said. "He's alright after all."

Ryan looked back at his freshly detailed Dodge Charger with jet-black leather interior. When he turned back around. Jake's dog jumped up and scraped his muddy claws on Ryan's green-and-white MSU Spartans jacket. *Oh hell no!* He screamed inside his head. *There's no way. I can't let the mutt inside my baby to tear it all up.*

Ryan looked down at the battered canine. A sad frown upon Bulko's face and a high-pitched whimper was all it took to rub that soft spot Ryan had developed in his sobriety. "Alright. Whatever, man. Get in." Ryan submitted against his better judgment and drove off with Jake and his dog to find Trevor.

Jake sat in the back with Bulko and smiled at Ryan in the front seat. "I think God brought you to my brother's house for a reason, Ryan Dugan."

Ryan chuckled and asked, "What's that? To give you two hundred dollars after we find him?"

"To repent."

Chapter 9
The Inventory

Trevor was nine years old the first time the shadow revealed itself in true form. It was in a dream buried deep in his subconscious.

Fourteen years later, when Trevor was twenty-three, the nightmare decided to resurface. A static white light beamed around all the crevices surrounding the pitch-black rectangle formerly known as his closet door. The cosmic bright glow forced the door open, spitting out a small rainbow-colored box that rolled to the corner of his bed like a die in a game of craps.

Trevor heard a rumbling thud that vibrated the joints under the floor. The distressed juvenile buried his head under his *Batman Beyond* wool blanket, but the light continued to blind his eyes. Suddenly, the brightness disintegrated and the air grew arctic cold. Young Trevor could see his breath.

He lifted his head from under the covers and saw the silhouette of a lofty, gaunt creature. White, pinhead-sized pupils gawked at the young boy trembling under his covers. Long, spear-shaped fingernails grew like a fungus rising up from slender hands.

Trevor slowly reached over to his nightstand and switched on the lamp. The creature recoiled and rushed back into the darkness of the closet. But it had been visible long enough for Trevor to see it wasn't a vile monster after all. It was just a withered, naked old man with pasty-white skin. His gray hair was ragged and twisted in reef knots. The crazed man appeared more frightened of Trevor than Trevor was of him.

7:00 p.m., Tuesday, September 22, 2020

After being knocked out, Trevor rose from his slumber, startled and confused, in a dark, new habitat. He was no longer in hotel room 202 upstairs. After his last stint of trying to escape, he'd found himself handcuffed to a metal pole and his feet firmly chained to massive concrete blocks. In the pitch dark, he had difficulty discerning his whereabouts, but his ears could hear the sounds of water dripping and chirping squeaks from the burning furnace. There were pipes creaking and the slow vibrating echoes calling out names too faint to hear. The sounds and smells hinted that he was in some type of basement or cellar.

A shred of light emanated from an unseen source. He looked down on the dirty concrete floor and gazed upon his own haunting sidekick, the shadow. At first, his shadow appeared to be casually stalking him again like prey. But after looking closer through the slim light, Trevor could see that the silhouette was up to something far more sinister.

Carrying some type of sharp dagger, the shadow lunged at Trevor, striking him in the chest. Trevor could feel the cold steel pierce his rapidly beating heart. But instead of feeling pain or death, he was in a state of euphoria. A polar opposite effect of what was to be expected, it was the most pleasure he'd ever felt in his entire life. *What kind of dark magic is this?* he wondered.

The high was only temporary, and Trevor could now feel the penetrating aftermath of his stab wounds. He held his chest as it bled profusely, blood streaming down his white shirt. As the pain escalated, Trevor peeked down and witnessed the shadow's knife repeatedly slicing through his heart. And then it was gone …

Trevor sat in silence for several minutes until his abductor returned, looming over him, diminishing any glimmer of light. Mr. X examined Trevor carefully and grew disgusted by the pathetic display of a human.

He knelt down next to Trevor while the young man gritted his teeth and sweat seeped from the pores of his forehead. The abductor leaned extremely close, pushing his burlap mask so close that Trevor could feel his breath wading through the thick, woven fabric. The soft hair on the back of the scared young man's neck stood at attention.

"Let me die already. Just get it over with," he begged the man.

Mr. X didn't respond to Trevor's groveling. Instead, he removed the burlap sack from over his head and threw it down on the cellar floor.

"Finally!" Mr. X exclaimed, getting to his feet. "That thing was too hot. I've been trying to figure out how to get the air to work in this place, but I can't. Probably because it hasn't been turned on in almost fifty years." The man paced around the cellar, panting and wiping sweat from his eyes.

The reflection of the slim light against the basement floor provided a semi-clear view of his captor. There was now a face to the man responsible for Trevor's torture. Trevor wanted to viciously rip off the man's flesh. But there was something distinctly familiar about his features, from his chiseled jawline to his dimpled cheekbones. The wrinkles over his eyes and fading gray hair that implied old age put to rest some of Trevor's rage. He wasn't dealing with a young monster. He'd been abducted by a pathetic, older, middle-aged man who looked familiar and happened to be jacked up on steroids.

Trevor took a deep breath and begged one more time. "Please kill me or find me an opiate. I don't care if it's oxy, morphine, fentanyl, or heroin." The urges transcended from detoxification to pure demonic possession. Trevor didn't know how long it had been since his last taste of heroin, but it had to be over a day. It seemed like eternity. He was so desperate for just one hit, one taste, one shot to get him moving.

The old man put his hands behind his back and walked in circles around the handcuffed hostage. "Let me ask you a question, Trevor. Who are you?"

Trevor paused to answer. His whole life he'd felt incapable of grasping his own identity. He saw himself as a seeker of truth, while others viewed him as an eccentric conspiracy theorist who was homeless and hooked on smack.

After his father left, Trevor had devoted his entire sanity to trying to figure out why. Something had happened after his dad abandoned him—something that devoured Trevor's soul the same way a stray dog devours meat off a bone and leaves it on the street. Trevor was consumed by Bill's absence, then he left home to eat scraps off the street. And the heroin was just his medicine to keep him going, to keep him eating off those streets.

Although Trevor was homeless and hooked on smack, he had incredible insight into the world. His conspiracies may have been delusional, but he revered himself as a junkie prodigy. After all, the greatest geniuses had their vices. Neurologist Freud had his cocaine, astronomer Carl Sagan was addicted to pot, and Bill Gates admitted to enjoying LSD and *Playboy* magazine. So naturally "woke artist, seeker of truth" Trevor Dugan had a tiny problem with the heroin that he was physically, emotionally, and mentally dependent on. But he still didn't know how to honestly answer the man's question.

The impact of Trevor's silence on the old man was visible. "You aren't getting out of this that easy," Mr. X growled. "No, you need to face your demons. It's the only pure detox that will haunt your soul and make you never want to pick up that poison again."

Mr. X was cruel, but he made sense. If Trevor ever wanted to get clean and stay clean, this experience had to be the most horrific and painful experience in his entire life.

"I'm not here to kill you, Trevor. I'm here to save you from yourself. But I need you here alive. No more running or trying to escape. Next time, I won't be so nice, and I'll nail you to the goddamn chair. You won't die, but you'll wish you were dead."

"Why do you care so much if I live or die or stay clean? And why am I in an abandoned hotel?" Trevor wanted to rip himself free from bondage and bite this asshole's face off.

"And we'll get to all of those answers. First of all, you can continue to call me Mr. X. I know that's what you've been calling me in that doped-up brain of yours. My real name is of no concern to you right now."

The man's carved chin glistened in the speck of light that snuck in, hiding somewhere beyond the dark of the basement. Trevor couldn't see the source, but he knew it was there. He hoped it would lead outside, away from this monster who apparently could now read minds.

Mr. X appeared to be in his mid-fifties. Not exactly old, but he was ancient in Trevor's eyes. He was slightly balding. He pulled out a pair of black-rimmed reading glasses that, when placed on his nose, appeared to enlarge his heavy, brown eyes through the thick lenses. Despite the nerdy glasses, Mr. X was built like a brick house and poured intimidation into the room.

"We're in a hotel right now because it was the only available location for your detox. It's completely off the grid, and no one will find you here. I demolished your cell phone, so don't worry about that. Besides, it was rotting your mind, and all of your old contacts, dealers, and associates were in that phone, Trevor. We need to find new people, places, and things to support your recovery."

"Like who?" Trevor couldn't believe what he was hearing. "Are you going to be my new support system? My sponsor? We're getting off to a great start. I imagine you kidnap and beat all the addicts you try to save." Trevor grimaced. He had no interest in whatever cult of recovery this psychopath was involved in.

"Why yes! This is where it all begins. We need to start the process of surrender. You have absolutely no control, but you do have a choice." Mr. X reminded Trevor of a motivational speaker with terrible prison tattoos who'd come to his high school seven years before. That man had been the epitome of "I used to be a drug addict, and now I'm here to scare you straight."

"What choice do I have right now?" Trevor asked as he tugged on his handcuffs, demonstrating the lack of apparent options.

"You can both participate in your recovery and enjoy the beginning of your new life, or you can fight this beautiful gift and sit there and rot. The choice is yours, I don't care either way. If you play along and try something new, then I'll make sure you're fed and have fresh water until it's time for you to go. If you make the other choice, you'll sit there tied up until you die of starvation and regret your miserable life."

Mr. X made quite a convincing case, but Trevor wasn't ready to surrender. He had some fight left in him even if it meant being treated like a dog, teased with fresh water and food scraps. He had almost changed his mind, but after deep contemplation, the actions didn't seem worth the rewards. This man wasn't to be trusted. The only option to live was to survive, and to survive was to escape.

He surveyed the room, searching through the speck of light for any possible weapon or means of killing this man. But there was nothing. So Trevor responded to Mr. X's ultimatum by building up a wad of phlegm from the back of his throat and hocking it in his direction, missing by mere inches.

Mr. X snorted, shook his head, and slowly walked up the cellar staircase. He hesitated in hopes that maybe Trevor would have a change of heart. From the top of the staircase he shouted down, "Have fun waiting to die!"

The cellar was now completely black. The light vanished in unison with his captor. *So what's our next move?* Trevor thought. His first impulse was to try to find a wire or something tiny and sharp to pick the locks to his handcuffs and chains. However, the absence of light made that task difficult. "Fuck it!" he screamed out, and he trudged ahead with all of his force. *I'm going to tear this metal pole down and use that cinder block to break the chain binding my feet.* He tried over and over again. But the pole held sturdy and didn't move an inch. He now homed in on the handcuffs. Roughing up the metal, he tried hard to squeeze his big hands out of the small steel cuffs. He thought that if he could get all the dirt on his hands to absorb the oil from the metal, it could help get the chains to bind up, but there was no friction. With his hands cuffed behind him, his struggle was only making his wrists bleed. But it wasn't enough to make him surrender. He wondered if his blood and the metal's oil could mix together to lubricate his escape.

Trevor sat in chains, bound. He thought about all of his options, none of which were pleasant. He placed bets in his mind about which would come first: starvation, dying of thirst, bleeding out at his wrists, or losing all touch with reality. Maybe he could just play along with this fool's "recovery program" long enough to get some food and water.

Taking in one last breath, Trevor hollered upstairs, "I give in! Help me! I'm ready for recovery!"

Mr. X's footsteps treaded down the stairs, one by one. He was surprised when he hit the squeaky stair in the center of the staircase that he'd forgotten about. But he expected that Trevor would change his mind.

A bright light switched on from the ceiling above. It blinded Trevor, as he'd adapted so well to the darkness. The new light revealed remnants of discarded furniture, loads of rusted scrap metal, and an old refrigerator. Mr. X pushed a broken air conditioner aside and stepped into the light under the ceiling bulb. The shadow of his bulk shrouded Trevor once again.

"I'm so glad you changed your mind. I had a feeling you would. So let's begin, shall we?" Mr. X strutted over to Trevor, pulled his fist back and planted it square into Trevor's nose. "Lesson one: change is painful and uncomfortable but so worth it! You're going to thank me someday for this."

The beating wasn't over. He jumped forward and kicked Trevor viciously in the abdomen. The pain was abrupt, sharp, and sudden. Out of instinct, Trevor's muscles tightened but added little shield for protection. He could feel the blow rise up and cause a temporary moment of paralysis. He'd had his fair share of beatings from elementary school all the way to graduating to the rough streets of Detroit, but this one kick to his guts put them all to shame. He quivered and begged for the attack to stop.

"Physical pain," Mr. X said. "Blunt trauma is nothing compared to the emotional and spiritual trauma you've inflicted upon yourself and others, Trevor."

"Fuck you. Can I just go back to dying in peace? I changed my mind over here." Frothy, blood-streaked phlegm crawled out from the corners of Trevor's mouth.

"Too late for that, son. Those wounds on your wrist look pretty severe. And your nose is bleeding out." Mr. X reached into his back pocket and pulled out a washcloth and alcohol pads.

The sting was ferocious, but Trevor could feel the alcohol cleanse once the burn subsided. Mr. X wiped the sides of his mouth, and Trevor spat up the remaining blood from the back of his throat.

"Yeah, that bleeding isn't going to just stop on its own," Mr. X said. He got up, moved over to a wooden work table, and grabbed a pair of black shears, some alcohol pads, and a white bandage roll from one of the cupboards underneath. He returned, then bent down and put a gauze around the base of Trevor's nose, applying pressure. "The first step is to admit you're powerless. Are you powerless, Trevor?"

"Yes." Trevor was dry heaving and gasping from having his lungs caved in.

"I can't hear you! I want you to say it." Mr. X squeezed Trevor's nostrils together.

"Yes, I am powerless." Trevor winced in pain, squealing at a high pitch.

"There, your nose isn't broke. The bleeding is stopping already." Mr. X stuffed the remaining gauze into Trevor's cartilage. "So if you realize that you're powerless, can you admit that you can't do this alone? Your own willpower isn't going to save your life, Trevor." Then Mr. X moved his attention to Trevor's wrists, pushing the handcuffs up and gently lathering his skin with alcohol.

The pressure stung but the burn was welcome. "Yes, I need help," Trevor admitted. "But I'm not sure if your idea of helping someone is holding them captive, beating the shit out of them, and psychologically torturing them."

Mr. X threw his hands up, feeling defeated from trying to emphasize his point. "You did this to yourself. Can't you see that? I'm here trying to help you. These past few years, you've been holding yourself hostage to this fucking poison and torturing yourself. It's time to free yourself from that. You have your whole life ahead of you."

"Okay, so who's supposed to help me if I can't even help myself? You? Ha! Give me a break." Trevor's expression went bleak. He felt like this intervention was going nowhere.

"I can only help you so far. You need to find that something else within you." Mr. X unraveled the bandage roll, cut nearly two-foot lengths for each wrist, and started wrapping Trevor's hands like a Christmas gift to himself.

"I thought you said I couldn't help myself." Trevor furrowed his brow.

Mr. X wrapped the last sheet of bandage over Trevor's wrist. Then he reached into his cigarette pack and grabbed another menthol. "Your own willpower, Trevor, is your worst enemy. There's a spiritual side to you, a power greater than you that lives in all of us that's going to see you through this mess." He stuck a Newport in Trevor's mouth and swayed his lighter back and forth until the flame connected with the tip.

"So you're a religious nut?" Trevor laughed. He'd seen this coming. He'd found that most religious people will hold you hostage if you talk to them long enough. "I don't believe in God." Trevor cringed at the idea of a higher power controlling his life.

Mr. X smirked, expecting Trevor would respond that way. "A thank-you for the damn cigarette would be nice!"

"Thank you, but I still don't believe in God. He didn't give me that cigarette that I needed. You did," Trevor replied with a smirk.

"I know you don't believe in God, but you better find Him now. Find meaning within the suffering. Without a purpose, we only serve ourselves."

"Self-service is the only reliable source of truth anymore, Mr. X. There's no magical man to take all this pain away from us."

"That's bullshit, Trevor! You depend on heroin to take all your problems away. Try depending on something that may actually save your life."

Trevor didn't believe in any type of higher power. Religion hadn't worked on him when he was forced into the church by his parents. And he would be damned if this whack job was going to save his soul. Was he supposed to let Jesus take the wheel and heal his wounds of addiction? He didn't believe in something he couldn't see. There was no evidence to back up religion besides the ranting of hypocritical fanatics. Heroin was tangible, something he could touch and embrace. He could feel all its euphoria and destruction. In Trevor's eyes, the Bible was a book of fairy tales designed to instill fear into the hearts of man. A poisonous manifesto from a false God used to judge and condemn anyone who dared bask in life's indulgences.

"You don't believe in God because you can't see Him, but you believe in all those whacky conspiracy theories that have never been proven legit." A thin layer of smoke trailed upward from Mr. X's lit cigarette, expanding into the ceiling rafters like a genie escaping a bottle.

Trevor's face went blank. "No, I've seen evidence." He was caught off guard by Mr. X's comment. "Government overreach is everywhere. It starts with public panic. The government controls the media. And the media control the sheep, who comply. The proof is beyond the current pandemic, and both sides are being played. Politicians are puppets, trying to push a mandated vaccine. A vaccine that is traced with a microchip that will grant access to goods, purchases, public areas, and bank accounts. Google Pay and scan cards on smartphones are already taking the place of money. Businesses suddenly have coin shortages and are refusing to accept cash. The chess table has been set up, and the queen is taking out all the pawns."

Mr. X kept watching his cigarette's smoke ascend into the ceiling as if he weren't even listening to the young man's political ramblings. "And Trevor, what's a good source for all that conspiracy you just spewed at me? YouTube?"

"No," he replied.

"Revelations, Trevor, is in that imaginary book you believe is made up. But you're so naïve, you blindly follow any link or podcast that aligns with your agenda, Trevor. It's no different than the so-called sheeple who follow mainstream media. We all have to follow something, Trevor. Even leaders have someone's trail in their sight. Why not follow God, who offers you salvation and light?"

Trevor's chest was starting to cave, his breathing sped up.

"You seem pretty worked up and anxious." Mr. X changed his tone. "Let's take a step back. I say we start the process with a mindfulness exercise." He sat down, crossed his legs, and put his hand on his chest.

"Mindfulness? What the hell are we doing here? Meditation?" Trevor cringed at the thought of cliché psychological, holistic bullshit. His mom had tried to force him into therapy after his dad left. He'd dumped coffee on the counselor's floor and was asked not to come back.

"Yes. Mindfulness, Trevor. A little trick I learned in prison. You need to stop judging yourself over the past and worrying about the future. Time is non-linear, and all we have is this moment."

Trevor arched his eyebrows and creased his forehead in irritation. "I'm tied up to a damn chair. That's my present moment."

The old man closed his eyes and resembled a jacked-up, tattooed sensei preparing to pray before he murdered someone. "That's the external world, Trevor. Focus and breathe into the internal world. Expand your chest out." The sensei inhaled a long, deep breath of wet basement air like a cool glass of water. "And out like a parachute. Woo!" Mr. X respired a faint, moist fog. "Slow your mind and observe your thoughts. Don't judge them, try not to fight or change them, just watch them grow and manifest. Remain neutral whether your thoughts are good or bad, for that's irrelevant right now. In this precious moment they just are ..."

Trevor's mind meandered off. He tried to imagine anything but his current reality of detoxing on the verge of death next to a spiritual guru on steroids. He truly believed he was going to die. And he couldn't shake the thought. There was nothing precious about dying. But beyond the fear of death, deep in the black hole of his mind, Trevor caught a glimpse of something else: a scared little boy. And the boy was playing with a multi-colored Rubik's Cube. Standing over the child was that glaring shadow. Trevor knew now that the shadow was just an old, frail man. He saw him with his own two eyes, but the skinny, weak man's shadow was much bigger now, almost as tall as a monster. He lurked over the boy and opened his mammoth jaws, ready to devour.

Trevor ran from the shadowy beast and jumped into a dark void. He felt like he was falling for eternity. Without warning, he landed smack dab on a glass floor. Unexpectedly, the glass didn't break. He looked through the glass and saw the abandoned house on the other side. When he looked closer, it resembled more of a hotel on top of a hill. It was surrounded with dead grass and tumbleweed. A narrow dirt road led right up to its door. *Is this where I am?* Trevor wondered. He winced and tried to get a closer look, but he heard a loud clap. The meditation came to an abrupt end.

"What did you think?" Mr. X asked.

Trevor took a moment to regain focus. "I think that this is all parlor tricks to groom me into Stockholm syndrome. A sick little game to play before you kill me." He didn't dare tell him about the shadow and the hotel on the hill. Trevor could feel another energy in the room. Nothing appeared in physical form, but he could feel an invisible illumination hovering in that basement between the two of them. A higher power.

The old man laughed at his response. "That's good, Trevor. Parlor tricks."

Trevor felt like his heart was dropping. Floodgates of past nightmares and visions of the shadow came pouring into his head. "I'm not laughing." His feverish tone aligned with his statement.

"Let me ask you, Trevor. You studied Carl Jung?" Mr. X didn't wait for an answer. "Carl Jung used a form of unorthodox therapy in his sessions with patients. He believed the true path to change was through confrontation, not submission. That confrontation took a metaphysical form of a shadow. And yes, I know you see your shadow when you close your eyes at night."

"Yeah, Carl Jung was a genius. You've done your research on me. Congratulations." Trevor would have fake clapped if his hands weren't bound. "And I don't know anything about this shadow figure you're talking about."

"You don't have to lie, Trevor. I know a lot more about you than just that. I know that other than psychology and conspiracy, you were a huge science nerd, obsessed with time travel, life on other planets, and Einstein's theory of relativity. You were an excellent writer at one time and always loved to write about supervillains."

This old man knows too much, Trevor thought.

"You had so many demons in your closet. I saw it with my own eyes. They're all here for you to face."

"Okay, this is some kind of sick joke. You must have talked to my mom or my brother, and they put you up to this as some kind of paid intervention to get me off drugs. Okay guys, your message is heard loud and clear. Come on out now!" Trevor screamed out, but no one answered.

Obviously, he didn't really expect his family to come running down the steps to put an end to this horrible intervention. But in this moment he needed some sign of hope to hold on to and get him through this hell. Oh God, how he would have loved for his mother to walk down those steps, shoot the old man in the chest, and save her beloved son. She could take him back home and make him a grilled cheese sandwich, and he would never return to heroin or Detroit again. His lesson had been learned.

Mr. X looked behind him and in all directions, shrugging his shoulders. "Doesn't look like they're here, Trevor."

Trevor stifled tears he wanted to drown in but didn't dare. He'd never felt so powerless in his life.

"Your demons are here though, Trevor, and we're going to check them out," Mr. X informed him. Trevor started to hear a buzzing sound from behind his eardrums, followed by a brief humming. Mr. X kept talking, his lips kept moving, but Trevor couldn't hear the words coming out of his mouth.

The humming ended and sound returned. "I'm starving and thirsty. You promised me food," Trevor said. The grilled cheese sandwich the man had offered had been devoured by the rodent. Trevor was going on forty-eight hours without any food. The stomachaches had turned into shallow growls, craving anything edible.

The old man veered his eyes up to the ceiling. He appeared deep in thought, but his cruel smile suggested otherwise. "I apologize. What kind of host am I? I did promise you food if you were a good boy even though you spat in my face. There really isn't a full kitchen in this place. Let me see what I can find."

"Great. You don't even know if any food is here?" The growls got heavier and Trevor's aches were sharper.

Mr. X walked to the other side of the basement to a near-empty pantry. Using a small, pointy flashlight, he dug around some of the old cupboards, searching for something to feed his starving hostage. Most of the shelves were vacant and coated with dust. But he managed to salvage a rusty old fork and a can of tuna fish. Mr. X knew that canned tuna usually has a shelf life of between three and five years. But he figured that if the kid was hungry enough, he would eat it. The tarnished blue StarKist can, with the funny blue fish wearing glasses on the logo, was covered in a sandy grime.

"Squatters and the homeless have been known to occupy this space from time to time," Mr. X said. "Or so I've heard. I'm sure this tuna is good." Mr. X went farther beyond Trevor's line of vision. Trevor heard in the distance a faucet squeak, followed by that familiar gurgling sound. The sink at The Hood Pack Mansion made the same exact noise. But right now, hearing the sound of running water damn near gave him an erection.

The old man returned with a dirty glass he'd recovered from the pantry. He put the water up to Trevor's mouth and told him gently, "Slow now, drink it slow." Trevor couldn't listen; he gulped too fast, and the overflow of water streamed down his face and puddled into the top of his shirt. Next, Mr. X pulled out the can of four-eyed blue-fish tuna and stabbed it with a small Swiss army knife from a satchel hidden under his belt buckle. Trevor devoured the tuna like he hadn't eaten in months, even though it had only been a couple of days. The old man patiently fork-fed him until the tuna was extinct.

Mr. X was growing tired of the pre-game show. The main event was coming. "Okay! It's time to face your past. Are you ready?" He took out a key and unlocked Trevor's handcuffs and the chain lock around his leg. Surprised, Trevor felt a momentary relief from his flesh no longer being ground against the metal. The joy soon ended, though, as his captor pointed his cold pistol against Trevor's throbbing temple. "Don't take advantage of my kindness this time. I'll have no hesitation blowing your pretty little head off if you try to run. But if you're a good boy, I can promise you there is freedom on the other side of this huge step." Mr. X raised his palm to Trevor in an upward direction.

"Freedom. You're going to let me go?"

Mr. X shuffled his feet, ignoring the question. "Your demons are upstairs waiting for you!"

Side by side, Trevor and the old man walked upstairs, breathing in the dusty fumes of the ancient hotel. Mr. X led Trevor out a stairwell on the other side of the hotel. They entered a new hallway that was slightly less presentable than the one Trevor had tried to escape from earlier. The carpet was still maroon but tainted with blotches of spilled blood and cheap carpet shampoo that someone had tried to use to remove the stains. The tacky paintings of lighthouses and beaches that hung crooked on the white walls were offset with mounted poster boards displaying cliché recovery slogans like *Sober for Today* and *Keep It Simple, Savage.*

Mr. X used the barrel of his gun to guide Trevor in the direction of the first room, or the first page in Trevor's inventory. Trevor hesitated, as he had no idea what was on the other side of the door.

"Go ahead, Trevor. Don't think about it. Just do it." Mr. X gently pushed him through the door with the back of his gun.

When Trevor entered, the space didn't look like an abandoned guest room in a deserted hotel. Instead, the room seemed to transport Trevor and Mr. X into a memory, almost like time travel. Trevor had given up trying to make sense of all of this. He knew this was beyond a microchip being planted inside him, and he feared it was only going to get worse.

First, he recognized a very familiar twin-size bed that was made perfectly with thin, rumpled Batman sheets, a cotton blanket, and a Transformers pillow that didn't match the rest of the bedding but fit flawlessly in a young boy's eyes. Action figures from both DC and Marvel comics were strategically positioned for battle on opposite shelves on the wall. DC figures—like Batman, Joker, Two-Face, Brainiac, and Harley Quinn—

were propped on the shelf on the right wall, while Marvel figures—like Thanos, Hulk, Wolverine, Carnage, and Venom—were gracefully lined up on the left wall's shelf. Timeless villains—with the exception of a few anti-heroes, like Batman and Wolverine—were the true inspiration for the troubled youth who lived in this room.

Present-day Trevor stood in the back corner of his old bedroom watching his younger self. He was only six years old then, and he distinctly remembered living in that house on Crestshire Boulevard outside Grand Rapids, Michigan. His parents had moved the family there for a couple years while Bill transitioned jobs from local law enforcement to the Drug Enforcement Administration before he ended up with Homeland Security. Trevor looked over past his bed and saw his goldfish, Eddie, still alive in his transparent, bubble-shaped bowl. Seeing Eddie alive narrowed down the timeline of his memory. Trevor called to mind the time he forgot to clean Eddie's bowl and accidentally overfed him. So his fish was abracadabra gone, and he remembered the stern whooping he got from Bill for not taking care of something that was his responsibility.

"Is this my demon, old man? Eddie the fish that I let die has come back to haunt me?"

"No, you were an idiot for Eddie. But look back over at the bed again."

Trevor gazed back at the babysitter, Megan McDaniel, lying in overtly provocative form, considering she was invading a six-year-old boy's bedroom. She was sixteen, and this was the first and last time his parents hired her to babysit. The regular sitter, Kelly Grosse, had called in, reporting symptoms of intoxication and bad decisions with a case of older boys hollering her name in the background of the phone call. But Megan McDaniel was ready to work, and she was the epitome of every young boy's fantasy babysitter. She'd left that part out of her ad in the paper. Bill had acted suspiciously interested and specifically sought her out.

Trevor could imagine why he would have been so interested. She had ocean-side blue eyes that looked at Trevor in a way no adult ever had before. Her bright, golden hair hung past her shoulders like a lion's mane. He didn't remember exactly what she wore, but he did recall that it wasn't much. Young Trevor's face had flushed and the pit in his stomach had flared up.

The date in time was Sunday, June 3, 2003. It was around seven in the evening. Ryan was at basketball camp, and their parents had gone out of town to visit friends from Bill's work. Oh, how Trevor wished they'd never left him alone with this sixteen-year-old perverted narcissist.

"What are you doing in my bed? It's my bedtime?" a six-year-old memory of Trevor asked.

"I know it's your bedtime, silly. But I wanted to play a little game." Megan sat up and leaned toward the young boy.

"Sure, I like games." Young Trevor became ecstatic. Games and a reason to stay up late called for such excitement.

"Okay. The name of the game is "I will show you mine, if you show me yours." So I'll go first." Megan lifted her sweatshirt over her head and exposed her lacy black bra.

Young Trevor's cheeks were blushed. The little boy turned away, as he'd been taught by his mother that "female body parts are bad until you're an adult and ready to make babies." She'd told him, "Just focus on school and being a good boy." His mother used to preach to him at night sometimes when he would ask questions about the magazines he and his brother used to find hidden in their dad's closet. Oh how he wished his mama had been there with him to make all of this go away. A frightened Trevor put his hands over his eyes.

"It's okay, Trevor. You can look." Megan pulled the bra off. Trevor uncovered his eyes and stared at her small, round bosoms. She was underdeveloped, but they were still the first pair of tits he'd ever laid eyes on. "You like that?" she asked, as she bit her lip and smiled. "Now it's your turn, Trevor. I want to see what you have underneath your pajamas."

Trevor was wearing his green Teenage Mutant Ninja Turtle pajama set. At this moment in time, he wished he were the ninja turtle Michelangelo so he could smack her head off with his nunchuck. "Wait. What?" Trevor was confused. What could she be referring to?

"I want to see your pee-pee, Trevor. What you use to go to the bathroom. This is how the game works. You don't have to play, but if you don't, I'll win." Megan remembered Bill telling her that if they played board games to always let Trevor win. He was a horrible loser. Bill also told her that the boy's favorite games were Battleship and Operation. "It's kind of like Operation, Trevor. I need to inspect you to make sure you're okay down there."

Young Trevor meekly laughed but trembled. All he wanted to do was run away. "This game isn't fun anymore. I don't want to play." He pouted and wanted to cry. But he choked back the tears. Even at six, he was already trained to suppress any sign of vulnerability.

Megan crossed her legs and uncrossed them like a trained gymnast, almost in one swift motion. "Oh, poor Trevor. Do you think Mommy and Daddy are coming to save you? They're gone all night, and I can call them right now. I can tell them how naughty you are. And I know your dad can be angry and hurt you. He will hurt you over the littlest things, won't he? I can tell him that you forced me to show you my bra so you could brag to all your little first-grade friends. Who do you think they're going to believe, Trevor? Now, do as I say and drop your pajamas." Her tone converted from soft to authoritative.

Grown-up Trevor couldn't bear witness to the shitshow any longer. He didn't care if the old man blew his brains out. Forcing back tears, Trevor made a break for the door and dived into the hotel hallway. He cried hysterically into his elbow, trying to shove the pain back inside. But he couldn't keep the hurt in any longer. The pain flowed out, along with the tears, cries, anger, and cursing. "Fuck you!" he yelled at Mr. X. Trevor didn't want to see what happened. This was a hidden memory that he thought he'd buried inside and would never see again.

The old man didn't shoot Trevor. Instead, he stepped into the hallway and picked Trevor up.

"Why are you doing this? Stirring up old trauma? It hurts!" Trevor sobbed into Mr. X's arms while beating his fist on the man's chest.

"It's okay, Trevor. Let it out. Let it out. Let the healing begin." Mr. X patted Trevor on the head, offering comfort and solace. "But you have to go back in. There's something in there that you've tried to forget. You shoved it down into your subconscious, but you must face it now."

"I can't." Trevor used his elbow to wipe the snot dripping from his nose.

The old man pointed his gun back in the direction of the little boy's bedroom.

Sniveling and wiping his eyes, Trevor stumbled back inside the room and back into his childhood home. His younger self ran right through him, and the wicked babysitter tailed him. Little Trevor knocked over a fake plant in the hallway to block her path.

Megan hopped over it and laughed. "Where do you think you're going? I just wanted to play a little game, Trevor."

The boy stormed through the kitchen, knocking over chairs and almost tripping over the old family dog's twenty-pound bag of Purina Dog Chow on his way to the basement door. Megan stalked behind like a slow serial killer in a B-rated slasher flick, toying with her prey. She grabbed a burnished chef's knife that rested on a cutting board next to the kitchen sink. Just in case the boy caused any trouble.

The basement was dimly lit with only a crease of gray sky sneaking in the ground-level window. There was a faint crack of thunder. Trevor scurried and hid behind the gas furnace, but he was still exposed from certain angles. The stainless steel door straight ahead of him was strictly off limits and padlocked shut. The furnace was the best hiding spot. He stooped low behind it and pushed his back against the wall.

He heard the clomp of her tennis shoes as she walked wearily down the stairs.

"So, are we playing hide-and-seek now?" Megan called out. "That's a boring game. Come out and let's have a chitchat about what just happened. I hope you know I was only kidding and would never do anything to harm you."

Megan saw his little feet shaking and recoiling behind the furnace. But she stopped in her tracks when she saw a static-white light emerge from under the padlocked door's bottom. A magnetic force reeled her in. She found herself trying to rip and pull apart the immovable door. She was panting but not out of breath when a crowbar from out of nowhere cracked the side of her head, crushing through her skull and killing her instantly.

Trevor gasped, blinked, and flinched simultaneously. His father, Bill, materialized from the shadows, dropping his rusted crowbar to the concrete. He hid most of his face under the hood of a wet black rain jacket. Megan lay lifeless below him, a thin creek of blood dribbling down her head. Eyes wide, she never saw it coming.

Bill pulled his hood down and shook the cold off himself. He made eye contact with Trevor and said, "Help me clean this up."

Chapter 10
The Inventory, Part II

And on to the next page of the inventory list. Mr. X pulled Trevor out of room 111 and opened the door to room 112. Waiting inside was an ordinary hotel room furnished with a king-size bed covered in checkered sheets, along with an oak nightstand that held two mints, a Holy Bible, and a brightly lit lamp.

Trevor blinked twice, and the hotel room transformed into a cluttered mess. There were dirty spoons and empty Taco Bell bags scattered on the tacky lavender carpet. The TV was smashed in from when his friend Jake had been so intoxicated that he'd mistaken the TV for a punching bag. Yes, Trevor remembered exactly where he was in this episode of *The Ghosts of a Dope Fiend's Past.* Jake, Mary, Trevor, and their old friend Gary Nichols had checked into the Motown Inn—one of the more luxurious suites the crew had become accustomed to. Motown Inn was a shelter for lowlifes, prostitutes, drug dealers, and junkies alike. The rooms were rented by the hour. Or, you could save twenty bucks and rent it by the night.

Gary Nichols was a year younger than Trevor and the rest. Mary had gone to school with him at the University of Michigan. He had oily auburn hair with dandruff flakes that avalanched out every time he shook his head. Rough pink patches of acne sprouted like wilted buds across the sides of his cheeks and traveled down to his back. Mary remembered sitting behind him in social economics class, terrified one of the loaded zits on the back of his neck would burst open and shoot her in the face. She'd mentioned to the fellas that back when they were in class together, he always bragged about how loaded his parents were. Gary had been bored one night and messaged Mary on Facebook, asking how things were and what she'd been up to lately.

Since Trevor had met her and introduced her to the lifestyle that he lived, Mary had transformed from a naïve and timid college student into a manipulating temptress of the streets. So Mary reported to Trevor and Jake that she had led Gary on a little bit and convinced him to come party at a hotel with The Hood Pack. She convinced herself it would be a good idea, contingent on one of his blackheads not erupting, forming into a monster of ooze, and attacking her. But the oily pimple head was loaded with more than just pus.

The kid possessed more money than he needed, which made him the perfect target. The mission was to get him to spend as much money as possible on drugs, let him pass out, rob him blind, and leave him in the motel. It wouldn't be a huge loss to him, as his parents would just reload his debit card the next day. Besides, this would give him an experience and life lesson that he would never forget.

It turned out to be the last lesson he would ever learn.

Mary easily convinced Gary to make several visits to the ATM that night in her old 1992 silver Chevy Corsica. The party started with a fifth of some off-brand rum called Captain Marko's and some weed sprinkled with cocaine. Jake had disappeared for a minute and come back to the room with a gram of crack cocaine—or the informally dubbed "Chasing Jason"—a tire pressure gauge, and a Chore Boy scouring pad. Gary watched Jake squirrel and fidget around with the crack-smoking instruments.

Jake took the tire pressure gauge out of its package, ripped apart a piece of Chore Boy, and assembled an impeccable crack pipe like an expert toolsmith fueled by cocaine and sleep-deprived adrenaline. "You ever try crack in Dearborn Heights, Gary?" Jake asked. He knew Gary's parents lived in the richest suburbs surrounding the city.

"No, but I saw a lot of female crack my freshman year," Gary joked back.

He'd lied. Gary never saw any female's backside besides his mom's on accident when she came out of the shower. The room got quiet but was soon followed by massive belly laughs in between heavy exhales of crack smoke. Gary's sharp humor amused Trevor. He almost second-guessed robbing the poor guy at the end of the night, but his addiction had already made that choice for him.

Jake disappeared again, but this time for an extended period of time. The three of them had run out of crack and were craving another hit. Mary started surfing the carpet, convinced she had dropped some dope out of the bag earlier. Trevor kept hitting the pipe even though the Chore Boy from the reservoir was completely roasted. The only fumes left were corroded and tasted like burned metal. Gary was in his own world, staring out the window through the blinds. He was convinced the FBI were watching him and that his parents had called them to monitor him due to his suspicious behavior. "They're onto me, guys. I'm telling you, they're out there."

"No, the FBI is investigating witnesses to the real Pizza-gate scandal. Not the fake one you probably read about on social media. The FBI don't care about you and your parents' debit card. They got bigger fish to fry," Trevor told him.

The door swung open and Jake sprinted inside, excited and eager to finally taste some of that sweet, precious heroin. All three of them pulled out their needles, and Gary looked around, confused.

"It's okay, Gary. I saved a fresh, clean needle just for you. This is the best high you'll ever experience." Jake reached in his knapsack, pulled out a new needle, and handed it to the anxious young man.

"I hope it's better than that crack shit we smoked, because that high didn't last long at all." Gary felt let down after his initial blast off the pipe left his ears ringing. Every hit after that felt like he was chasing that first high. But he kept telling himself one more hit would do the trick. He discovered that the first hit was too intense, but a thousand hits after didn't seem enough to satisfy the craving.

Jake plastered a sinister expression across his face. "No, Gary. Crack is whack, and we just did that shit for fun. This is the real shit right here. The high won't leave you, and the feeling is so smooth, dog. I can't really describe it. And I didn't even have to pay for it. Our dude was out, but I met this guy a few blocks from here, and he gave me this to sample in hopes I would come back to him for more." Jake licked his lips. He then put his thumb, middle finger, and index finger together for a magnifico kiss. "H is for heaven, my man."

"Wait. Our dude was out, so you just copped from a random stranger? Jake," Trevor said, "I thought I taught you better than that. We can't take any chances. So many undercovers out here waiting to bust our asses." Trevor's heartbeat increased with paranoia.

Then he reached for the bag to inspect the powdery content. The color was ice-white instead of brown. There was no vinegar or acidic odor. Trevor smiled in glee. White and odorless signified purity. "I should be the one to test it out."

"No, I want to try it. I paid for everything else. I want the first hit." Gary rolled his sleeve up and smacked his arm like he imagined a trained junkie would.

"No, Gary. This stuff looks really pure. You should let me sample test it first," Trevor said.

"Not if you want me to spend any more money with you tonight. I got dibs on first," the rookie insisted.

"Just let him go first, Trevor," Jake said.

"Whatever, man. It's your funeral. Do you even know how to do it?" Trevor reached under Mary's purse for a spoon.

"No, Trevor. I want you to do it for me."

Trevor sighed in defeat, tied Gary's arm up with his belt buckle, and injected the poison into his deep-purple vein. But the dope was a little too pure, and as soon as it entered his blood stream, Gary closed his eyes forever.

Jake shook Gary to try to rouse him. "That must have been some killer shit right there."

Trevor checked his pulse. "Guys, I think he's dead," he said, holding Gary's hanging, lifeless arm. "Fuck. What do we do?"

Mary started to tear up. She felt the most responsible, as this was her acquaintance she'd lured to this seedy motel to overdose and die. She started clawing at her eyes, tugging on her hair. "We should call 911. I reckon this is all my fault."

Mary went to pick up the room phone when Trevor grabbed her arm. "We can't call 911. And I'm the one who shot him up, Mary," Trevor said. "We have to think rationally because we could all end up in prison for this."

"This isn't right, Trevor. Tell me this a bad nightmare, baby." Mary's sobbing elevated.

Trevor pulled her close, offering warmth but no reassurance. "Let's see. We checked into the motel on his credit card. He went into the lobby to pay for the room by himself. None of us joined him, which is good." Trevor was retracing all their steps to figure out what could and couldn't be used as evidence against them in a court of law.

"We can be seen on all the security cameras in the lobby and parking lot." Jake was pulling his short curly hair. His long, unkempt fingernails dug into his skull, leaving light traces of blood.

Mary pushed away from Trevor. She started to pace up and down the room, frantically pulling on her own curly hair. She was mumbling to herself in some panic-induced Tourette-like language. "I did this, fuck, shit, should have stayed down South. Smoke crack, heroin bad, shit-cock fuck life. Fuck Michigan. Damn Yankees. Sorry, Gary. My bad. Hell is where ya'll going. Everything over."

Trevor shot stern eyes toward Mary. "Mary, calm down. The only thing we can do is somehow get his body in the trunk of your car. We take him to Ambassador Bridge and drop him off the ledge. It'll look like a suicide if anyone ever even finds him. If anyone watches the motel security camera footage, we can always say we left the motel and Gary wanted to stay the night by himself. We just came to visit him for a while and took off."

Jake was now breathing in heavy, unsteady pants. "Nice plan, but there are too many holes, dawg." He slowed down his panting to a smooth hum. "Ambassador Bridge is the busiest bridge in Detroit. You don't think anyone isn't going to notice three shady-looking characters like ourselves dumping a body over that huge bridge? Second, the toxicology report will show he had heroin in his system. And third, if there are security cameras, not to mention other witnesses nearby, how are we going to transfer Gary's body from the room to Mary's car? Man, sweet Jesus, forgive us for our sin." Jake closed his eyes, quick-crossed his chest, and tapped his forehead.

Trevor eyeballed the two of them. "Good thing we're on the second floor. That's only one flight of steps. The car's parked right out front. We can pick him up like he's drunk, Jake and I carry him shoulder to shoulder. If anyone asks, then we say he's too wasted to walk and we're helping this drunk fool out. The hard part is when we have to place him in the trunk of Mary's car and pray to God no one sees us."

Jake grew manic and couldn't stop biting his thumbnail until it bled. "Why does he have to go in the trunk? We're a few miles from Ambassador Bridge. We put him in the back seat. If a cop pulls us over, either way we're fucked. We can tell them he's just really drunk and passed out, like you said. Then we get to the bridge and find the perfect opportunity to throw him over. But what about all the camera footage they may or may not have here?"

"I reckon I can take care of that." Mary lowered her heavy sobbing to a light whimper. "I'll go downstairs and deal with the clerk at the desk. Just get him out of here and let's get this over with."

Jake and Trevor looked at each other, nodding in agreement.

Mary tiptoed her way down to the main lobby. She knew she had to put on her sweet and innocent face and imagine that the last half hour of her life never happened. "You got this, Mary," she told herself. She pulled up the hood on her blue-and-gold Wolverine jacket in an attempt to hide from any cameras. She then grabbed a tissue out of her purse, scraped off dried tears, and placed a piece of Doublemint chewing gum in her mouth as an oral flirtation device.

A Middle Eastern man with a long nose and brown turban was stationed behind the front desk, playing on his smartphone and giggling to himself.

"Whatchya looking at, Ravinder?" She took notice of his name tag, marched up to his desk, and dialed up a sweet smile for him.

"Oh, you know, some funny YouTube videos of people doing dumb shit," he said with a thick accent.

"I fucking love YouTube. I bet you could make some awesome and hilarious YouTube videos with the security cameras around this place." Mary relaxed the back of her hoodie and twirled her hair underneath. Ravinder took brief notice of her as she chomped her chewing gum, shooting him those seductive "sweet innocent Mary" eyes.

"Yeah, except the only security camera we have is in this lobby, and nothing exciting ever happens in here." The clerk directed his eyes back down into his phone.

Mary sighed a breath of relief. "So the only camera is in here? Well that makes sense. All the shit you could put on YouTube from what goes on out there would probably get your customers arrested."

"I guess." Ravinder shrugged his shoulders, not giving Mary any more attention. His eyes had homed back in on random YouTube videos of parents being beat up by their children.

Mary pretended to look at her phone real quick. "Oh shit, I have to go. My ride is waiting on me. Nice to meet you, Ravinder."

She returned to the room, giving a nod to go ahead and carry on as planned.

Jake and Trevor placed Gary's dead arms over their shoulders and guided the body down the motel steps. An older Black gentleman wearing a gray sport coat and reciting obscenities to himself passed them on the steps. He didn't stop to give any attention to Jake and Trevor's helping a dead guy walk. Trevor pictured Gary as the dead guy from that movie *Weekend at Bernie's* and him and Jake being the Larry and Richard characters who pretended to carry their drunk friend home.

Finally, Jake, Trevor, and Mary were able to direct Gary safely to the car without any onlookers.

Mary drove her old Chevy, which had 221,850 miles on it, with Gary's corpse in the back seat. Trevor rode next to her in the passenger seat. Jake, who'd originally objected, agreed to sit in the back seat next to the foul carcass. He held his nose against the musty, mothball-like odor of death. The longest ten minutes in their lives went by before they made it to the bridge. It was three o'clock in the morning and traffic was slow, but there were enough cars out to cause them paranoia.

Present-day Trevor was not physically part of this memory. He was still back at the abandoned hotel but completely engulfed in this memory like he was really there. He recalled how they pulled the car over on the side of the bridge and put the hazard lights on. Jake pretended to change the tire while Mary kept watch for oncoming traffic. It was during two minutes of no traffic that Trevor grabbed Gary's cadaver and tossed it over that ledge. And he could never forget peering down into the Detroit River, feeling his body temperature decline. His body stood still like he was stuck in time, unable to budge a muscle. And that was when he saw her. For first time since 2003, he was staring at Megan McDaniel's cold, dead eyes. She was resting on top of a rock in the water where Gary's body should have been. He heard the distant voice of his father. "Help me clean this up."

"Come on, Trevor, we have to get the fuck out of here!" Jake was slapping his arms on the driver-side door, trying to get his attention.

Megan McDaniel's image faded and the lifeless body of Gary Nichols remained. Trevor snapped out of his trance. "Wait, he's still on top of the rock. We have to go down there and move him into the water!"

"You're crazy!" Jake shouted back. "The current will wash him off the rock soon enough."

Jake was right because when Trevor looked back down, Gary's corpse had floated away. He reached in the side pocket of his pants for the tiny bag of deadly heroin he'd almost forgotten in the room. Jake continued to pound on the car door, impatiently waiting on his procrastinating friend. Trevor ripped the heroin baggie apart and let the powder dive into the river to join Gary.

"Did you just throw that out?" Jake asked, still hollering.

"It was going to kill us," Trevor replied.

"That means it's the good stuff. Come on, let's just go."

No one learned if the body was ever found or not. There was nothing on the news. The police never came snooping around for answers, or at least not in their direction. The tragic night was about a year before, and Trevor had had so many drug acquaintances pass away from the disease of addiction in the meantime. But none of them ever affected Trevor the way Gary had. Maybe it was because Gary trusted him to shoot him up for his first dose—the one that ended his life. Maybe it was just further proof that Trevor was a piece-of-shit human being.

Trevor's mind flashed back to present day. He was wheezing and sweltering. Room 112 was clean and appeared just as it had before.

Mr. X crept up behind him and patted him on his shoulder. "Are you okay?" he asked. "I know that was a lot to see in there, Trevor, but do you see why this is so important for you to heal? You have made a lot of careless mistakes, but you're not a bad person. You watched your father murder someone, so it made it easier for you to do the same. But the time has come for change."

Trevor wiped saliva residue from around the side of his mouth. "My father saved my life from that psychopath babysitter, and I didn't kill Gary Nichols. It should have been me that took that first shot, but he insisted."

"Keep telling yourself that, Trevor."

Trevor turned away from the old man, fighting his words. But they resonated firm. "Tell me about this hotel," he said. "How are we able to travel memories and time-hop? None of this makes sense."

Mr. X took a deep breath, as he'd expected this question. "Follow me." Mr. X guided Trevor with his pistol against the back of his hip. They traveled down the left-wing hall that led to the main lobby. They stopped at the reception desk, and Mr. X reached under the counter.

"Look at this." He handed Trevor a framed black-and-white portrait. A group of around twenty people posed like statues on opposing sides of an institutional building. On the right stood a line of expressionless men and women wearing white scrubs and dark-blue lab coats. The left side of the picture showed a string of happy and sad faces. The men wore matching dark trousers and white button-up dress shirts while the women were clothed in long black skirts and ivory blouses. Front and center was a tall man in a dark leather jacket, bearing white whiskers and a gray top hat. The curious fellow looked like a mysterious character from a children's book.

"What is this?" Trevor asked.

"That's the staff and residents of The Detox Hotel back in 1973. I found this when I first came to the hotel a few weeks ago. The picture hung lopsided on the wall, so I took it down and did some research on it."

"What did you find out?"

Mr. X pointed upward past the timber-wood ceiling rafters to a Palladian window depicting an image of an unknown saint in a black coat, white beard, and gray top hat. "The hotel was built in the 1800s and was originally a psychiatric hospital. It shut down in 1918 for undisclosed reasons. But I imagine something terrible happened. And then in 1971 this addiction specialist and entrepreneur bought the building and renovated it. As you can see, he was a bit eccentric and thought highly of himself. He turned the asylum into a rehab center for drunks and addicts.

Sadly, most of those people in that photo died. One of the few missing from that photo is your grandfather, Randolph Grey. He was a resident under the hotel's care."

A strong, cold wind forcefully whisked through the room, planting a malign energy that lingered in the dead air. Trevor grew chills as he scanned the lobby windows, which were sealed shut and offered no logical explanation for the sudden gust. Then he was greeted by a frigid breeze. Something malevolent was present with them. Although Trevor couldn't see him, he knew his old friend, the shadow, had made another grand entrance.

"How did they die?" Trevor wasn't convinced that Mr. X was telling him everything he knew.

Mr. X shifted his posture as if dodging an invisible deity. He had a shadow of his own. "No one knew what happened to them. But as you can see, the ghosts and demons of its past never left this place. After the hotel shut down in 1973, some of the surviving patients made a garden memorial out past the pool for those who died while in The Detox Hotel's care. Legend has it that the building was purchased to house patients—to treat them as hotel guests but also inflict malicious methods of detox interventions. So it earned the nickname 'Detox Hotel.'"

"And whatever happened to the guy on the ceiling? Was he the crazy owner of The Detox Hotel that you mentioned?"

"Yes. His name was Lance Burrows. And you could say he found his new forever home." Mr. X lifted the pistol from Trevor's side and placed the steel against his own head. "Boom." He made a popping sound with his tongue and cheek.

Chapter 11
The Recovery Inn
(aka The Detox Hotel)

June 21, 1973

Fear is a sly devil wearing so many masks: anger, jealousy, greed, depression, and even joy. In the end, the entrepreneur Lance Burrows knew that all those façades boiled down to fear. But the entity of pure love is free from the burden of fear. True love holds no expectations or ulterior motives. Nor does it need to control anyone or anything into believing in it. Although the two entities, love and fear, are polar opposites, they have been known to feed off each other and destroy the hearts of man.

Lance Burrows was going to manipulate love and fear to save Randolph Grey's lost soul by breaking him down first.

Randolph Grey was still puzzled by this tall, strange man's overt generosity. The Volkswagen appeared to be no more than three years old. This Lance gentleman wore formal attire and spoke with a proper tone unlike most of the heathens Randolph had encountered on the streets of Detroit.

"So where exactly are we going?" Randolph asked from the back seat.

Lance looked back at his new passenger through the rearview mirror. "I call it The Recovery Inn, but it has many different names. You'll be safe there. It's beautiful. I can't wait for you to see it. We're almost there."

When Randolph first saw the hotel, he imagined it as a paradise for the lost who were looking for sanctuary, a place to recover from their demons. The former psychiatric hospital was about a century old but somehow had managed to hold sturdy weight at the top of the hill. It was surrounded by woods that would be demolished fifty years later, transforming the landscape to barren land. But when Randolph arrived, the building's fifty guest/patient rooms, stacked on top of each other like a house of cards, each had a view of the majestic forest and sky.

Lance drove on the only road leading up the hill. The entrance to the property was safeguarded from the rest of society by a massive iron gate. The opening consisted of a dirt path that led to a shiny bronze statue of Lance Burrows himself. It then split in two and joined behind the figure to point to the front door of The Recovery Inn. From the exterior, the building was elevated, thin, and built out of solid bricks with a coarse texture. Climbing plants grew around the building, zigzagging around the drain pipes and competing for sunlight.

Lance parked the car in the back and led Randolph inside. The main building preserved the ambiance of an institution while maintaining a hotel environment. The lobby included newly installed flowery wallpaper and a sparkling chandelier that brightly lit up the room, extending Randolph a cordial welcome into a safe haven where he could heal and begin his journey into recovery. The ceiling lights were blinding and allowed no shreds of darkness to enter the hotel—a warm reminder that the grim world he once knew was behind him.

Randolph had a sour, musky smell and seemed to have surfaced from under a garbage can like Oscar the Grouch. When they finally entered the hotel, Lance sent Randolph to the locker room to relish his first shower in days. The water and Ivory soap felt like liquid bliss as Randolph scrubbed the layers of filth from his skin. Then Lance gave the derelict a fresh outfit of beige trousers and a button-up white dress shirt.

Once Randolph was clean and dressed, Lance gave him the grand tour. And Randolph was sold on the tour from the very beginning.

Lance Burrows was a knowledgeable and charming guide. He first showed his new guest the sauna located on the other side of the shower and locker room. The residents of the hotel sat on a wooden bench, dripping in boiling sweat, detoxing the poison of trauma and substances from their pores. Randolph took a step inside to feel the rising warmth from the bin of steaming rocks that released vapors deep into his lungs and his mind. Some of the men were meditating in the midst of the scorching air. Randolph's body temperature elevated. He couldn't comprehend how anyone could meditate in this hotbox. But somehow the men were floating in serenity. Randolph wanted to look like them: at peace.

He also noticed that there weren't just men in the sauna. Also present were women wearing only towels wrapped on their heads like buns to keep their hair up and away from interfering with the full experience of detoxification. Randolph found it difficult to not stare too long at the exposed breasts and wide variety of private parts. There was one particular woman wearing no towel on her head or anywhere else on her immaculate body. She had dusty-blonde hair, shimmering blue eyes, flawless fair skin, and medium-size breasts. This naked stranger drew his quick attention.

When cleaned up and groomed, Randolph was an attractive, middle-aged man. He didn't resemble the gaunt, disheveled skeleton the streets of Detroit had come to know him as. For a short moment, Randolph and the beautiful blonde goddess locked eyes, and the energy of mutual attraction eclipsed the room. Lance sensed it as well and was quick to move Randolph along to the next attraction on the tour. However, Randolph had already found his attraction.

"And the outside swimming pool is right next door. It's the most convenient location for cooling off after sweating the all the poison from your soul." Lance gently nudged Randolph out of the sauna. "I know she's lovely to look at, and there will be plenty of time for that later. Right now, you need to focus on getting better and refrain from any distraction or temptation that could interfere. Fraternization is strictly prohibited here at The Recovery Inn."

"Is it The Recovery Inn or The Detox Hotel? I heard a resident on the way in call this The Detox Hotel. Which one is it?" Randolph asked. "I like Detox Hotel better."

"Yes," Lance said slowly. "*Detox* is a new term addiction and health specialists are throwing around to describe the process of withdrawal. I have considered changing the name of The Recovery Inn to The Detox Hotel to adapt to the changing times. This is a safe place to detox not only from the substances but the trauma and mental illness attributed to addiction. And in this safe place, I have enforced a very strict rule that there's no romantic relations among residents and/or staff at this facility!"

"Then why do you have men and women in the sauna together, walking around flashing their unmentionables?" Randolph wrinkled his nose and raised a brow. He wanted to go back and talk to that woman but refrained.

"Because it's a true test of how serious you are about recovery. Look at it as a way to weed out the weak and lustful." Lance opened the door to the outside swimming area.

The deck was made of pressure-treated light oak wood that complimented the clear, blue tranquility of the adjacent swimming pool. It was far from what Randolph's grandson would witnesses forty-seven years later. The garden was open in the grass behind the concrete swimming area. The wooden fence that Trevor had seen separating the garden from the pool was non-existent. In the seventies, there were two gardens divided by hedges on stilts. The closest was full of rose bushes, a variety of blooming organic flowers. The parallel garden featured assorted dill leaves, squash, pumpkins, strawberries, and other fruits and veggies that contributed to the botanical paradise. The only thing missing were the crucifixes, but that part of the tour came later.

"Far out … Can I get a closer look at the garden? I love nature, man," Randolph said.

"Later, my friend. There will be plenty of time for that. But I must introduce you to some good people and show you your room." Lance deflected Randolph's attention away from that garden, spiking his curiosity even more.

Randolph followed Lance inside for the rest of the tour. A long, narrow hallway guided them toward several rooms reserved for group therapy. They passed an assembly hall decorated like a cathedral, with pinewood pews sitting on top of polished hardwood floors, that was reserved for twelve-step meetings and mass fellowship. "This is where the magic really happens," Lance told him. Individual therapy sessions happened over in the right-wing corridor. An enormous lounge room with giant black leather couches, upholstered wooden furniture, and a brand-new color TV called out to Randolph. It had been so long since he'd melted away in a nice, clean couch and got lost to some old black-and-white episodes of *Perry Mason*. Now he had a chance to watch Raymond Burr defend the innocent in color.

On the other side of the lounge was a game room with a bar-size pool table, air hockey, and foosball tables. Two male residents approached, wearing beige trousers and matching white shirts that coincided with their bleached white smiles. The outfit was identical to the one Lance had given Randolph to wear.

"Hey, you're the new guy, right?" a man with a name tag that read *Steven* asked. Randolph looked around and discovered that all of the residents were wearing name tags except for him.

Lance picked up on his confusion. "Ah yes, I forgot your name tag. All residents are required to wear one. It's actually waiting for you in your room, Randolph. Forgive me for not introducing you to two of our finest residents here at The Recovery Inn. This is Steven and Jacob. They'll be graduating the program soon, and we'll have a huge celebration for them tomorrow night."

"Nice to meet you both." Randolph had been taught to always have manners when being introduced to new people, even if he didn't really care to meet them. He was still fixated on the beautiful naked blonde back in the sauna.

"Now we make our way upstairs to your room. The first ninety-four hours are considered the quarantine stage of detox. You reported your last use of heroin was about eight hours ago, so I reduced your hours in quarantine. You now have eighty-six hours remaining. You'll be isolated and medically monitored by our nursing staff. However, don't ask them for any controlled substances, as they're mandated to report that to their superiors. If you ask for anything like that, your visit here at The Recovery Inn will be terminated. Security is very tight around here. If you try to escape, another day of detox will be added to your itinerary. There are guards at every exit. If you try to escape more than twice, you'll be immediately discharged from the program," Lance warned.

Randolph nodded in agreement but thought, *If this place is voluntary why would anyone try to escape?*

"You don't want to lose your chance at paradise, do you, Randolph?" Lance asked.

"No, of course not."

Randolph was ushered to the second floor and down another slender, endless hallway. He could see across the wing to the north corridor. The doorway was boarded off and wrapped in yellow caution tape.

"What's over on that side? Why is it closed off?"

"It's under construction. This place hasn't been open long, and actually it used to be a psychiatric hospital."

Lance told the partial truth. The building had been a mental hospital and technically was still under construction. The corridor itself wasn't under construction, but the residents who wound up over there were in need of extra structure.

"Now I need to be completely honest and transparent with you, Randolph. The initial detox is going to be brutal, but it's necessary." Lance put his hand on Randolph's back, prompting him forward. "If we were to pamper your complete experience here, then it would be too easy to return to your old ways. Spare the rod, spoil the child, as it says in the Good Book." Lance lifted a pocket-size Bible out from under his jacket. "You a follower of the Gospel?" he asked Randolph.

"No, sir. But I am open to all kinds of teachings," Randolph lied. He had no interest in learning about the Lord and Savior. When Randolph was a boy, every time his mom force-read him psalms and excerpts from Revelations, he would get diarrhea.

"Change is uncomfortable," Lance went on. "Pain is uncomfortable, but the two are parallel here at The Recovery Inn. We haven't been open that long, but our success rate is drastically higher than traditional rehabilitation found in prison or hospital rest centers. There are great rewards for hard work and surviving the horrors of detox. But breaking the habit won't be easy, and you'll get your chance to see. I hope you make it through. We're all rooting for you."

Lance handed Randolph over to two "hotel wardens" who dragged him down the long hall, which now more resembled an asylum rather than a hotel.

"Wait. Is this exactly necessary? I don't know if I like this. Lance, I need a word!" Randolph shrieked. He'd been blindsided by the shifted energy. This wasn't exactly the warm welcome he'd received downstairs.

The two wardens cloaked in white scrubs under navy-blue lab coats shoved Randolph into what would be his new room for the next eighty-six hours: room 202. The cold steel door slammed behind them. The echo of the dead bolt clanging shut rang like metal bending inside his eardrums.

Randolph examined his new environment. The room was nearly empty with the exception of a brand-new iron radiator installed below a wide, steel-barred window that reminded him of an upscale medieval dungeon. Floors were laminated with amber cherry wood. A ceiling light, centered above, flickered on and off. He noticed a vintage painting of a fruit bowl containing an assortment of fruits hanging on the wall. Below the painting, a corner piece of the recently installed Victorian-style wallpaper hadn't stuck and was folded over. Randolph drew closer out of curiosity and lifted up the corner piece of wallpaper to reveal *TJD was here.* He had no idea who TJD was, but he assumed TJD had undergone the same disrespectful treatment he himself was receiving. On the same note, he wondered if the harsh methods cured TJD and maybe could cure him.

Forty-seven years later, Trevor Dugan would be held captive and forced to detox in this exact room. But unlike Trevor, Randolph Grey had volunteered himself into this environment. Randolph didn't understand why this room didn't resemble a hotel room or patient room in a psych ward. It was just an abandoned bedroom with nothing in it, not even a bed. There was no sign of the name tag that Lance had promised or anything remotely comforting like the color TV for *Perry Mason* reruns or the leather couch to sleep his withdrawal away.

"This wasn't in the brochure, man," he muttered.

Randolph had been stripped of everything except the defaced penny that he'd begged the hotel staff to let him keep. Lance allowed him to bring the coin inside, and Randolph was now rubbing it for good luck. Shortness of breath, an accelerated heart rate, and muscle spasms abruptly intruded Randolph's physical self. He braced for the agonizing symptoms to run their course. This wasn't his first rodeo. He'd spent many sleepless nights outside in the cold Michigan winters, freezing while itching his way to another hit.

The insides of his mouth felt hardened from dehydration. He screamed out for water, but no one came to his rescue. Where were the nurses? The medical staff? A proper detox needed to be medically monitored. Randolph already knew there was going to be nothing proper about this detox.

Out of desperation, he coughed up some of his own saliva in a failed attempt to quench his thirst. Except he'd forgotten that saliva's saline concentration makes you thirstier if you drink it. He knew this fact from previous failed attempts, but his mind wasn't operating at baseline level.

A faint zapping noise directed Randolph's attention to the moth circling the sputtering ceiling light, which had almost dimmed out. He was intrigued by the moth but not as fascinated as he was with its close relative, the butterfly. When Randolph had tried detoxing in the past, he always imagined himself as a caterpillar trying to earn his wings. The caterpillar would spin itself into a cocoon. This was the natural process of transformation—a metamorphosis, like recovery. But Randolph always gave up in the cocoon or detox. He wondered if the caterpillars that couldn't finish the metamorphosis were downgraded into dust-scaled moths. The unfortunate truth was that the moths lived in the shadows of their flamboyant butterfly cousins, never measuring up to the other Lepidoptera in the insect kingdom.

Randolph made due with having no couch or bed and took an uncomfortable nap on the hard floor, dreaming of moths and the history of their addiction to light. A few hours later, the sound of keys jingling next to the door roused him. *Finally, they send someone to check on me. I'm dying over here*, he thought.

When he first glanced at the nurse in a surgical mask entering his room, he couldn't see anything except her eyes. But he automatically knew they belonged to the woman from the sauna. There was something different about her. The fact that she had white nurse scrubs covering her previously naked body may have been a key difference. But her demeanor and energy were off-kilter. She didn't look at him the same way she had downstairs in the sauna. Now she could barely make eye contact as she handed him two painkillers and a Styrofoam cup filled with water.

"Thank you," he said.

"No problem. I'll be checking in on you every couple hours or so." Her voice came out flat.

"Don't you remember me from the sauna? My name's Randolph. What's your name?"

The woman from the sauna did not provide a response.

"Fine, don't tell me who you are. But I saw the way you looked at me downstairs. Don't you remember?"

When she didn't respond to return his interest, Randolph slumped his shoulders. He'd always caught feelings for women early on, but this was an entirely new level of obsession.

"My name is Doris," she finally said. "I'll be your one of your nurses on staff during your stay in The Detox Hotel."

Her stoic indifference cut through his heartstrings like razor wire. But she didn't really owe him anything. They had no history.

"Okay, so you don't remember me. That's fine. But I saw you in the sauna with other residents. Do they let all the employees swim and lie around in the buff downstairs?"

Doris turned away and pitched the water cup in a tiny disposable bag she was carrying.

"I got dragged by the guards to this room, but I came here of my own free will," he said, trying to appeal to her sympathy. "Shouldn't I be able to leave on my own accord?"

Randolph's muscles were aching, his head was ringing, and this woman of no help was draining his patience. But he was still fascinated by her, and it wasn't just her beauty. There was something about her eyes that made him feel at peace, like they could stare into his soul.

Doris turned back toward Randolph. "It's okay," she finally replied. "I understand you have a lot of questions, and this place was confusing to me as well in the beginning. However, once you learn and understand Lance's vision for recovery and treatment, it will all make sense. For now, you just have to trust the process."

She finally engaged in direct eye contact once again. Randolph felt the caterpillars in his stomach merging into that sweet butterfly, or maybe it was the outcast moth. He couldn't tell the difference. Doris's voice of reassurance settled him down, but he still believed something was off about this place.

"I know you have a job to do, Doris, but I also know you felt that energy downstairs just like I did. Free-spirited love is in the air."

She slightly giggled before clearing her throat and walking out of the room.

"Wait!" he shouted before she shut the door. "How do I signal to you if I need help?"

"You don't," she replied.

Time didn't exist in his guest room at The Recovery Inn. After a while, the ceiling light diminished after glinting one too many times. The moth had found a new home. Randolph was shivering as his body temperature fluctuated from steaming hot to frigid cold. Painstaking, disorganized thoughts flooded his mind. His heartstrings had been pulled apart by the woman he'd fallen in with love with at first glance. A sad song crawled up inside his head and the chorus refused to leave. Randolph sat in the darkness and recited the gloomy lyrics to the King's "Heartbreak Hotel." Elvis wasn't on the top of his personal musical playlist. He tended to favor more obscure and psychedelic artists, like Dylan and the Grateful Dead. But although he didn't care for mainstream pop music, there was something about the song "Heartbreak Hotel" that always caught his fancy. And now being inside The Detox Hotel, the irony of unfolding events made it impossible to refrain from breaking out in song.

Eventually, the singing got old and the room grew too dark for him to find any means of escape. In desperation and rage he began to slam his fist into the drywall. At first, his fist just bled, but he kept going. The wall soon began to slowly crack open with wide, gaping holes. Randolph was now thrusting his entire body into the cracks, creating his escape.

He heard keys jingle again and thought, *This is how to get Doris's attention.* But to his surprise, unless Doris had transformed into an obese, bearded man in a white warden uniform, Doris wasn't coming to his rescue. The burly man stormed into the room and grabbed Randolph by the collar of his shirt. Violently, he shoved Randolph onto the wooden floor and began to pulverize his face and abdomen. Randolph always identified as a lover, not a fighter, but the physical pain being inflicted upon him became a useful distraction from the horrific withdrawal symptoms.

"Come on, you hit like a girl! Is that all you got?" Randolph shouted, antagonizing the uniformed bully. The guard flipped Randolph over on his side and continued to kick his backside. With each thrust of the guard's foot, blood trickled down Randolph's mouth and chin, splattering on the laminated floor under him. The fat ward unleashed more fury until a tall man in a dark leather jacket entered the room: Lance.

"Adam, that's enough. I think Mr. Grey has learned his lesson here. Also, tell the construction crew that I told them time and time again to add reinforced steel to these walls. Drywall is too cheap and easy to damage."

Adam let out a disgusted grunt and left the room.

"You just added another day here, Mr. Grey. I told you the penalty for trying to escape. Don't worry. I'll have the nurse come in and clean you and this mess up." Then Lance was abracadabra gone.

Randolph passed out or maybe he fainted lying down. There was a drop in blood flow to his brain. He remembered going fast into a dark hole. When he finally regained consciousness, Doris was there tending to his wounds. She wiped and sanitized the abrasions around his lips and jaw. Also, she wrapped the right side of his head due to the massive swelling that most likely was connected to a concussion.

"You suffered a pretty bad blow to the head," she said in a professional tone. "There could be some internal bleeding or damage. I'm just going to have to keep a close eye on you. A licensed physician, Dr. Goldberg, will be here tomorrow to examine you. Just try to take it easy and get plenty of rest."

Doris gave him a brief smile but stopped herself as if she was afraid someone would see her. Randolph interpreted it as a sign of hope for their love to blossom, but he knew they had to keep it a secret. "Here's something for the pain." Doris discreetly slipped him a syringe of about 15ccs of morphine. "Shhh. I'll be back. Try to pretend you're still in pain. No one can know."

The medicine was like a small wet dream inside the nightmare chamber of torture for Randolph. The morphine was enough to take the edge off, but he had built up quite a tolerance when it came to opiates—or to anything for that matter. He still felt some periodic amounts of agony when the medicine began to wear off.

Doris snuck in a few more times throughout the night to give him a little extra bump to hold him over. So much for detoxing cold turkey. Randolph had failed every stone sober withdrawal attempt without something to soothe the pain. A couple years before, he'd gone to a local clinic in Detroit to get daily doses of methadone to curb his opiate addiction. He got kicked out of the program for trading his methadone for heroin, but "medically assisted turkey" as he called it was so much more tolerable than cold turkey.

The next morning, Doris wheeled Randolph in a rickety antique wheelchair to Dr. Goldberg's office for his evaluation. On the way in, Randolph caught a glimpse of the taped-off north corridor. "What's really behind there?" he asked.

"I'm not a hundred percent sure, but those who have come out are completely different. It's bizarre." Doris looked around in all directions to make sure no one was listening.

"What about the others?"

"Well, some don't come out at all. I'm not sure if they get discharged or what."

"So they're doing more than just remodeling back there?"

"Oh, they're remodeling something back there," Doris replied. She knew something either glorious or sinister was happening behind those walls.

Two wards passed them by mid-conversation. Abruptly, Randolph and Doris tried to act normal and sealed their lips, which actually made their interaction more awkward and suspicious.

During the examination, the doctor had Randolph look at some pictures of random exotic animals, like zebras and snow leopards, and identify what he saw. He took a vision test, and his blood pressure results came back normal.

"There could be some internal bleeding in the head," the doctor said. "But we have no exact way of knowing. Just take it easy for the time being, and I would like to see you back here daily to monitor symptoms."

"Thanks, doc. So nothing too serious? Just a possible brain hemorrhage? I'll be just fine." Randolph wiggled his ear. A sarcastic tic.

Over the next few days, Randolph and Doris ended up having several interesting conversations during her "routine check-ins." She revealed that she was a recovering addict herself. Lance had found her waiting for a bus after she'd been fired from Detroit Metro Hospital for stealing painkillers. Doris had nowhere to go, so he took her in. After she successfully completed the residential treatment program, he hired her as his head nurse. Randolph discovered that all the employees had their own personal sauna time. And the hotel's rehabilitative residents weren't allowed into the reserved area. They had their own separate, designated times for the sauna, hot tub, and swimming pool, which explained the first time he'd laid eyes on her in there.

One day on the way to the doctor's office, Doris pulled Randolph into the corner of the hall, out of everyone's view, to deliver an important message. "I have to warn you, Randolph, about Lance and this place. All the residents and staff here are very free-spirited, but Lance takes recovery very serious. Sometimes, he takes it too serious. And there have been some scary stories that happened in here. To be honest, I didn't think it was the place for me, but I have nowhere else to go and I'm on Lance's good side. You don't want to get on his bad side."

Doris snarled. She raised her upper lip and widened her nostrils. "Rawr." She laughed and fell onto Randolph's chest.

"Doris, I already know there's something off about this place. I got knocked out and thrown in an empty room. And with that being said, I don't think I'm on Lance's good side."

"I'm going to be completely honest with you. No, you're not. Others have received worse punishments. But I think you have to learn how to get on his good side and find your way out." She brushed his shaggy hair back behind his ear. Doris had a smile that could tug at a statue's heart. "But I can make your stay as pleasurable as possible. We just have to keep it hush."

Randolph held the side of her face in the palm of his hand. "I want you to come with me and leave this place."

She blushed but had no words.

Doris continued to visit Randolph daily to help him to the doctor's office. No one got suspicious until Doris decided to wheel Randolph into the custodial maintenance closet. Stripping off her white scrubs, she pounced on top of him, knocking over one of the standing mops and causing a commotion that they would later regret. But it was the best three minutes of both of their lives. *Pure sexual euphoric heaven,* Randolph thought. This was the nurse who loved him, and he returned the love. Doris became his supplier of sedatives and orgasms.

Randolph's initial eighty-six hours got extended by another two weeks for minor violations like scoffing at the guards, flirting with Doris in public, and hocking loogies on the floor just to piss off the guards when they had to clean it up. Besides the additional days in detox, there were other consequences for Randolph's behavior. The ward staff, as directed by Lance, would leave him to starve for days. The wheels of dinner-tray carts squeaked by his door, leaving him malnourished and bitter. But Doris would always sneak him in a grilled cheese sandwich fresh from the cafeteria and a cup of orange juice, always with two ice cubes, just as he liked it.

She began to visit him more frequently, and staff had already taken concerned notice. Not long after the janitor closet incident, the big, bad boss received word of the forbidden relations. A nosy maintenance man witnessed some of their affair and snitched the couple out. Also, some of the other nurses noticed morphine vials that were reserved for high risk medical patients were randomly disappearing. It was then Lance decided to visit Randolph for a one-on-one intervention.

An orderly unlocked the door and followed Lance into Randolph's room.

Lance took his jacket off, handed it to his orderly, and walked over to the drapeless, barred window. He peered outside, breathing in the view of soaring pines. Glimmers of sunlight snuck through cracks in the cloudy sky, reflecting against Lance's specs.

"Mr. Grey, have you ever heard of the mythological figure Addictus?" Lance didn't wait for Randolph to answer. "The term *addiction* was first coined from his Latin name. According to legend, Addictus was a slave who was released from his master and allowed to roam free, but he was so conditioned by his chains that he chose to leave them attached. He wandered many lands with these chains on and could have removed them at any point. But he chose to keep them on because he grew used to being a slave. He didn't recognize his own freedom when it was offered."

"So Addictus was the first addict addicted to chains?" Randolph rubbed his chin and laughed. He looked over at Lance's orderly henchman, who stood against the wall with a poised look on his face. The moment got awkward and silent. Finally, the orderly snuck a quick smirk before Lance glared in his direction.

"I suppose so, Mr. Grey," Lance continued. "But like him, you were offered an opportunity to have your chains removed. You have been enslaved to your addiction your whole life. But this woman, this lust, has become your chain that you refuse to let go of." He walked a slow circle around Randolph.

"I don't see how I'm free when I'm locked up in here. She's the only thing that gives me hope in here. It's true love, and you can't deny that, man."

Lance continued to circle and went on. "Just over a year ago, I found this desolate state hospital that had been sitting here vacant for years, decades. I sought and traveled a lifetime searching for the perfect sanctuary where addicts, junkies, and drunks could sober up. But I never intended for them to just sober up, Mr. Grey. I wanted them to recover. Someone took a chance on me, so I wanted to return the favor to the helpless and hopeless much like yourself."

"This is a fabulous establishment you created here, sir. I'm very impressed, but I think things got out of hand." Randolph inched back a little from Lance.

"I wasn't finished." Lance's tone sharpened. Wrinkles on his aging forehead tightened from stress. "You're right. Things did get out of hand for you." He sized Randolph up, looking him up and down, confirming that he had his attention. "In the early 1930s up until the 1950s, the cure for addiction was locking the addict up and removing part of their brain. Lobotomies and electroshock therapy were standard procedures. I came here with a vision to change that—to offer addicts and alcoholics freedom from active addiction without punishment and despair. Some people naïvely think that recovery will be sunshine and rainbows. No, Randolph, you have to work for it. Morphine, sex, and deliberately breaking rules is not the best way to begin your stay here at The Recovery Inn."

Randolph stared back, with wide eyes and a crooked smile. "I believe in love, man."

"I know you do, and so do I. But love comes with a price. In order to find love, we must overcome our shadow," Lance went on. "The shadow is the part of our soul that holds the deepest secrets, trauma, and pain. AA and NA adopted many of the ideas from the shadow in the twelve steps but limited the spiritual experience with anonymity and watered-down step-writing. These so-called sponsors never really lived the spiritual awakenings that they preached about. The mission here at The Recovery Inn is to allow our guests the opportunity for an authentic and raw spiritual awakening. Our guests crawl in here like dirty caterpillars but leave these walls as beautiful butterflies." Lance opened his grinning mouth wide, closed his eyes, and extended his arms up toward Heaven. "However, some end up like moths and won't make it out alive."

Randolph took another step back. He was thinking about the moth in his room and how he knew it died as soon as the light flickered out.

"I know you may find this hard to believe, Randolph." Lance's voice heightened like a preacher's warming up for the climax of his sermon. "I used to live in Detroit, but I moved somewhere far, far away. But I came back here looking for you. I can't explain how or why. It's like I knew you from another life. And when I stumbled upon you on the filthy, drug-ridden streets, it wasn't by accident. God led me back to find you, and there you were. You could possibly be dead if it weren't for me. I came here to save you. I came to offer you salvation, Randolph. And this is how you repay me. By sleeping with one of my nurses and using morphine behind my back."

Oh God! Another religious nut trying to seek redemption by saving the poor and helpless, Randolph thought. The signs of a cult were everywhere. Everyone wearing identical outfits, residents and staff barely allowed to speak to each other, awkward glances from other guests when he passed them. He felt like their eyes were telling him to run. And the megalomaniacal persona that Lance exhibited, with him as the light bulb and all the residents his little moths.

"Okay! Stop!" Randolph was genuinely laid-back and mild-mannered until pushed to the point where his voice could shake a hotel's foundation.

"Excuse me?" Lance was taken aback. No one had spoken to him in that tone since he opened the hotel.

"No, No, No! Excuse you. I have sat here and listened to your crap." Randolph aggressively moved closer to Lance.

The ascetic orderly standing against the wall started to advance toward Randolph. Lance raised his hand. "Stop, Edward. Go on, Randolph. I'll listen. I hope this is good."

Randolph let out a heavy sigh. He started speed walking in circles around Lance. "Thank you for taking me in, but I think my stay at The Detox Hotel has expired. I need to leave. This is some kind of weird, sick cult." He slowed his march down. "You obviously have some kind of messiah complex. You're no fucking Jesus. I know your kind. You offer the weak and poor refuge, food, shelter with this promise of curing their addiction. In reality, you brainwash them into thinking you're God. And the ones who defy or disobey are beaten and tortured. Did I defy you, Mr. Burrows?" Randolph's speech was tangential and manic. His voice echoed the strains of a man who was tired and fed up with being gaslighted. "I want out of here, and I'm going to take Doris with me! She doesn't need to work for an egomaniac like yourself." Randolph moved toward the door, but Edward the orderly blocked his exit.

Lance laughed, exhaled deeply, and looked up at the ceiling. "Doris doesn't love you, Randolph. She's just a nurse, and I hired her to keep tabs on you, to seduce you and see if you would cave. I saw the way you two looked at each other. And you caved, Randolph. You failed your recovery. Besides, if she did leave with you, you're homeless. Where are going to take her? Under your bridge, Randolph?" Lance drew a lopsided smile across his arrogant face.

Randolph gritted his teeth. He was stung by the reality that in thirty-six years, all he'd accomplished was owning a duffel bag full of clothes and a dirty spoon habit. "That's a low blow, Lance. I thought you were supposed to help people like me. But you're here for your own sick gain."

"Now, the morphine was her idea, and it's completely against the rules." Lance interjected, ignoring the accusation, which bore truth. "Doris was instructed to report her seduction and your responses directly to me. But our sweet nurse spy kept things secret, or tried to keep things secret between the two of you. So she will be fired and stripped of everything. You, on the other hand, get to visit the renovations on the north corridor. I'm going to show you exactly what you wanted to see over there. It's glorious, but it will be painful. The pain will only hurt temporarily. The freedom behind the pain will be eternal. You're right: I have found the cure for addiction, and you're about get it."

Randolph's pale face transformed into a shade of crimson. "You're going to kill me, aren't you?"

The old man's posture tensed. He fidgeted with a loose thread on his jacket, continuing to avoid eye contact. "Sad as it may seem, I had higher hopes for our relationship. But this is the way it has to be. I came here to try to change your fate, but I was so naïve, thinking you would take this serious. Change or be transformed. You aren't going to die, Randolph, but you'll never be the same again. I bid you farewell."

"I'll see you in hell," Randolph said.

"You aren't going to hell, Randolph. It's somewhere worse. Keep this safe from me while you're there. It'll come in handy, too." Lance pitched a multi-colored hexahedron that landed in Randolph's lap, then he turned away. He winced like he always did, fighting to hide a teardrop that he almost shed.

Lance motioned to Edward. "Take his wheelchair and grab some wards on your way back. We need some insurance in case he tries to escape."

Randolph kept staring down at the rainbow-like cube. He was transfixed by it, almost oblivious to his certain doom drawing near. *Why does Lance want me to keep this safe*? he asked himself. *And what powers does it behold?* he wondered.

Randolph was wheeled off to the north corridor. Once the door shut behind him, it was never opened again. A crucifix with his name tag was planted in the garden to honor his graduation from The Detox Hotel. He was "cured" and never had to suffer another day in addiction.

Less than a week later, Doris was terminated from employment at The Recovery Inn, or The Detox Hotel as some called it. However, she was spared the horrors that many of her fellow staff experienced when fired. Rumors spread among staff and residents that she was with child. Lance was a demon, but even he couldn't bring himself to carry out murdering an innocent baby. Instead, Doris was sent out into the cold streets of Detroit.

Months later, Doris got her own apartment and a part-time job at a thrift store, where she met a handsome man looking for some camouflage army pants. His name was George Dugan, a Vietnam War vet. They got married and Doris gave birth to William George Dugan on March 17, 1974. Bill didn't learn about his biological father until his twenty-first birthday. Doris took him out to the bar to get drinks on her, and her drunk lips tattled on the affair and the lies to her husband, Bill's presumed father. She explained to Bill that although she loved Randolph, she'd had to carry out a façade of indifference.

"We were just a one-night stand. He was a junkie and he overdosed. He never would have been a good father," was the lie she told George, but she spilled the true beans to her son, Bill. Lance had hired Doris to seduce Randolph, she'd ended up falling in love with him anyway. It was an occupational hazard that Lance hadn't considered, but he knew why it was meant to be.

Bill didn't know how to process his mother's confession. He wanted to deny it. *How could she lie to Dad?* he wondered. Anger consumed him, and he resented this Randolph character he never met. As far as he was concerned, his mother could have made all of this up. However, Bill was curious and had to research his biological father. But he found little after years of research and stumbling down the rabbit hole of government cover-ups. There was no announcement of Randolph's death. Limited Google searches resulted in headlines that read "Local Detroit Homeless Man Missing," next to a black-and-white photo of him taken in a methadone clinic in 1970. Bill came to his own conclusion that his father was still residing in The Detox Hotel.

So when the ghost of Bill appeared to Trevor, he had to warn his son about the ghost of his grandfather, Randolph Grey.

Chapter 12
Triggered

6:00 p.m. Tuesday, September 22, 2020

An overcast sky of gray clouds drained the city of its evening light. To Jake Johnson, Detroit had always seemed like a bleak, hollow shell brimming with unemployment and toxicity. He once adored the town, but it seemed the longer he lived there, the more it resembled a Babylonian city of evil. His chauffer, Ryan, was morbidly interested and fascinated by its elements but grateful to live far away from the city.

Jake gazed at the vacant and condemned houses lined up like domino blocks ready to collapse. Then there were the pedestrians, mindless drones who were bitter and hardened by the demons of the only home they would ever know. On the corners of intersections and crosswalks were Stop signs spray-painted with *BLM.* Black Lives Matter was more than just a brand against systemic racism and police brutality that had plagued Detroit since its birth. For Jake Johnson, it was the only life preserver, with the exception of God Almighty, to instill any sense of hope in his own upbringing.

Jake sat in the back seat of Ryan's Charger with Bulko, giving directions and smothering the dog with abundant hugs and kisses. He also wanted to make sure the dog didn't chew up Ryan's leather interior, even though the mutt would later mangle the back seat anyway. Jake prayed that Trevor was home so he could he ditch the White man, take his two hundred dollars, and run far away from everyone—everyone except, of course, Bulko. He had two days of sin left before he got right with the Lord and checked into detox.

At the next stoplight, Ryan turned around to face the back seat. "Are you sure he's going to be here?"

Jake paused his tender, loving smooches on Bulko, sat up, and rolled his eyes. "Ryan, answer an honest question for me. Why are you really doing this? Searching for your brother after all this time?"

Ryan sighed, turned back around, and adjusted his rearview mirror. The mutt's backside was obscuring important view space. "Can you get that dog a little under control for me?"

"Hey, down, boy. Lay down." Jake put his arm around Bulko and gently subdued him into a resting position.

"Anyway, to answer your question, our dad passed away. Mom wants me to bring Trevor home for the funeral."

"Well, that's honorable of you after all this time, to obey your mother's wishes. To go searching for your brother, who you haven't spoken to in forever, lost somewhere in the ghetto of Detroit." Jake directed his attention out the window. He glanced across the business loop at the panhandlers begging for change and holding up crudely scribbled cardboard signs. They too most likely had brothers they hadn't spoken to in forever.

Ryan pushed on the gas, weaving in and out of traffic, veering too far to the left. "Look, like I told you, I sent that check to your brother's address. I was trying to help out any way I could. Trevor called me begging for it. I knew he would probably blow it on drugs, but I sent it anyway."

"Oh, the failure funds. I remember that. Yeah, he actually spent that on a phone, believe it or not, and added a data plan so he could keep up with all those damn conspiracy videos connected to your dad's work. He really believed your dad was some kind of hero, a seeker of truth, as he called him. But he mentioned that he had to disappear to save his family from harm's way."

Ryan sneered. "Yeah, our dad was a coward, but I don't want to get into that."

"Well, he must mean something to you if you're coming all this way, even if you say it's for your mom. And by the way, I'm sure Trevor thanked you for the money. But the rich can't just send money to write people off. My grandparents had bank-loads of cash and felt bad for my parents being deadbeat crackheads. They refused to take me in, and they let the system adopt me out to abusive families. But they wouldn't forget to send me a couple hundred dollars every birthday and Christmas. That was their way of saying, 'We don't love you enough to come see you or help raise you, but here's some money so you don't think we're total assholes.' But they were total assholes. So maybe that's why you're here: you don't want to be a total asshole anymore."

"No, I'm not an asshole. Relationships are a two-way street. My mom and I tried our best to help Trevor after Dad left, but he chose his own path. We all have our own paths to choose."

Jake leaned up closer from the back seat. "Maybe God has chosen for you to go down this path. A path to healing and amends. A chance for both brothers to reconcile and put all this behind them."

"That would be nice." Ryan glanced back and noticed the cross on Jake's silver necklace, which was resting on top of his black Adidas hoodie. "I notice you been mentioning God a lot. From what I remember in high school, you carried a backpack with an upside-down cross patch sewed on it."

Jake exhaled, thinking of his past, and even current, demons. "Like you said, seven years ago. I'm working on becoming a better person now. I ain't gonna lie—I still struggle with sin. But Jesus will see me through this, I know. After I go to treatment on Wednesday, I'll be a new, sober Jake."

Ryan turned back to look at Jake. "Good for you. I wish Trevor would check himself into treatment."

"He will when he's ready. Be there for him, and don't give up on your bro." Jake patted Ryan's shoulder.

"Yeah, if he doesn't die first," Ryan muttered under his breath.

"God has a plan for everyone. We can't always see it for what it is until it happens. He just works like that. Sometimes he takes away the people we love the most. I'm sure you may wonder why he took your dad, but everything happens for a reason. Your dad's probably up in Heaven smiling down at you for trying to help your brother out now."

Ryan struggled to digest what he had just heard. "I doubt my father is in Heaven. He killed himself. I'm pretty sure that's one unforgivable sin."

There was a prolonged moment of silence. Jake was a new believer in Christ and hopefully optimistic, but even he had no words. Suicide was a defamation toward God. It was giving up any chance of salvation.

Ryan entered a trance, and his mind and car went on autopilot. He almost missed Jake directing him to take a left to The Hood Pack Mansion. Jake had to shake him back into focus. The Charger's tires came to a screech as Ryan swung a hard left, barely making his turn.

The home wore a darker shade of empty than the other houses on Ryan and Jake's voyage. Ryan pulled into the dirt driveway, not surprised at the Condemned sign he noticed plastered on a broken door that hung ajar from its hinges. As soon as Ryan came to a stop, Jake opened the door and Bulko leaped out from the back seat. The big mutt scratched some of the flawless black interior leather with his razor-pointed claws on his way out. The damage was minimal, but the rips were visible enough for Ryan to spot, and they caused internal tears.

Jake led Bulko to a gnarled oak tree in the backyard to unleash a streaming marathon of piss. Ryan waited in the car, drumming his fingers on the steering wheel. He felt awkward, out of place, and just wanted to find Trevor. Finally, Jake and his dog reappeared and then vanished inside the eyesore house. They were gone only a few minutes, but it seemed like hours to Ryan. When Jake returned, Trevor wasn't with him. In his place was a blonde, slightly gaunt woman. Her face was riddled with a few subtle scars and meth-induced acne, but it was beautiful nonetheless.

"This is Mary, Trevor's woman," Jake said. "And this is Ryan, Trevor's brother."

Mary studied Ryan's pride-and-joy vehicle before acknowledging his presence. "I've heard a lot about you," she said.

Ryan grinned and replied, "That's funny, because I haven't heard anything about you."

Mary peeked her head inside the driver's window, intruding on Ryan's personal space. She examined the scratch marks in the back and eyeballed the loose change in the console. Unimpressed, she turned back outside to the lovable presence of Bulko, the great fighting dog who'd been saved by his tormented owner, and started to pet him. "Aww, cute dog! He's a little beat up, but he's precious. Yes you are! You're so precious." When she locked eyes again with Ryan, her voice switched to a harsh tone. "And what do you want with Trevor, mister?"

"We need to go bury our dead. And I'm kind of in a hurry."

"Who died?" she asked.

"Our father."

"What makes you think he'll even go with you?" Mary's eyes rolled in disbelief.

Jake sensed a little tension between his blunt friend and his best friend's brother. He tried to change the subject. "Look, Trevor isn't here, but he could be back at any time. We could wait here. Or, Mary says she may know where he might be."

"I vote for going to find him. I don't know if I can wait around too long around these parts. What do you say, Mary? Will you help me find my brother?" Ryan squinted his eyes and faked a smile.

"Depends. I'm kind of hungry. I was wondering if you could buy me a hamburger, mister." Mary crossed her arms, impatiently tapping her foot on the ground.

"Sure thing, darling," Ryan replied, imitating her Southern twang. "But only after you help me find my brother." Ryan was a businessman, and everything came with a price.

"Deal," she agreed. Mary was a sucker for a juicy, sweet cheeseburger.

The trio made their way north to a rough district known as the "Red Zone," located in one of the most dangerous zip codes in the country: 48205. Two young White folk accompanied by a young African American in this neck of the woods raised as many concerns as Ryan's drunk Uncle Ronnie bringing a flamboyant Black stripper over for Thanksgiving dinner to break bread and play board games. The feast was rather awkward, and Ryan had seen his uncle only once since the fiasco. Of course, Ronnie denied he knew she was a stripper and claimed a friend from work had introduced them. Ryan felt bad for his uncle, but his parents never looked at Ronnie the same way again. Ryan was uncertain if it was more because she was a stripper or because she was Black. But like that poor, drunk African American woman stumbling into a White, conservative Thanksgiving dinner, Ryan's rich White ass driving deep into the Red Zone" spelled out t-r-o-u-b-l-e. But no one was playing board games in this neighborhood. They shot dice and used up all their "get out of jail free" cards.

Ryan accelerated down Gratiot Avenue, where they received a broad assortment of puzzled and intimidating expressions from the locals. *You don't belong here* was literally spray-painted on one of the decrepit houses they passed. Ryan thought of it as an omen indicating they should turn around, but he kept going. He pulled the Charger over three houses down from Anton Cole's residence but left the car running. Mary insisted on going in alone.

Jake agreed and ducked down. He managed to hide most of his face under his hood. "Shhh," he whispered to Bulko.

"Why are you hiding? You're starting to make me paranoid now. Do I have something to worry about?" Ryan asked.

"You notice how Bulko here is all beat up?" Jake asked.

"Yeah, it was kind of one of the first things I noticed about him, but I didn't want to say anything. None of my business and all."

"Well, I stole him back from a dog-fighting ring. I was strung out pretty bad and sold him right after I found him alone in an alley. It was a dope-fiend move, and I'm trying to make it right now. But the guy I stole him from, his brother owns that brick house that Mary just went into to go find your brother. So yeah, I'm a little paranoid." His heart fluttered.

"Great! Are you going to get me killed as well if they find you?"

"No, they won't even recognize me. I don't think they got a good look at me when I snatched him. And if they do, they're only after me, so don't worry about it."

"So is that what happened to your leg there?" Ryan pointed toward the blood leaking through Jake's Adidas track pants. "It doesn't look too good. You may want to get that checked out at the ER."

The swelling around Jake's wound was expanding instead of decreasing. But even so, he said, "Yeah, I'll be okay." Jake fidgeted with the automatic car window, persistently rolling it up and down.

"Would you stop that?" Ryan sensed something wasn't right. Jake's eyes had gone almost blank.

"Hey, Ryan. I kind of need that two hundred dollars now." Jake itched his nose and his insides shivered.

"Well," Ryan said as his mouth fell open. He knew the warning signs of relapse—or in Jake's case, active addiction. He knew why he needed that money early. "We haven't found Trevor yet, and I thought the deal was—"

"We had no deal, Ryan," Jake interrupted. "I got you this far, and I'll help you find him. I just would feel more secure holding onto that cash, man, in case something happens."

"Something happens?" Ryan didn't like the way he said that.

"Look, bro. Just give me the money," Jake said with bass in his voice.

Ryan fumbled with his wallet and handed Jake two crisp hundred dollar bills.

"Please watch my dog for me. I'll be back in like five minutes," Jake said.

"Wait, what? You're leaving?"

Bulko whimpered as his owner jumped out of the back seat and ran up the street.

"Where the fuck does he think he's going? This is insane," Ryan said to the dog. He knew he shouldn't have given the kid the money already. "Ugh, damn it, Ryan." Bulko rested in the back seat, a sad look drawn on his face. "I'm sorry, bud. I don't know what your master is up to, but I hope he comes back okay."

Jake hiked up the street, making a sharp left down Tacoma Street, leaving Anton's house behind him. He gripped the two hundred dollars in a tight fist. The thought of checking into treatment, being stripped of his medicine, and forced to take new medications—isolated and quarantined on Wednesday—was no longer that appealing. God could have a different plan for him. Maybe it was time he left Detroit and started anew somewhere else. There seemed to be nothing left here for him. Besides, he knew it would only be a matter of time before Andre hunted him down and he ended up as another chalk outline on the sidewalk. Of course, he would have to go back and grab Bulko. Perhaps they could move out to the country and hunt wildlife. He could find a job at a deli, live a simple life away from all the chaos of the city. But for now he was stuck in the Red Zone of Detroit—full of snitches, killers, cops, and ruthless hustlers.

As an addict who had survived Detroit long enough, Jake had developed a keen awareness of how the streets operated. He studied all the passersby with experienced knowledge of how an undercover cop walks. He could recognize their swagger and body language. So when the Caucasian man in a flamboyant pink sun hat peeked his head out of a teal Buick station wagon hollering for his attention, Jake kept on trudging, paying no mind. Everyone knew station wagons belonged to either a narc or someone's grandfather. *Not today, Officer Grandpa*, he thought.

Jake raised his black hoodie up over his head so that it covered his eyelids. He turned in all directions looking for the right guy—the guy who could make his next two hours a complete escape. Ironically, Jake found a guy, but not quite the someone he was hoping to see.

A man with knotted locks and a pitch-black complexion, and sporting a white tank top with a mustard stain on the left shoulder strap took a pressing notice of the man who'd stolen his dog. Jake took a minute, but he identified the man from a side view. His first thought was to wonder why someone would wear a tank top on a chilly September day, unless maybe they were selling drugs. But by the time Jake realized the man in the white tank was no ordinary dealer, Andre Cole had already signaled his posse in a silver-and-black Escalade to turn around and help him trap Jake.

Jake limp-sprinted his way through a small crowd dispersing from the liquor store. The swelling of his infected bullet wound gave him momentary paralysis. But, too stubborn to give up, he grabbed his legs, thrust them forward, and moved as quick as he could. Somehow, through the panic-induced sweat that draped over his eyelids, he managed to see a desolate alley two blocks from the nearby market. Andre was nowhere in sight. Jake turned into the empty alley and collided with a brown dumpster in front of a tall, wrought iron fence. Behind him, footsteps kicked aside loose gravel.

"Hey, crackhead, you have my dog! I want him back. I know that was you at my crib last night!" Andre yelled.

Jake turned to face Andre, staring down the barrel of a Magnum steel berretta pistol. "Look man, I don't have your dog. As you can see, I'm just out here looking to score, okay?" His voice trembled.

"Why did you run then, bitch?" Andre's voice dialed up a few notches.

"Look, man. Put the gun down. I got two hundred dollars. Just let me keep the dog and it's yours."

Andre looked over his shoulder, trying to catch any bystanders in his rear or peripheral vision. No witnesses were around besides Andre's crew, and nothing was heard except the rumbling subwoofers of the Cadillac behind him. "Let me see the money," Andre said.

Jake shuddered and pulled two crinkled-up hundred-dollar bills from his back pocket.

"Bring it to me!" Andre barked. He maintained the gun's position toward Jake's head. Jake slowly walked forward and handed Andre the wrinkled cash. Andre looked down at the two bills and laughed. "Well, thank you, sir. But that's still my damn dog!"

The blast leaving the gun's barrel left little sound in Jake Johnson's ears, but an angelic voice in his brain screamed that it was time for him to come home. Andre's bullet punched its way through Jake's neck, excavating a gaping hole that quickly filled with blood that streamed down his flesh like strong currents collapsing the crest of a dam. He fell to the ground, a pool of blood forming around him and soaking into his clothes. His body squirmed and flopped around like a fish out of water until he ran out of life. The distinct metallic odor of blood lingered over his corpse. Before long, he'd be just another chalk outline.

Bulko was sensing something bad had happened to his owner. He was smart like that. Ryan heard the blast from the gun and tried to brush it off as a warning shot or the cops shooting a bad guy who deserved it. Then he remembered what Jake told him about the police and his own lifestyle. In the eyes of the law, Jake was the bad guy.

Bulko whimpered with a high pitch.

"What's wrong, pooch?" Ryan asked the dog. "It was probably just fireworks. I wouldn't worry too much. Jake will be back any second, I hope." Ryan reached in the back and rubbed Bulko's ears. He wanted to believe the story he told himself.

Bulko let out a short growl before burying his head into the cushioned leather back seat.

Locals in the neighborhood walked by Ryan's car and shot suspicious stares his direction. "I hope Mary and Jake do hurry up," Ryan said to

Bulko. "I keep getting weird looks from people. I don't think they take too kindly to us around here." He turned the car off to save gas.

There was no acknowledgement from Bulko this time, but a sharp tap on Ryan's driver-side window caught his attention. An unmasked, light-skinned police officer with muscles that bulged under his tight-fitting blue uniform demanded Ryan's attention. He wore a pair of tinted Ray-Ban sunglasses and was gnawing on a half-chewed toothpick that he'd snatched from the Chinese buffet hours earlier.

"Am I doing something wrong, officer?" Ryan dripped bullets of sweat. His hands fused together like a clam. He didn't know why he already felt guilty except for the fact that he was sitting outside a well-known drug house that was most likely under surveillance.

"Do you know where you are right now?" Officer Half-Chewed Toothpick smelled Ryan's stench of fear.

"I think this is Detroit." Ryan tried not to be sarcastic, but that question made it difficult.

"Okay, smart ass. But this is the Red Zone, and I can almost guarantee you aren't from here. So, I don't know exactly what you're up to around this way. But I have a good idea, so I'm going to warn you: start your car and head back home to the suburbs before these wolves out here eat you up. Because trust me, they will eat you alive." The cop lowered his sunglasses, revealing stern, deadpan eyes.

Ryan peered at Anton's brick house and looked back at Bulko, trying to formulate a logical reply that wouldn't make him sound overtly suspicious. "I'm waiting for my girlfriend. She left her headphones at her grandparents' house down there. As soon as she comes out, then we're out of here."

"Your girlfriend? Her grandparents? Down there?" Officer Half-Chewed Toothpick wanted to make sure he was hearing the bullshit correctly. He took his sunglasses off and stuffed them in his shirt pocket.

"Yes, sir, officer. That's what I said."

"Sounds like *grandparents* is code for *drug dealer*, and *headphones* really means *crack* or *heroin*. Or *weed*?"

"Absolutely not, sir," Ryan said in a compliant tone.

"Get the hell out of here. I'm not going to ask you again," Officer Half-Chewed Toothpick ordered.

"Yes, sir." Ryan started his car back up and took off. His heart started pounding inside his chest. He did a circle around the block. Officer Half-Chewed Toothpick was scoping him like a trained sniper who'd given his victim a running start and couldn't believe the idiot kept coming back for more.

Finally, Mary made her way outside and strutted down the sidewalk on Queen Street. The cop glared her down. Ryan looped around and waved at her to get in.

Ryan's Charger took a left on Tacoma Street, where he'd last seen Jake running. "No Trevor?" he asked Mary. Her pupils dilated and the subtle twitch gave her away. "And you're high as hell?"

"No, and yes," Mary replied.

At least she's honest, Ryan thought. He could respect that to a certain level. He was disappointed, but he'd expected it. "There's a cop on our tail who already told me to get out of here. If he pulls us over, tell him you're my girlfriend and you went to your grandma's house, but your headphones weren't there," he said.

"Huh?" She was toasted from the meth and heroin swimming in her bloodstream and moving up into her cranium.

"That cop is tailing us, Mary. Do you have anything on you?" He raised his voice. Mary's lack of response was enough of an answer. "Shit, Mary. Come on now!"

"Don't worry—I stashed it up my 'you know.' That cop won't find it unless he wants a sexual harassment charge. We're good. Um, where's Jake?" She looked in the back seat. Bulko was sad asleep.

"I don't know where he went. He just demanded that two hundred dollars I promised him and took off out the car, leaving his dog behind. Did you at least get a lead on where Trevor might be?" Ryan glanced in his rearview mirror. Officer Half-Chewed Toothpick was keeping right on his ass.

"Wait. You gave him two hundred dollars? What about me?"

"You asked for a burger. Just forget about that, I'll help you more if you just tell me if you know where my brother is."

"I have no idea where but ..." she paused, vision narrowed to a pinprick and eyelids fastened together. Each time Ryan hit a rocky bump on the street, her eyes would pop back open, startling her. "We can drive around and find him or some shit." She kept spacing out and stumbling over her own words.

"If we get pulled over, leave all the talking to me," Ryan snapped.

Mary nodded both in agreement and from the heroin. The cop took the next turn on Monarch Street and flicked his red-and-blues on to bother someone else. Ryan's nerves calmed, but he also realized he'd just lost his safety net. Maybe Officer Half-Chewed Toothpick had been tailing to protect him, and now he and Mary were open targets. Ryan turned left on Gratiot Avenue and passed a collage of police lights, ambulances, and masked bystanders gathered around a body bag on a stretcher. "I bet that was from the gunshot earlier."

Mary wasn't present at the moment. She just sat there, slouched over and slipping in her own fuzzy euphoria.

"What if that's Jake in the body bag?" Ryan asked anyway. The probability sunk in, and he could feel that empty pit in his stomach churning over. He wasn't positive, but deep down in his newfound sober instinct, he knew that Jake Johnson was dead.

"You ready for the burger yet?" he asked Mary.

Mary popped back up from her slumber. "Hell yeah." She went to say something else but dissolved back into her drowsy abyss. "Heroin and burgers with a Diet Coke" was what she meant to say.

Chapter 13
Room 106

11:00 p.m., Tuesday, September 22, 2020

"I need to show you room 106." Mr. X motioned forward. Trevor was hunched down in the hall, looking up at the hotel's drab designs. A white wall was covered with slashed graffiti that spelled out *Welcome to a new kind of hell, recovery begins here at the Detox Hotel* in rustic, red letters. Another warning begged Trevor to escape. But the old man kept his pistol in sight, reminding Trevor that trying to run would be foolish.

"What's in room 106? More trauma?" Trevor asked.

Mr. X learned forward. "Ha! This is a fucked-up memory you haven't experienced yet. It's an alternate reality that would have existed if I hadn't saved you from the bathroom stall."

"What do you mean?"

"Let's go take a look."

Trevor thought the old man had a few screws loose, but there was obviously something supernatural going on inside this hotel. He was frightened but also wanted the freedom the old man promised him. So he grudgingly followed Mr. X down the dim and narrow hallway.

"I have a bad feeling about this," Trevor murmured. "I don't trust any of this." His paranoid ideation finally had some credibility.

Abruptly, the two of them stopped at room 106. Mr. X fumbled through several keys clanging together around a metallic key ring until he spotted the one he was looking for. After he unlocked the door, the old man's pointed fingers invited Trevor to enter first.

The room was black, void of any form. There was no ceiling, no floor, no walls, no windows, and no bed—just empty darkness. Trevor could feel the old man's presence behind him. Every deep breath he took made Trevor's skin crawl. He heard a flick.

The light was blinding but soon fizzled out, going completely dark until a new, brighter light emerged. Trevor found himself in a trashy restroom littered with empty cigarette boxes, disposed surgical masks, and orange plastic needle caps. It was the same metro bus station he'd overdosed in almost two days before. Trevor kicked the second stall door in to find himself nodded out, eyes rolled to the back of his head. He tried to wake himself up, violently shaking his shoulders and slapping his own face. "Wake up, motherfucker, wake up!" He didn't understand that he was just a ghost in this alternate world. There was no way to intervene. He just had to watch events unfold.

An elderly, drunk, homeless man, wearing a tattered brown raincoat, wrinkled and stained, aimlessly wandered in. He was holding back a flood of intoxicated urine that needed to be released. The vagrant came upon Trevor and tried to shake him awake. The man yelled "Help! Call 911!"

Paramedics soon arrived and administered a shot of Narcan to revive Trevor. Then they took him away on a stretcher and placed him in the ambulance waiting outside to take him to Detroit Metro Hospital. The feeling of watching himself get carried away in a lifeless condition was too surreal. The shadow was there, too, standing against the wall, watching and waiting just like always.

Trevor was no longer just a spectator in this universe. He now integrated into the alternate version of himself. His invisible spirit migrated into this reality's version of Trevor. He would see the upcoming events play out from his other self's eyes with no control.

Trevor woke up cold and withdrawn, alone in a strange bed, garbed all in white. *Where the hell am I?* he wondered. Then he looked around. Judging by the IV he was hooked up to and the constant dripping sound that intensified his headache, it was apparent that he was in a hospital. Wearing only a delicate hospital gown, Trevor felt naked and sat up in the bed. "Where are my clothes? I need to get the hell out of here."

"Sir, you need to relax and lie back down. Your clothes are safe," said a nurse who'd come running in from the hallway.

Trevor ripped the IV out of his arm. "No, I need to leave." He found a grocery bag of his dirty clothes wrapped up under one of the guest seats in the room and ran into the bathroom. Quickly, he changed into his derelict attire of red flannel shirt, dusty cargo jeans, and the faded Reds baseball cap. He then proceeded to storm out of his room.

The attending nurse chased him down. "Sir, just sign some discharge paperwork. Your brother is here to pick you up."

Trevor came to a halt. The squeaky echo of his shoes across the newly polished tile floor made the hospital staff plug their ears. He turned to take another glance, another listen, to make sure he heard her right. "Excuse me?"

"Yes, just sign here. He's out in the lobby waiting for you," she told him.

"Here, give me the clipboard." He signed his John Hancock and staggered down the hall to the elevator. Just as the nurse promised, when the elevator doors opened, Trevor found his brother, Ryan Dugan, sitting in the main lobby reading an outdated copy of *Sports Illustrated.* The issue was dedicated to the legend Kobe Bryant, who happened to be Ryan's favorite athlete in the world.

"The prodigal son returns," Trevor said as he trudged off the elevator, still disoriented and loopy. "Prodigal son" was one of many nicknames he had for Ryan. (Also included were "Mr. Perfect," "Asshole," and "Douchebag.")

"And the black sheep has risen from his slumber. Nice to see you too, brother." Ryan laid the magazine down, stood up, and took a moment to study the train wreck that was his only sibling.

"What do you want?" Trevor asked, clearing his throat. Dehydration had scratched his voice.

"I need you to get sober and go to Dad's funeral with me."

Trevor paused. "Wait. Dad's dead?" He'd always known it would only be a matter of time.

"Yes, and the funeral is Thursday. Department of Homeland Security shipped his body back to Marlin. Mom wants you there. So will you get in the car with me and head back home? I'll let you dry out at my place. Wife and kids are gone, anyway."

Trevor pooh-poohed the idea of going anywhere with Ryan. "No thanks. I'll pass." He limped his way out the ER lobby, holding his back and pretending it was sore. His back didn't hurt, but that wasn't what he was going to tell the urgent care doctor across the street.

Ryan fetched his Charger from the parking ramp while Trevor slowly escaped down the sidewalk. Trevor had almost made it out of the parking lot before Ryan pulled up next to him from the opposite direction. Ryan leaned his head out the window. "Come on, Trevor. Where are you going to go? You have nowhere to go. Oh wait, you're going to go find some more poison, the same poison that almost killed you."

"Yup, I sure am, and it's also none of your business." Trevor kept walking straight ahead, not even turning in his brother's direction. "How did you find me, anyway?"

Ryan started to drive backward to keep up with his brother. "When your friends didn't know where you were, we checked all the local emergency rooms for any overdose patients."

Thick clouds marched like a parade into the horizon. Sharp gusts of wind swooped in, blowing Trevor's greasy hair back from hanging over his eyes. A sharp crackle of thunder rumbled from above, and light drips of water spit on Trevor's hands and head. The gentle rain transformed into rapid, heavy pellets that stung like piercing paintball blasts. Trevor's sole wardrobe was drenched.

"Shit." Trevor jumped in the passenger seat of Ryan's car. He resented his brother but hated rain and had nowhere else to go. "Let it be known that I'm only going for Mom. I'll do the funeral and then I'm gone."

"Whatever you say, Clever Trevor!" Ryan had his nicknames for his brother just as Trevor had some for him. He hadn't called him that in almost eight years.

"One condition: you have to let me score some dope, or I'm going to get sicker than sick, and it won't be good for me or you." Trevor could feel a slight headache and sniffle coming on again. Sitting in the front seat, his legs started to twist. The junkie junkie shakes.

"Absolutely not! You need to come to Dad's funeral clean. When you start getting an urge, just rub this for good luck." Ryan reached in his middle console and tossed Trevor his AA serenity chip. *To Thine Own Self*

Be True was etched on the gold-tinted medallion. Trevor thought about throwing it out the window to set his serenity free.

"So, I'm just supposed to rub this thing when I get triggered and all the cravings just disappear? That's not how it works, Ryan." Trevor shook his head and flipped the coin back into his brother's console. For a minute, he wondered why his brother had a serenity coin to begin with. But he was too dope sick to even care about that now.

Ryan sensed his brother's resistance, but he had everything mapped out. He'd prepared his home for Trevor's detox with appropriate caution. He'd stocked up on ibuprofen, orange juice, ginger ale, and chicken soup. A friend recommended getting Trevor into a community mental health organization to see a psychiatrist who could prescribe a medication, like Vivitrol, to reduce the urges and cravings for opioid use. Ryan had done his research, placed vomit buckets all around his house. He'd also installed a new, solid dead bolt to his guest room where Trevor could sleep. Locking him in that room was a last resort but an option he had to consider for a successful detox.

Trevor started thinking about his father, and his mind spiraled potential conspiracies, premeditated motives, and questions. *Who killed him? What did he know? Did his bootleg witness protection plan fail him? So who was it that took Dad out? FBI, CIA, Department of Homeland Security, domestic terrorists?*

He doubted Ryan would know the answers to any of these questions but figured he would ask anyway. "Anyone allude to or mention anything of the FBI, Department of Homeland Security, or any government involvement?"

"He overdosed on a full bottle of Seroquel and stabbed himself in the chest. Dad committed suicide."

"So whoever it was made it look like a suicide. That makes sense."

Ryan detected uncomfortable tension and started dialing through all the radio stations that still had a signal. He stopped at 105.3, *The Rox*, cranking up the bass and treble to max watts. The heavy yet delicate sound of Mudvayne's "World So Cold" traveled like mechanical waves transporting a high-pitched melody beyond their ears and into the marrow of their memories.

During a time when they were younger, before all the turbulence, Dad had purchased the album *The End of All Things to Come* for the two of them. They would blast the tune, maxing out the volume on Ryan's subwoofers. Bill even showed Trevor how to play some of the chords to this song on his Les Paul 100-rhythm guitar. The boys got so addicted to the song and guitar that they would stay up way past midnight, learning new chords and singing the song over and over. Bill had to the cut the electricity off from the breaker to get those two weasels back into bed.

Trevor took a moment and smiled, remembering those days. He started tickling his stomach, dancing his fingers across imaginary frets and softly mouthing the lyrics. Ryan joined in, nodding his head to the beat, and in unison their melodic growls complimented each other. The younger Dugan brothers were back. Even if it was short-lived, they were back. *Cut the electricity off now, Dad*, they both thought.

Ryan lived in a pricey home on the outskirts of Marlin. Trevor had never been there before. For Ryan, it was a basic contemporary home, but to Trevor it was a visual masterpiece. The house itself rested on a hill surrounded by several acres of grassy fields. The sharp, red-tiled roof arched skyward. Silver-struck aluminum siding barricaded the house against outside vagrants and thieves like Trevor. There was no white picket fence, but Ryan pulled his Charger into a three-car garage that screamed prosperity.

Inside, a clean but disorganized living room with beige carpet was flooded with Legos, a pink rocking horse, Nerf guns, and a pair of overstuffed Incredible Hulk boxing gloves. The toys sat motionless, abandoned by Ryan's children, who on a normal day would be having Nerf wars and grueling superhero boxing matches with each other while Mom and Dad cuddled on the couch watching animated Netflix movies.

The gray plastered walls served as a domestic gallery of picture-perfect family portraits aligned in precise columns. Trevor grimaced as he fixed his gaze upon a happy family vacation photo with Lake Michigan in the scenic background. His niece, Lucy, and nephew, Lukas, looked so innocent, so protected from the Dugan family curse. He adored but envied them. If he weren't such a horrible train wreck, he could be involved in their lives. Uncle Trevor could take them to the beach and take cheesy selfies to post on social media.

"So make yourself at home. Just don't steal anything. I'll make us both some coffee," Ryan said.

"Ha! Funny. So where are Jessica and the kids?" Trevor pushed a frame a smidgen to the left, on an angle, ruining its perfect position.

"Gone."

An uncomfortable hush fell over the room. Trevor looked over Ryan's shoulder at annuals in soiled pots resting on the window sill, waiting for the sun to bring them warmth. Unwelcome nostalgia reminded Trevor of his mom and her obsession with plants.

The silence grew more intense. Trevor left the kitchen and took the liberty of giving himself a brief tour of his brother's suburban fortress. He took his focus back to the photos and discovered that in the back of the living room stood a china cabinet that resembled a mighty shrine with several more pictures. Most of the framed photos were of Ryan in junior high and varsity football, including one gold-framed portrait of his freshman Michigan State football jersey number 86. Next to the shrine, almost behind it, hid a small, framed snapshot of two brothers playfully wrestling in the backyard of the home outside Lansing they'd resided in for a couple years. They couldn't have been over ten years old. The pure, guiltless expression on their faces was a far cry from their current state of despair.

This particular house wasn't his and never would be. But Trevor fantasized that it was his childhood home because he didn't have a childhood home—he'd just visited several foundations where his family dwelled throughout his youth. His family had never settled long enough to consider any of the dwellings a home. But the energy, the smell, of this home reminded him of Mom and Dad, just a watered-down scent.

All of Ryan's possessions and evidence of success made Trevor wonder if, if he could travel back in time and undo his past, he would choose a different path? Would he be married and have beautiful children he could drive to softball practice and tuck in every night? That was a different life, but someday, if he ever got his shit together, maybe it was possible. Then he remembered Ryan's present situation. He glanced back at his brother in the kitchen, preoccupied with cleaning out his Keurig coffee maker so he could fix up a fresh cup of black brew. Ryan looked like he was worried and scared. Trevor had never seen him like this.

"At least you have a beautiful home. I could only imagine what living here feels like." Trevor went back in the kitchen and helped himself to an empty mug, waiting for Ryan to offer him coffee. The Keurig wasn't cleaned out yet.

Ryan filled the coffee maker's reservoir halfway with vinegar and the other half with water. "Well, I'm on the verge of probably losing this home." He started the machine and placed an empty bowl underneath to catch the liquid. After the cleansing process was finished, Ryan snatched Trevor's mug from his grasp and a K-Cup pod from behind the paper towel holster to brew his brother a cup.

"It's obvious I'm a mess," Trevor said, "but what the hell is going on with you? AA sobriety chips, losing your home?"

Ryan ignored the question. "I don't have any cream for your coffee because I drink mine black. We have milk but it's outdated."

"My life is expired, so I think I'll be okay," Trevor said with a smirk.

"Let me show you where you'll be staying." Ryan mixed a small shot of milk in the black coffee and handed it to Trevor.

Ryan led Trevor past the kitchen and showed him his guest room so he could unpack. The room was small with clean, white walls; a twin bed; a desk with an Alcoholics Anonymous textbook sitting on top; a closet with sliding doors opposite the bed; and a thin, beige shag carpet.

Ryan threw some of his old but clean clothes from the laundry room on the bed: a Michigan State jersey, black skinny jeans, and a pair of white socks. Trevor looked back at the AA book on the desk and discovered right next to it a pile of loose change. The amount couldn't be much, but it was enough to twist Trevor's mind a little and make his stomach growl. He was hungry but a hundred miles from a dealer, and ten bucks in quarters wasn't going to get him anything more than an ass kicking and a gun to his temple.

"You need a shower. Go get cleaned up and we can talk." Ryan snapped Trevor out of his trance. He pitched Trevor a freshly dried Michigan State towel.

I bet this guy has a Michigan State penis pump hidden somewhere in this house, Trevor thought.

Trevor took another sip of his coffee and jumped in the shower. The sensation of the steamy water calmed him into tranquility. He knew that soon the withdrawal would peak and any chance of serenity wouldn't exist. But for now he'd soak all of it in.

He came out of the bathroom in his brother's fluffy white-and-green Michigan State bathrobe. "Can I get another cup of coffee?"

"Already one step ahead of you." Ryan handed him another cup of hot, steaming joe.

Trevor thanked him and sparked a menthol-100 cigarette right in the kitchen.

"Um, you can't smoke in here, dude." Ryan waved the smoke from his face. The rancid smell of tobacco made him nauseous.

"Oh shit! Sorry, man." Trevor opened the sliding screen door to the back patio and stepped outside.

Ryan accompanied him outside and passed him his coffee. "And no, I don't want a cigarette, in case you were going to ask. Just wanted to make that clear."

"Good, because I wouldn't give you one anyway. And I'm also out." Trevor tapped ash from his cigarette.

"I know you're out because I watched you pick that up off the ground outside the hospital, idiot." Ryan chuckled and shook his head.

"Can we make a supply run? I'm going to need a carton of cigarettes and some weed to take the edge off. Also, Pringles. I crave Pringles when I'm withdrawing." Trevor glanced up to the sky. The rain clouds were dissipating, and the sun was pushing its way into sight. "Why aren't you writing any of this down?"

"Yeah, I'll get right on that." Ryan snatched his brother's cigarette to try a gross taste.

"What the hell, man? You can keep it." Trevor started to get mad, but he couldn't resist laughing at his brother gasping like it was his final breath.

"I got two days to keep you clean, and that means no weed either, man," Ryan said between struggling hacks.

Trevor scoffed. "In two days, I'll be a walking nightmare. If I were you, I'd really think twice about the weed. It calms me when my nerves are shot."

"Weed always gave me cotton mouth and the munchies."

Trevor laughed at the thought of Ryan raiding the fridge in his mansion in the middle of the night and drinking gallons of water, paranoid about waking his wife and kids.

"You know, on second thought, weed will just make me want to go find the hard stuff anyway."

"I'm glad you're able to finally admit that, little brother. Believe it or not, I care about you."

For a moment, Trevor felt like he had his brother Ryan back. The same Ryan who would stay up past their bedtime, hiding under covers and telling him yo' mama jokes into the beam of a flashlight. Considering they'd shared the same mother, Trevor was always a little confused, but he laughed along anyway. Or the Ryan who taught him how to clean and gut a trout, mix hot peppers into the fish meat, and watch their dad wince and gag after taking a few bites.

Ryan led Trevor back inside, into the living room. "Can I get you something to eat?"

"Not just yet. Thank you though." Trevor's appetite was still restoring itself.

Ryan put on a documentary called *Social Media Takeover.* Trevor became glued to the TV. The program showed testimonies from anonymous FBI and NSA personnel admitting to monitoring citizens' movements via technology. Trevor explained to Ryan how he always used a fake name on social media accounts but that even then the government had ways to collect all your data, your Google search engine history, and the records of how many shoes you bought in order to target future advertisements on your Facebook page.

"It's targeted consumerism through social media," Trevor explained to Ryan. For the past seven years, since his paranoia had increased and his addiction had minimized his funds, he'd carried a Boost Mobile prepaid phone with disposable SIM cards to limit the government's monitoring capabilities. He'd started subscribing to YouTube conspiracy theory channels that warned the sheeple of America that the military was kidnapping, trafficking, and experimenting on children in the United States. The podcast *Jungian Hour* suggested that the government was soon going to plant surveillance technology into humans while still in the womb to monitor their subconscious thoughts.

Ryan listened to Trevor rant for a while but then debunked his wild conspiracy theories. Although Ryan was aware that technology was invasive, probing human fetuses with microchips seemed a little extreme.

"I love you, brother, but you took Dad leaving us to a new level of paranoia and combined that with drugs. You melted your brain," Ryan joked. But it wasn't really a joke. Trevor's mind was fried like scorched bacon.

Trevor hit the pause button on the remote. "I was the only one who took Dad's leaving us serious," he said. "Mom just cried nightly but did nothing to try to keep him around. And you acted like it didn't bother you. Dad left to protect us, but he also left behind little bread crumbs, like a picture of a Rubik's Cube attached to a letter."

He pulled out his phone and showed Ryan three different pictures of the cube that was left in the basement of their old home in Marlin. "The letter was addressed to a Lady Phantom. It was written in code, but I did see that it mentioned *Save The Children* like all the future right-wing hashtags on social media. Dad and Lady Phantom were ahead of their time. But the interesting part was Dad directing this Lady Phantom to 'steal back technology' from the lab and telling her that 'E.T. needs to phone home.' Dad was trying to send a message. So I engrossed myself in researching that cube, which led me down a rabbit hole. But all my paths kept getting blocked. I believe the cube had something to do with the technology he was telling Lady Phantom to steal. But he never mailed that letter out. He must have forgotten it before he left." Trevor slurped the last few drops of his second cup of coffee.

Ryan held his palms over his ears to drown out the irritating sound of liquid being slugged down. He had a condition, misophonia, where certain sounds, like loud chewing, cracking joints, slurping, tapping, sniffling, crunching, tongue clicks, and even heavy breathing, could trigger in him exasperated moments of homicidal ideation.

Trevor turned to Ryan, eyes protruding like they were clawing their way out of his sockets, tired of seeing the world through his chaotic lens. "Save the Children, ET phone home or go home, whatever, steal the technology, Rubik's Cubes, what did it all mean?" he asked frantically. "And who was Lady Phantom? Based on my own assumptions, I gathered the government was experimenting on children or implanting alien technology into unborn fetuses. The Rubik's Cube could have been coincidence or a vessel for such technology. This is what I believe Dad knew, and he was going to destroy the experiments and needed to get out. He had to leave to save us from what he was going to do or try to do."

Ryan stood up, walked to the kitchen, and threw his coffee mug into the sink. "I'm sorry to be the one to tell you," he called to Trevor, "but now that he's dead, it doesn't even matter. Dad never met with a guy to make him 'disappear' or even leave to go be a hero. That was just his ploy. He left us and Mom to go move in with his new, twenty-two-year-old, redheaded partner he was assigned to. Or as you came to know her, Lady Phantom. The aliens, Rubik's Cubes, and children? Well, I'm sorry, but that sounds like more Dad bullshit to keep your head spinning and give you hope. Mom and I found out about Lady Phantom later on but didn't know how to break it to you. You loved Dad so much, we knew it would crush you."

Trevor sat up and swung his head toward the kitchen. "Liar!"

"There was no FBI or Homeland Security cover-up. Dad wasn't a whistleblower for experiments on children or implanting microchips in fetuses. It was all bullshit. Dad was a cheater and made up this ridiculous lie claiming he had to join some underground witness protection program to keep us safe when really he just wanted to move into his partner's apartment and bang her without being bothered by his family."

Trevor's blood pressure heightened. He knew the caffeine was ramping him up, but these new lies were pouring kerosene on his central nervous system. "Maybe that's what he told you and Mom because you're too weak-minded to know the damn truth. Dad would never do that. You would probably do that your wife, but don't you dare put that on Dad." Trevor sat up from the couch and slammed his empty mug down on a wooden coaster. "I'm tired. I think I'm going to go to bed now. I can't believe you invite me here and pull this shit about Dad."

Ryan's calm demeanor quickly dissolved. The Dugan rage took the pilot seat. "Go ahead and run to sleep, Trevor. Why are you so quick to defend Dad? He beat the bricks off you when you were young and treated you like gum under his shoes. But you don't remember that part, do you? You only remember him when he felt guilty for his shit and tried to make it up to you by making you feel like you would be his little secret agent sidekick. It was all bullshit to give him an out and not completely ruin you. Sorry the truth hurts, but you had to face it sooner or later."

Trevor slammed and locked the guest room door behind him. He immersed his head in the closest pillow, letting tear floods flow like Niagara Falls. All the buried trauma, resentments, anger, and fear had surfaced, and he wanted to submerge it back down with some numbing heroin. His mind kept racing. Was it really all just lies to hide his dad's infidelity from his mom? Trevor's nerves jittered. But what about the letter? Snot poured down from his nostrils in an uncontrollable fashion. He could detect the pressure of a small gas bubble forming. The warm, slimy feeling of the backdoor trots slid down his thighs, and the excrement seeped through his bathrobe.

He remembered that the toilet in the guest room's bathroom had been clogged when he went to piss in it earlier. Disoriented and anxious, Trevor pushed his way out the door and scouted for the nearest shit-bucket. Ryan had disappeared, but Trevor saw between the kitchen and guest room a staircase leading to the basement. He made his way down into the basement, but he couldn't make it in time, and the soil made its complete exit. Trevor stripped himself bare and saw another shower in the basement restroom. He freshened up for a second time that evening.

Ryan still hadn't appeared to see what all the ruckus was about. He was upstairs, reliving in his mind the hurtful exchange he'd had with his brother moments earlier.

Trevor ejected a little bile down in the wastebasket. He didn't quite make it to the toilet. He started to mount the steps when something in his periphery caught his eye. A shiny metal lockbox rested comfortably on top of a flimsy ironing board. A hodgepodge of blue jeans, sweaters, and other valuable getaway clothes shrouded the metal box. In Trevor's addict mind, he had hit the jackpot.

He grabbed a pair of blue jeans and a plain black t-shirt off the ironing board and put them on in a hurry. Void of logic, he grabbed the lockbox and raised it up high above his head. Using all his adrenaline-fueled power, he smashed it down on the dusty concrete floor. The combination lock was still in one piece. *You weak son of a bitch, try harder!* he mentally scolded himself.

After about four or five cracks, the damn lock still didn't want to budge. Trevor grew furious and kicked the safe forward, sending it straight into the concrete wall. He looked down to see that the combination lock had split into two cracked pieces. He scurried over and opened it up. The box was full of crumpled-up newspaper and gift wrapping paper, but there appeared to be something heavy underneath. He viciously ripped the paper out of the lockbox and beheld an early birthday gift to himself. A gun.

Anton had said he needed .38-caliber pistols. Trevor snatched the pistol up, cradling the barrel against his chest like it was a precious newborn baby. He didn't care if he had to walk back to Detroit. He'd found his ticket home. *To hell with detox and Dad's funeral,* he thought.

A door flew open and heavy footsteps marched down the basement stairs. "Trevor, what the hell are you doing down here?" Ryan was panting. He hadn't run that fast since college football.

Trevor struggled to get up and positioned himself straight, pointing the steel weapon at his brother. "Get back, Ryan. Give me the keys to your car! I'm not going to Dad's funeral. And unless you want Mom to visit your casket, give me the keys and all the cash you have on you."

Ryan's eyed widened. He stopped and slowly moved closer to his brother. "Now, Trevor. Let's take it easy. We don't need to do anything stupid. I can give you a ride back to Detroit, but I can't let you steal my car. So put the gun down and let's talk about this. I know you're upset about what happened with Dad," Ryan said with a calm, soothing voice.

Trevor took a step in reverse. His hands were trembling, swaying the gun back and forth. "I don't want to do this. Just let me go. I'm serious," he said with a whimper. He stiffened up and leveled the pistol at his brother's chest. "Don't come any closer."

Ryan held both his hands up in the air. "Trevor, don't let this happen. Don't let this fucking disease take you here, take us here! We can talk about this. Maybe I came off a little rough about Dad. You could be right and there's more to the story than any of us know about."

Ryan fought back waves building up under his eyelids. He wanted this to all be over and to have his brother back, like the good old days before dope and conspiracy ruined everything.

But it was too late. Trevor's fingers were quaking as he felt the cold metal grow heavy within a split second. He didn't consciously mean to pull the trigger. This wasn't his exact intention. He merely wanted to intimidate his brother into letting him go.

The old déjà vu sting returned. Trevor watched his brother holding his chest. There was blood seeping through his hands as Ryan tried to cover the expanding wound under his sweatshirt.

"You shot me, brother." Ryan muffled the words as he fell down in disbelief.

Trevor flinched. His ears grew deaf. He didn't even remember hearing the gunshot blast.

Ryan collapsed onto the floor, but there was still some life in him. "I'm sorry." He was gurgling on his own blood. To the average ear it would have been hard to make out the words, but Trevor heard them clear as day: "I'm sorry I failed you." The light left Ryan's eyes, color drained from his face, and his heart stopped. His battle was over.

Trevor kneeled over his brother's lifeless body, sobbing. "Wake up, motherfucker. I'm sorry. This isn't happening. We have to go to Dad's funeral. I'll get clean, brother. This isn't happening!"

Ryan's blank eyes glared back at Trevor. Trevor jumped back in terror and picked up the cell phone to dial his confession.

"Nine-one-one. What is your emergency?"

"I shot my brother and I think he's dead."

Chapter 14
Parole Mission Amends

Trevor was dragged from room 106 and transported to the year 2045 to see his fate. This was where he met a peculiar fellow by the name of Sherman Jackson.

4:00 p.m., September 20, 2045

Sherman Jackson was a twenty-five-year-old Caucasian male diagnosed with schizoaffective disorder (severe) with psychotic features and opioid use disorder (severe). He had a slight limp from falling off too many ladders as a young roofer. But the falls hadn't been accidental. Those little voices that made word sounds in his brain told him to jump. He belonged in a psychiatric facility, not the state penitentiary in Jackson, Michigan. But there he was, among a gauntlet of criminals being led by an obese guard, who smelled like vinegar and Axe body spray, down the walk of shame. Some of the turnkeys, or prison guards, had titled that hallway the "walk of shame" because life was about to fuck every last one of the prisoners.

"Fresh meat!" a heavyset burly man with a Nazi insignia branded on his forehead hollered out. This was a ritualistic catcall to alert the other inmates of new blood coming into their new home. Sherman cowered and felt paralyzed from fear. One of the guards who was ready for his shift to be over pushed him forward from behind.

A loud buzzing sound echoed. A different stout guard, one with gray hair parted down the middle like a teenybopper from the 1990s who'd grown old and bitter, nudged Sherman into cell B86, his newfound home. The cold iron cell door slammed shut behind him.

Sherman nervously ran his slender fingers through his unkempt ginger hair, studying the dimensions of the vault: six feet by eight feet. He examined the white walls and estimated that he was surrounded by 132 square feet of reinforced concrete. Sherman was a bit of an intellectual and great with numbers, even though the voices told him otherwise. They told him he was an idiot and reminded him that this was his harsh new environment for at least the next twenty-five years. The life outside that he once knew no longer existed.

Trevor Dugan, now forty-eight years young, rested comfortably on the bottom bunk, squinting his eyes through the new specs he'd finally been able to purchase through the commissary. It had taken him only three weeks of hard trustee labor to be able to afford this new pair of reading glasses. Three long weeks before he could properly be fascinated by the newest edition of *Garden Variety* magazine. Biweekly he would take on a new horticulture project. This week's venture was the Patagonian Groundsel, also known as *Baccharis*, an ideal shrub that could survive through harsh winters. They required patience, as Trevor read they were slow-growing but reached heights and a spread of nine feet with strong, binding roots. He'd ordered the seeds through the commissary, and they were due to ship any day. In fact, his latest shipment tracking estimated another two to three business days. He was eager to get out in the garden and merge his hands back in the soil, planting new lives. His rose bush from two weeks before was already showing early signs of sprouting.

"Hi, I'm Sherman. How's it going?" The new chum smiled while his forehead drowned in perspiration.

Trevor didn't look up from his article. He was absorbed in studying photos of a Groundsel in full form, monumental and divine. He wasn't really in the mood for the good old "welcome to life in prison" monologue.

"My toothbrush is the red one. If you touch it, you die. Touch any of my shit, you die. And courtesy flush before you're done shitting. If you can manage all that, then there will be no problems," Trevor said. The revised welcome speech was short, blunt, and to the point. "Also, don't jerk off and moan loud while I'm trying to sleep. That shit gets really annoying."

"Courtesy flushes and jackoff-free zone or quiet jerking off. I think I can handle all of that." Sherman strutted toward the small sink to sanitize his mitts before touching anything in his new bedroom/bathroom. His jokes may have been dirty, but he always made sure his hands were clean.

"Not much of a sense of humor? Or much of a talker?" the idiot chatterbox continued. "That's okay. I get it. I'm the new guy, and you probably been in here forever. Here I come along, talking your ear off and trying to tell jokes. But everyone needs to hear jokes. Comedy makes the world go around."

Sherman waited for a reaction from his new cellmate but there was nothing. Trevor kept his eyes glued to his magazine, ignoring the pet jester and hoping he would take the hint to shut up. Sherman wasn't good at taking hints. "*Garden Variety*, huh?"

"You can read. Congratulations."

"Hey, why was the gardener so embarrassed?"

No acknowledgement from Trevor.

"He wet his plants. Get it?" The newbie snorted like an obnoxious swine before more silence hushed his laughter. Sherman was known to be the only person to find his own jokes funny. "Did you know that one of the very first human emotions and responses as a newborn is laughter? It's a hardwired response that has no boundaries when it comes to language or race. Obviously, crying, which is caused by fear, is the first human response. Most infants enter the world that way. They're afraid of this strange, new world being thrown into their reality." Sherman paced the white cell like was he was giving a fantasy TED Talk on the topic of humor.

Trevor continued to ignore his presence.

The TED Talk continued. "Before, it was the soft comfort of their mother's womb. Now, it's like, 'Sorry, buddy, we're kicking you out. Now you have to go live in this fucked-up world ruled by fear, money, sex, and corrupt power.' They never asked to be here. So fear comes first, and the laughter follows. It's a tradition that we carry with us into adulthood. But we're able to get more control of it."

Trevor peered up from behind his magazine. "Wow, you're a walking encyclopedia of useless knowledge. Thanks for the educational portion of this program."

"Fair enough. I get it. Shut up new guy! Roger that." Sherman started unpacking his toothbrush, toothpaste, deodorant, shampoo, body wash, notepad, and pen. He whistled as he made his bed more than three different times to make sure the sheets and blanket were lined up to perfection. Eventually, he grew silent as he lay on the top bunk. He just blankly stared at the ceiling, pondering all the tragic events that had led to this moment and listening to the voices. *But we need to forget them, Sherman.* Rambling on seemed to be an effective distraction to block out those memories. *But you can't block them out forever, Sherman. They always come crawling back.* He wondered if the doctors in prison would prescribe him his Haldol to quiet those damn voices down.

Trevor smiled, embracing the peaceful stillness. He continued to read and marvel at horticulture until his eyes grew blurry and he drifted off into an oblivious slumber. Sherman joined him from the top bunk, slipping into his own personal dreamland. The inmates slept maybe an hour before their power naps were interrupted. Between the prison guard's baton rattling against the iron cell bars and his bunkie sawing wood, Trevor was startled back into consciousness. It was chow time.

Upon release, Trevor and Sherman walked through the first set of cells and headed down to the dayroom. "Now what?" Sherman asked with naïve curiosity.

"We wait for that door to open, then we go eat," Trevor replied. Some of the inmates turned back to get a peek at the newbie asking all the questions. They were sizing him up.

The prisoners stood in a single-file line and waited for the chow hall door to allow them entry. Trevor liked to eat alone. Some days he would sit with the Aryans. He despised their ideology but they protected him. In exchange, he made them shanks, or weapons, to murder anyone and everyone. Today Trevor wanted to sit alone, but Sherman hovered over him like a lost puppy dog, oblivious to all social cues.

"Sit down," Trevor hissed. "Listen, don't make it too obvious that you have no idea where or who the fuck you are. It doesn't matter that you're new. If they see you looking around, asking too many questions, they'll assume you're vulnerable. The last thing you want them to think is that you're weak. Keep your eyes focused straight ahead. If you absolutely have to ask a question, don't draw too much attention. The more you lay low, the easier it'll be on you." Trevor grabbed Sherman's wrist and his jaw clenched with the severity of his words.

"Okay, I got a question. How the hell did we end up with fried chicken this good? Because this is not what I expected the food to be like in prison." Sherman broke the tension again with humor, but this time Trevor couldn't help but laugh. And it was true. Their prison food wasn't as nasty as what's shown in the movies. Although there were days when the budget was tight and they were fed stale cornbread and dried beans. But that day's menu included tenderized green beans, mashed potatoes, and crispy fried chicken with a cup of freshly squeezed lemonade.

The two of them got to talking, and Trevor discovered that Sherman was possibly not that big of an idiot after all. Trevor still labeled him a dummy, just to a lesser degree. Additionally, Trevor learned they had one major similarity: both suffered from addiction, and in the grips of its holy hell each had taken someone's life. Sherman had killed his best friend in a drunken stupor.

As Sherman explained, "We were grappling on the bridge, and he went for my knife, and I pushed him over, fighting over a measly twenty dollars." Sherman hung his head low and sucked back tears before they could even think of surfacing. He knew what would happen if he was caught crying, but he missed his best friend.

Trevor empathized with Sherman's situation. He imagined the scene in his head and pictured his brother's face on Sherman's friend. The image drained his energy, and he slouched back in his chair and disclosed a few small details of his conviction. But every time it had been brought up in the past, he'd relived that moment of putting the bullet in his brother's chest. He refused to talk about it unless absolutely necessary. "Yeah, I killed my brother on accident. It was the fucking dope, man," was the usual brief summary he recited for people who needed to know. But not many people needed to know.

"Wow, man. I'm sorry to hear that," Sherman replied. "They need to reform the system. Addicts like us belong in treatment centers. And for me, well, with all the voices I hear, I belong in a hospital or asylum somewhere. Maybe a nice one with an arcade and candy dispensers full of psychotropic medications." Sherman furiously gnawed down on a fried chicken leg and spit out a slice of bone that had almost settled between his front teeth.

Trevor positioned himself upright and looked across at his new bunkie with slight pity. "That's optimistic, but that's not the kind of world we live in. We committed violent acts in the mist of our addiction. They don't take lightly to that, and they won't give us special accommodations, either." Trevor didn't consider himself a pessimist. No, he was a realist.

After chow, the Michigan Department of Corrections' finest guards escorted the men outside to their prison-ground recess. A wire fence with densely interwoven, jagged barbs shielded the prisoners from even a fleeting thought of escape. Two stone brick watchtowers stood on the north and south sides of the yard. Prison guards with scoped rifles strapped over their shoulders paced in circles around the tower's ledge like medieval knights preparing to protect their empire of criminals from themselves. Their job was to monitor the flock of segregated inmates below. The races and nationalities were separated from each other. They all huddled in their own corners of the yard and plotted against one another.

One of the nations, the Aryans, were eyeballing Trevor and his new companion. Trevor gave a hand signal, a single stroke across his receding hairline, to the Aryans. This communicated that Sherman was "okay." In response, most of the Aryans turned away and dismissed their concern for the time being. By no means did Trevor's declaration offer Sherman protection, and he would still have to figure that one out on his own. The mountain-sized, Nazi-branded nut-job who'd catcalled Sherman earlier kept his eyes locked on the fresh meat. Sherman picked up on the White supremacist's invasive energy. So he kept his eyes locked straight ahead just as Trevor advised.

Trevor needed a new spotter for weightlifting. The last one had been shanked, wound up in the medical unit, and was still recovering. Sherman was frail, but Trevor imagined he could at least catch a bar if it slipped. Today, Trevor was going to attempt to bench a solid two hundred and fifty pounds. He'd managed two hundred and forty and almost dropped the bar on his head after one rep. Sherman graciously agreed to help him.

When Trevor pulled the sleeves of his blue-and-orange uniform up to his elbows, Sherman enjoyed viewing his ripped forearms. Trevor was favorably built with a balding head. Underneath his uniform, his flesh was riddled with a vast inked display of entangled vines wrapping their arms around a two-headed dragon that shot a sword of flames down the veins of his forearm. His elbows were nothing more than elementary spider webs, each cob representing another year he'd spent in the cage. Above his biceps, a trail of Chinese emblems crawled up to his neck.

When Trevor clenched his fist around the steel barbell, Sherman took note of the bold letters *D-R-U-G F-R-E-E* tattooed across his knuckles. The poor boy tried to keep his eyes straight ahead like he'd been told, but they kept getting distracted by Trevor's hunky physique. There was one dark secret Sherman couldn't let out of the bag. But in the joint, it eventually gets ripped out one way or the other.

Following recreational time, the prisoners were led to the shower room for their daily cleansing. Trevor always accelerated his bathing experience. Even after twenty-five years, he still didn't feel comfortable getting naked around sixteen psychopathic criminals. Afterward, he retired to his bunk, picking up the Stephen King novel *Revival*. He'd left off on Chapter 3 the previous week. Minutes transcended into over an hour or more, and Sherman had yet to return to the cell. Trevor stayed up a little past his normal bedtime to see if he'd come back. He figured maybe the guard had moved him to a different cell or the inmates had killed him already. Either one wouldn't be surprising, after all.

About an hour later, Sherman's natural, subtle limp had transformed into a bow-legged hobble as he made his way back into cell B86 with that all too recognizable mortified expression scribbled on his red face. Trevor didn't even need to ask what had happened. He already knew because it happened to almost everyone. Trevor had had his turn. Granted, for him it hadn't been the first night, but the dehumanization still occurred.

Sherman kept quiet as a mouse, climbed to his upper berth, and retired for the evening. Although his eyes were peeled wide open and he didn't sleep a wink, he had checked out that night. Trevor felt brief empathy for his new bunkie's brutal initiation—just another routine hazard of life in prison. Despite his concern, Trevor needed all the sleep he could get. Tomorrow was his big day in front of the parole board.

9:00 a.m., September 21, 2045

It was judgment day. The parole room was dimly lit, with shards of sun shining through dusty white blinds. The Unites States and State of Michigan flags hung from chrome poles next to a window to freedom—a freedom Trevor Dugan hadn't seen in over twenty-five years. In the center of the wall, above the window, a sculpture of a bald eagle rested on a wooden mount. Trevor was uneasy, as he felt like the bird was casting luminous eyes directly at him.

He returned his attention to the panel and counted ten members, not including the short Latino patrol guard with a red Bluetooth speaker in his right ear who was circling the room and slapping his baton across his palm. He kept mumbling into his earpiece like a schizophrenic mall cop reporting for duty. Trevor believed that if he wanted to, he could take the guard out.

The panel consisted of five criminology experts with PhDs and published books; a lawyer; the warden; a parole officer; the almighty Commissioner Marble; and Trevor's case manager, Clint Rollins. Trevor liked his case manager. Clint was disorganized and scattered-brained. He had a flimsy toupee that always slid off when he got too overwhelmed and a cheesy detective mustache that always had a trickle of mayo left over from his lunch. "I'm saving it for later," he would joke with Trevor. Despite some of his unprofessionalism, he'd worked hard to present Trevor's case. Trevor had received no tickets in almost two years and attended all his AA and NA meetings in the library. Hell, he'd even found a sponsor. But above all, feeling remorse for his crime was the most important piece Trevor had to sell.

Two of the criminology experts were drop-dead gorgeous. Trevor hadn't felt or even seen female skin that soft-looking in decades. They were probably half his age, and he had to be careful not to stare too hard. His life was depending on this.

The warden was old and looked preoccupied. The parole officer was a middle-aged African American man with a flat effect. The slender prosecuting attorney, sporting oversized, black-rimmed bifocals, was texting on his phone and oblivious to everyone else in the room. If only the prosecutor could have texted an offer to the judge for a lighter sentence or a more reasonable plea bargain during that horrible trial twenty-five years before, Trevor might have scratched a deal. But an eighteen- to twenty-five-year plea bargain wasn't any more appealing than twenty-five to life. He'd taken his chances on trial, trying to use the "remorseful addict needing treatment" ploy. Needless to say, it hadn't worked, and here he was.

Clint had told Trevor that Commissioner Marble was the wild card on the panel and the most important one to convince. The commissioner had that deadpan stare reminiscent of the superintendent at Marlin High when Trevor got busted selling catnip to his naïve, curious classmates who'd never even smelled marijuana in their lives. Marble was skimming through some paperwork, which Trevor assumed was part of Cliff's report on his progress.

Trevor rested timidly in the hot seat, centered straight in front of the panel like a convicted Stormtrooper sitting before the Galactic Empire. He kept scooting his chair back and forth, screeching it on the tile floor beneath him. This was one of the several nervous tics he'd developed over his time in prison, and it was painfully obvious that the warden was growing annoyed. But Trevor couldn't control it. He finally was able to minimize the scoot to a low howl, inching slightly forward.

"Are you Trevor Dugan?" Marble asked.

"Yes," he replied.

"I'm Commissioner Marble. Present also with us today is prosecuting attorney Mr. Gobles. I'm sure you remember him." The snake Gobles hurriedly put down his phone and perked up with a smile.

How could I forget that asshole? Trevor thought. But he nodded at the group.

"Now, you're before us today as an initial applicant for parole release. You're presently serving a term of twenty-five years to life for murder in the first degree and possession of an unregistered firearm, is that correct?" The commissioner peered down, shuffling through the mountain of unorganized paperwork that Trevor's case manager had assembled. But he finally looked up to see the inmate's response.

Trevor coughed slightly and said, "Yes, sir." His voice cracked.

"We've reviewed your central file, Mr. Dugan, and looked at your prior transcripts. You're going to be given the opportunity today to correct or clarify the record. We're not here to retry your case. We're here for the sole purpose of determining your eligibility for parole. We offer your discussion of the facts of the case, and if at any time you need a break in the proceeding, then you'll let us know, okay?"

"Okay." *Can we move this shit show along?* Trevor said inside his head.

"For the reasons I've given, it's entirely up to you to proceed. You understand that?"

"Yes, sir. I understand."

His case worker, Clint, was jotting down notes in a black notepad.

Commissioner Marble continued, scrambling through some more paperwork. "Do you feel you're a risk to the community if released?"

"I feel I'm no risk whatsoever." Trevor surveyed the panel one more time. Their eyes beamed lasers of anticipated judgment. He felt his hands get clammy and turn pale. His mind went blank. The whole speech he'd scripted and recited countless times alone in his cell was erased from his memory—abracadabra. He took a long moment to practice a mindfulness technique he'd learned from prison therapy—radical acceptance. Four deep breaths in, four deep exhales out, focus on the here and now, watch your thoughts drift around, but don't judge them.

Once composed, he took the plunge. "It's no secret that I was an addict. I have a few charges of possession and retail fraud on my record. The fact that I was an addict was no excuse for what happened."

Now that he'd gained some clarity, he scanned the room to study expressions. He was pretty keen on reading body language. Sometimes in prison it was the only way to communicate. But everyone on the panel looked blankly inscrutable. So he continued.

"When I found my brother's gun, my intention was to go back to Detroit and trade it for illicit substances. A wrench was tossed into my plans when my brother came downstairs. I was focused on getting out of that basement with the only thing I'd found that I could pawn to get my drug of choice: heroin. I pulled the gun on him and decided I needed to take his car because I had to have a way to Detroit. He refused to get out of my way. I got nervous and pulled the trigger. There hasn't been a night that's gone by in the last twenty-five years that I haven't pictured the life leaving his eyes on that fateful night. But I'm not a cold-blooded murderer."

Trevor was glad he'd scrapped his speech. This was all perfect improvisation. Case manager Clint paused in his notes and proudly looked up at Trevor. Trevor made sure to look again at all the panel members dead center in the eye. Liars, with the exception of sociopaths, have difficulty looking people in the eye. But he was just an honest sociopath, reformed.

"The disease of addiction brought me to my rock bottom. Immediately, I took responsibility and called 911, confessing my guilt. Since this tragedy, I've remained drug-free, gone to almost all of the AA and NA classes offered here in the library and dayroom. I plan on continuing to maintain my sobriety, and I want to contribute back to society."

"And how exactly would you contribute back to society, Mr. Dugan?" Gobles, the annoying prosecutor, chimed in.

Trevor cleared his throat before answering. "I would find some work, maybe a place that gives felons a second chance. My sponsor told me in Michigan they have some non-profit organizations that hire recovery coaches or peer supports to help people still struggling with addiction. I believe that's one way I can make my amends to society—by giving back. And to be honest, I feel like I paid my debt to society by being here the duration of the last twenty-five years."

"And can you report any progress on your fascination with conspiracy theories, paranoid ideation, and beliefs that the prison staff was going to experiment on you or abduct inmates' children to test out alien technology in the basement of the prison?" The commissioner returned to conducting the interview.

Trevor rubbed his forehead and stared down at the tile floor. "I have undergone therapy and realize now that my wild allegations and conspiracy theories were only acute side effects from opioid- and meth-induced psychosis. I never dealt with my father's abandonment properly, so I created these fantasies in an attempt to make sense of it all."

"Thank you," the commissioner replied. He turned around to his colleagues, who were scattering murmurs. He turned back around to face Trevor and dipped his chin to his chest. "Here's the deal. Although you've made incredible strides in the past two years ..." He stopped and shuffled through Trevor's paperwork again. "This so-called disease of addiction is no excuse for murder. And what you did and admitted to was murdering your brother."

Trevor's heart sped up. "But—"

"I'm not finished yet, Mr. Dugan. And that's not all. There's also the fact you've been caught with weaponry contraband after being trusted to work for the prison. One of these weapons you designed that you traded for snacks or whatever was used in the murder of an inmate. What do you have to say for yourself?"

Stern, curious looks across the board closed in on Trevor.

Trevor swallowed the dead air. He paused long and hard before answering. "Sir, when you're in prison, the world you knew out there no longer exists. Inside these walls, no one cares about your life, your feelings. Some days I didn't know if I was going to wake up the next morning or not, constantly sleeping with one eye open. So, yes, I did provide contraband that was used to end someone's life. Do I regret it? Would I do it again? If I had a choice between my life and his, I honestly don't know. I had no protection. And in here, if you have nothing to offer the other inmates, then you're as good as dead. I learned my lesson and haven't sculpted any sheet metal since the horrible tragedy."

He knew that was a lie, but the less they knew, the better. "Not to make excuses, but the guy was a known pedophile who didn't belong in general population. He was dead if I made that shank or not. Whoever threw him in general population killed that guy, and in my eyes he probably deserved it."

The warden scoffed, knowing he was the one who decided to throw that child molester in general population. He'd known what would happen to the guy in there.

There were other mutters among the panel until the commissioner banged his fist like a gavel on the boardroom table. His face flushed florid even though a part of him agreed. That child molester did deserve to have his balls chopped off.

"Consequently," Marble began, turning to his colleagues. "We have officially denied your eligibility for parole."

The words stung like one of Trevor's homemade shivs through his kidney. "However," the old commissioner said. He wasn't done yet. "There's an alternative choice." Marble cleared his throat and loosened his burgundy tie. "I would like to excuse the panel, with the exception of Mr. Rollins. The formalities of this hearing are over."

The attractive criminal justice students/experts (whoever they were) fled first. The rest followed slowly and proceeded out in a single file. The vertically challenged guard hovered around until Marble motioned for his dismissal. Trevor's heart raced with a toxic combination of hope and stone-cold fear.

"You said you made a lot of amends with the people you hurt, right?" Rollins finally spoke once everyone was out of the room.

"That's correct, sir."

Marble took back the floor. "But you never got to make amends to your brother, Ryan, did you?"

"Well, he's dead." Trevor struck a blank stare. He wondered where they were going with this.

"What if we told you we discovered a way to change your fate?" The commissioner's eyes grew sharp.

Trevor felt a tad bewildered. "I wouldn't know what to say … I guess I'm lost here."

Rollins chimed back in. "What if you could relive the past twenty-five years of your life with freedom and your brother lived?" His eyes widened.

Trevor took a long moment to process everything he was hearing. "I would give anything to turn the clock back and do things differently."

Rollins and Marble looked at other and smiled in succession. "With traditional parole, you may get released but would be branded a felonious murderer for the rest of your life. In that scenario, you may be lucky enough to get a studio apartment and part-time work in some dead-end factory job," Rollins said. His eyes bored into the convict. He was offering Trevor salvation, redemption, and a once-in-a-life time opportunity. "What if in this parole mission—let's call it parole mission amends—your brother gets to live, but it's not going to be an easy task?"

"Before we tell you any more, this is highly classified information, and we have said too much already," Marble interrupted. "We need to know if you're willing to accept this offer. A chance to redeem yourself and to finally make things, right."

Trevor was visualizing himself jumping in a DeLorean with a flux capacitor and leaving Jackson State Prison in the dust. "Just so we're clear," he said slowly, "you're talking about some crazy time-travel shit?"

Rollins and Marble glanced at each other with cautious excitement. Rollins turned his attention back to Trevor. "Are you in?"

Trevor stroked the gray stubble on his chin. "Hmmm, let me think … Ugh! Hell yeah!"

"We'll send for you in a few days. Have everything prepared," Marble said.

11:00 p.m. September 25, 2045

Trevor spent his final moments in Jackson State Prison contemplating this crazy proposition from the parole board. Could this even be real? Marble told him to have everything prepared. He wondered what exactly you could take with you in time travel. A lunchbox with a peanut butter and jelly sandwich in case you ended up famished in the Dark Ages? Maybe he needed a toolkit for survival and some weapons. He considered grabbing the shank hidden under one of the cracks in the shower room but left it behind. He knew he had to think outside the box, on the off chance that during his travel, he accidentally landed in the middle of Iraq or even worse, the wrong side of Detroit. He also questioned if the commissioner just meant emotional prep time. To bid farewell to prison life—say his goodbyes to all the murdering, psychotic convicts who had either attempted to kill him or thought about ending his life. He was content with skipping that part and was ready to leave. But the idea of leaping through time was beyond his conceptualization. He wondered, *Was this one of the experiments my father had been running from? Did they send children like guinea pigs through time and now they've progressed to ex-cons?* At this point, Trevor didn't even care if he lived through it or not. He needed a way out.

As far as all the other prisoners were concerned, Trevor was being transferred to a remote maximum security facility across the state. Like a child being abandoned, Sherman sat up on his top bunk, wrapped his arms around his knees, and watched Trevor pack up his belongings.

Trevor felt bad for the little guy but told him, "Keep your eyes straight ahead. Find some folks in here to protect you. Find something you're good at and use it as trade. It's the only way to survive. Be strong."

Sherman had some specific talents in mind, but he didn't care to disclose them to Trevor.

After spending his last hour saying his goodbyes and contemplating life beyond the walls, it was time for his departure. A deputy with a crew cut and military stature entered the cell. "Booking number?"

"X2159007," Trevor responded.

Blindfolded, Trevor was taken in a wheelchair to the murky basement of Jackson State Prison. At least he thought it was the basement. Without sight as a travel guide, he could only sniff the air. Mold and the odor of rotten eggs narrowed down his location to most likely somewhere close to a boiler or water heater overgrown with bacteria. Abruptly, the blindfold was stripped off. Rollins and Marble glared down at Trevor. Cloaked in white lab coats and wearing black, vented radiation goggles, Trevor could all but see the lunacy in their eyes. They sensed the new parolee's vulnerability and confusion.

"Trevor, I know you're a bit confused, but this is where we send you off," Marble said.

Disoriented, Trevor tried to listen but heard only the crackling of oxide gas melting into the dry air and the ever present furnace rumbling heat to the old prison.

"A boiler room? We're in the basement. My conspiracy theories were right all along. You guys spent so much time washing them out of my brain, when I was right the whole time." He smiled in elation. In front of him there was a bland shower curtain connected to busted copper pipes dangling like nooses from the ceiling. A divine light radiated through the curtain's edge, almost blinding Trevor.

"There was a little truth to your claims, but we couldn't have you riling up all the other inmates with manic rants. But there's so much more in this boiler room." Rollins broke a wide grin. "Wait until you see what's behind the curtain!"

"Let me guess. It's either a death torture chair or the wonderful Wizard of Oz." Trevor's elation decreased. A shade of worry fell over him.

"I can sense your fear, Trevor, and it's completely understandable. But let me show you the creation. Or the discovery, shall I say." Rollins pulled back the curtain, exposing a black hole entangled with endless spirals of marvelous light.

"Einstein-Rosen Bridge is your ticket home," Marble said. He was almost bulldozing over his own words.

"Is that a wormhole?" Trevor asked, shocked. "That's impossible. Wormholes don't exist. And if they did, the law of gravity would only allow such a continuum to exist only in space, not on Earth." Trevor knew these guys were quacks. The black hole had to be some kind of digital hallucination.

"In the last twenty-five years, scientists discovered a way to create a wormhole and use it as a time machine. I know it sounds insane, but the resources and knowledge in the future have become infinite. The experiments started in my lab." Marble paused and tapped his forehead, looking up at the ceiling.

"Our lab," Rollins butted in.

Trevor grew even more baffled the more he listened to this pure madness. This was the same kind of madness he'd been obsessed with twenty-five years before. He thought he'd outgrown that delusion, but here it was smacking him in the face like a gate made of pizza. "So you two are from the future?" He wanted to make sure he was hearing them correctly.

"Yes, twenty-five years from now," Rollins explained. "The commissioner and I are scientists who worked for a private sector of the government that we can't identify. But we secretly partnered with NASA. Most importantly, we traveled back through this man-made vortex to offer prisoners a chance at redemption. Specifically, we wanted to give addicts/alcoholics a chance to make amends, save lives, and be offered salvation." Rollins devilishly rubbed his hands together and stood on his tiptoes to emphasize the godlike capabilities he was playing with. "We created false identities with false documentation to convince the prison to hire our alter egos: a struggling prison social worker and an ethically torn politician."

Marble cut back in. "For the past two years, we both worked here, surveying all the prisoners for potential candidates."

"You mean guinea pigs?" Trevor interrupted.

"We're the guinea pigs, Trevor," Marble said. "We traveled first to find the ideal candidate. We were impressed with your story. You felt remorse and had a lot of insight and intellect, which made you unlikely to consider this crazy. Your obsession with conspiracy actually saved you this time."

Marble was doodling in his black notepad. He lifted it up to show Trevor a roughly drawn spiral with chicken-scratch equations lapping over squiggly lines. "A wormhole is conceptualized as a tunnel with two ends at separate points in space time. According to Einstein's theory of relativity, our hypothesis to manipulate gravity, which defied general relativity and the laws of gravitation, was improbable. But special relativity pertains to physical phenomena void of gravity. The speed of light could be accelerated if contained in a vacuum in the absence of gravity. Thus exists the wormhole. But its potentially infinite limits ended in space. It was only possible in space. There was no way to contain a force without gravity on planet Earth. Where Einstein gave up, Dr. Rollins and I discovered you can lower Gs in high speeds within a controlled room. It wasn't enough, but it was a start."

Marble took a deep breath and a chug of bottled water he'd hidden in his lab coat. Revealing his life's work to a stranger always accelerated his anxiety to light speeds.

"I know a little about physics, but you guys are speaking a different language to me," Trevor said. The reflection of the shimmering light from the vortex began to burn his eyes.

Rollins sensed his confusion. "To put it in layman's term, we finished Einstein's work for him, but it wasn't completed yet."

Marble handed his water to Rollins and interjected. "You have to hear the rest of this out. It may not all make sense, but it's important you know. Slowing gravity wasn't enough to create negative energy density. This is the only material that could be used to stabilize the wormhole. So this is where the real research began. What kind of material can we develop to contain this quantum realm?"

"Electromagnetic fields?" Trevor answered for Marble. Another lesson he remembered from physics class.

"Precisely, Mr. Dugan. See, you are following," Marble said. "However, the electromagnetic fields couldn't hold enough energy. So we asked ourselves how much negative mass we needed to build a wormhole. Well, according to Einstein's theory of relativity, in order to open a wormhole one foot in diameter, you'd need roughly one Jupiter-sized planet's worth of negative mass."

Trevor's mind was spinning like the basketball-sized time hole six feet from him. He was relapsing on conspiracy when a thought occurred to him. "How is that wormhole not swallowing us and this entire planet whole?"

"We're getting there" Marble said.

Rollins, his trusted partner, retrieved a small multi-colored Rubik's Cube from the front pocket of his lab coat. He tossed it in Trevor's direction. The cube caught Trevor off guard when it landed in his lap. Perplexed yet intrigued, Trevor examined the kaleidoscopic puzzle, trying to understand its role in time travel.

The Rubik's Cube from my dad's picture. The one from my dream of the scary old man in my bedroom when I was six, Trevor thought but didn't say out loud.

"Go ahead and figure out the first algorithm." Marble grinned with excitement. He was fully confident in Trevor's abilities.

In a matter of seconds, Trevor had crossed the first layer of blue, crossed the corners, and completed the second and third layers. He didn't even look down when he matched the final corners. The algorithms had never left his memory: Front, right, up, and left. The spiraling wormhole expanded into a hole of blinding light. Trevor's eyelids stretched out wide as the Rubik's Cube began to vibrate and opened up. In a blink's time, the wormhole dissipated inside the cube like a penny sucked up by a vacuum hose. Trevor's knees grew weak as he held the weight of a galaxy in the palm of his hands.

Marble lightly clapped his hands together and jumped in delight. "I already know what you're asking yourself. 'Did I just see an entire black hole sucked into a Rubik's Cube?' Yes, you did. How? Well my partner and I stumbled across something extraordinary. Now, this will sound even more insane, but in twenty-five years, although it seems a short amount of time, the world has completely changed. In 2070, an unidentified flying aircraft crashed in Tulsa, Oklahoma. It was the second landing after Roswell, and there were no survivors. But, we did find something alive." Marble licked his lips. He was acting odd and jittery. "We found extraterrestrial DNA. We took it to our lab, studied, examined, and experimented. After a few years of trials, we almost gave up until the son of one of our scientists snuck into the lab. He slid into the main testing room and completed a perfect algorithm on his little toy. His father caught him, and the boy dropped the pint-sized Rubik's Cube before running away from his dad. Although he didn't know it, that little boy opened the key to time travel. Upon impact on the floor, the cubelets disconnected and, like a magnet, sucked in the alien DNA, thus creating the opportunity to contain the wormhole. So here we are, Trevor!"

"E.T. phone home. Abracadabra gone. My dad was trying to tell me this the whole time." Trevor's words came out flat as he stared at the wormhole in a dreamlike trance.

"Time is non-linear, Trevor. In a past timeline, this opportunity was given to someone else in the seventies. He was a homeless drug addict. Randolph I believe his name was, and he rejected the gift of amends, which made our mission go haywire. He refused to change his old ways and was sent to another dimension in time. And unfortunately, because of his failure, the government didn't trust the first amends time travel experiment. Instead of second chances, science and military focused on more preventive measures. Ultimately, lives were lost, children who were convicted of crimes in the future were tortured and experimented on as your father did witness. Some were even killed. But we're back with a second chance to erase all of that." Marble shuffled his feet while gulping down more bottled water.

Although Trevor seemed to be under a spell, he heard Marble's words, and they resonated with him. The seemingly infinite possibilities of the parole mission were beyond his comprehension. Alien DNA, time travel, wormholes, all contained in a tiny Rubik's Cube. This was a chance to change the course of history, to truly save his brother. Trevor was on board with the mission, but the intensity in Marble's and Rollins's words and their strange behaviors frankly frightened the shit out of him. Something was off about all of it.

Trevor snapped back to the present moment. "So why was time travel so important to you guys? Why are you offering convicted prisoners redemption?"

A shade of sadness fell over Rollins's face. His posture slouched. "In 2018, my father killed my mother inside an abandoned hotel and went to prison for life. I was only five years old when it happened. I never got to know my mother, and my father was gone. But I wanted to help my father. As much as I hated him for what he did, he was an addict just like you. It didn't justify the fact that he ended my mom's life. If only I could discover a way to turn the clocks back and change it, I would. And I did."

"So what happened next?" Trevor asked.

"Well next, I traveled back to 2018, and the fifty-five-year-old me found my drunk father in that abandoned hotel. I held him hostage in an old guest room or patient room, as the hotel actually was some weird cult rehab center—the perfect place for an alcoholic's redemption. When my mother came looking for him after he texted her in a rage, she never found him. After detoxing my father, I never identified myself. I kept a mask on, and he was scared to death. But I tell you what, Trevor, my friend, I instilled the fear of God into him, and he never drank again. My dad never went to prison. I got to grow up and have a mom. They divorced shortly after, which was a disappointment. But it was far better than the alternative. I grew up in two different realities."

Trevor scratched his head. "So you lived happily ever after? This sounds great and all, but there could be serious repercussions as a result somewhere in the universe. I didn't see it at first, or maybe I saw it and didn't want to admit it because I was so ready to leave prison and save my brother. But we can't just manipulate fate and reality without catastrophic consequences, can we?"

"Trevor, we're talking about saving your brother's life and saving the lives of those children. You have to ask yourself if they're worth the risk of possibly changing a few small details in time versus saving your brother and the future horrors of addiction through your brave act of amends." Marble tilted his head and his eyes blinked in rapid succession. His breath was heavy, and he leaned in closer to Trevor.

Rollins stepped up and motioned his partner back. "Marble and I have time-jumped a few times. The last and final time jump was two years ago, when we took on new names—Cliff Rollins and James Marble—and ended up back in 2018 once again to prepare for this very moment. Our original names are Hunter Clinton and John Rancid. Our twenty-three-year-old selves are growing up in two different parts of the country and won't discover their fates until the time is right."

"And when will the time be right?" Trevor asked.

"Time is non-linear, so the time could be right now or it could be in a thousand years. The answer will always be the same." Rollins pulled out a pencil from his lab coat pocket and tapped it against his chin.

"And what about you, Marble, or John?" Trevor asked. "What was your investment in all of this time travel and redemption?"

"Hunter is my best friend, and we grew up together. Then we worked for NASA together until we got pulled into a confidential sector of the government. If this was important to him, it also meant the world to me. I believe in redemption."

"I don't know man," Trevor said.

The two scientists tossed their hands up and shook their heads, feeling defeated.

Rollins clawed the back of his neck. "Look. We're here offering you the same opportunity. But if you're having second thoughts now, it's kind of late. You already agreed and you know too much. Solitary confinement with no communication with the outside world doesn't sound like a fun way to spend your remaining years."

Trevor rolled his eyes. He knew he was out of options, but it all sounded too good to be true.

Rollins leaned in close and locked eyes with the prisoner. "Of all the prisoners here, if anyone deserves a chance at redemption, it's you. Think of the last time you looked at Ryan alive."

Trevor sat on these words for a minute. He kept thinking of the look on his brother's face when the bullet entered his chest, the good times they'd spent together before high school ruined them. Hell, Ryan came to rescue him from his addiction, offered up his home, and Trevor couldn't stop picturing the life leaving his brother's eyes.

Marble took his turn to lean in close to Trevor. "And don't forget about Mary Hopkins. Wasn't she only twenty-six or twenty-seven when she committed suicide?" The words hissed like a den of snakes slithering out of his mouth.

"Had a two-year-old boy she left behind, I believe," Rollins intervened, pushing the manipulation button.

Trevor recalled that Mary had come to visit him in prison a few times, but he never got to be in the same room with her again because all the visits went virtual. After a while, the visits stopped, and he didn't hear her name again until he eavesdropped on some prison mates bragging about how their buddies on the outside would "pass her around." In the street world, she was known as a "bust-down chick." "That bust-down chick committed suicide," he overheard one of the Aryans mention to his old cellmate. Trevor knew she was dead, but this was the first time he'd heard anything about her having a son.

As he wiped the sting from his eye, Trevor's heart dropped. The manipulation worked. "I need to know where I'll end up. And some kind of instruction pamphlet would be nice."

Marble nodded at his compliance. "You're making the right choice. There's one other Rubik's Cube resting in 2020. Rollins left it behind at that abandoned rehab center in Detroit. This will be where the wormhole will take you. We left some supplies for you to discover on your way. This is a journey and you're a smart guy, so I'm sure you can figure out how to fix your fate."

"Yeah, because I'm known for setting my own perfect path in life." Trevor held back a sarcastic laugh.

"We have faith in you," Rollins assured him. "But I have to warn you, there are some side effects. Nothing too extreme, but the first time I jumped, I took digital memories from my present life into the past, and they were projected for my father to see. It confused him terribly, and I was tempted to reveal my true identity. But you have to remember: it's vitally important that you not let your past self know that you're him."

Alarmed, Trevor sat up straight. "Nothing too extreme?"

"I know, but it's not as bad as it sounds. Trust me. Now, there's a change of clothes in a bag we packed over there for you. There's a burlap sack in the bag. Please wear that when you time-jump, as we've traveled without it and the warp speed of the jump left some facial scarring." Marble pointed to the small, scaly time-travel stripe across his left cheek that Trevor had wondered about. "Also, wear the sack as a mask in case your twenty-three-year-old self somehow recognizes his forty-eight-year-old self. That could compromise the whole mission. Do you understand, Trevor?"

Trevor nodded. He spent his last few minutes in 2045 praying to God, the almighty Father. Over the last twenty-five years, he'd renewed his faith in religion and owed his recovery to Jesus Christ. As Trevor physically, emotionally, and mentally prepared to dive headfirst into a Rubik's Cube containing a wormhole composed of alien technology, he needed Jesus more than ever.

Chapter 15
Character Defects

10:00 p.m. Tuesday, September 22, 2020

Mary Hopkins devoured the double-bacon cheeseburger with green olives and extra mayonnaise like it was her first meal since Obama had been president. The disposable mask drooping under her chin served as a bib, intercepting splatters of ketchup and mustard. Ryan Dugan sat in a contained rage, restraining himself from jumping across the table and choking his brother's girlfriend each time she chomped down and smacked her lips. His appetite had been depleted by not only her rabbit-like gnawing but the lingering thought that their friend Jake Johnson was in that body bag they'd driven by earlier. Mary had dismissed the idea, claiming people got killed every day in Detroit and it likely wasn't him.

"He's prolly vein deep in some dope or one of his lady friends. God knows he has plenty of them. And you, mister, shouldn't have given him that two hundred dollars so soon." Mary shot Ryan a brief glare before sinking her teeth back into the fat, greasy sandwich.

"Yeah, it's all my fault." Ryan sucked back on his teeth. "Maybe we should save some food for the dog, now that he's our responsibility." Ryan was picturing that mutt chewing apart the back seat of his precious Charger while he sat in Marv's Diner listening to the monstrous chomps of a starved junkie.

"I need to go use the restroom first." Mary excused herself from the table. Before she rushed off, Ryan caught her attention and motioned toward her upper lip. Laughing at herself, she wiped off the pinch of mayo from the corner of her mouth.

"Just don't fall in," Ryan said. He was a little taken aback by her behavior, almost embarrassed, but he was trying to push through it. Under normal circumstances, Ryan would object to someone going to spike some heroin in a public waste box. But on this very day, after all the recent events, he gave zero fucks. He was tired and just wanted to find his brother so he could leave this shithole of a city.

Someone in a booth behind him coughed, and dead silence swept the restaurant. Ryan adjusted the collar on his shirt. He was imagining tiny coronavirus particles swimming toward him, ready to attack his lungs and slowly kill him. He decided it was time to get the check.

Mary emerged from the ladies' restroom and rejoined Ryan. A waitress with a Betty Boop face mask and thick eyebrows that looked like a child had colored on her forehead with a black crayon passed their table. Ryan signaled her for the bill. She looked back and shook her head at Ryan's table, which was scattered with two empty plates, balled-up napkins, sprinkles of loose ketchup, and wasted cigarette butts that sprawled over the checkered tablecloth.

"There's no smoking in here!" Her hoarse voice cackled when she yelled.

Mary peeked at her purse, which had toppled over on the table, dumping all of the half-smoked cigarettes that she'd put out with the intent of saving them for later. "I'm sorry. We weren't smoking, and they aren't lit, anyway."

Ryan slapped a hundred-dollar bill on the table, seized Mary's wrist, and dragged her out the door. The bill was only twenty-five dollars, but the extra seventy-five was for Mary's toddler-proportioned mess.

The two drove off in the Dodge with no leads on where to find Trevor, just the open road. No words were exchanged. Mary stuffed her mouth with some Doublemint chewing gum. Her lips smacked. Ryan considered finding a bus stop or, better yet, a ditch in which to drop off his burdensome, noisy passenger.

"Where are we going?" Mary finally asked.

The sound of her voice scratched like nails on chalkboard. "These are my character defects showing," Ryan accidentally said out loud.

"Huh?"

"Nothing, never mind. It's getting late. This is your town. Any ideas where Trevor might be?"

"When I was in the bathroom, I called all the local emergency rooms to see if he may have overdosed again, but none of the hospitals had him checked in." Mary began twisting gum around her finger, another one of her many tics.

"That's what you were doing in the bathroom?" Ryan asked sarcastically. "Any other bright ideas?"

"My guess is as good as yours at this point. He wasn't at Anton's. We can go back and check our place out again. Maybe he returned."

"You mean your crack house," Ryan joked.

"Fuck you." Mary giggled playfully and belched. That burger and Pepsi had done a number on her.

Ryan slouched down in the driver's seat. "I'm sorry. That actually is a good idea. Let's try there."

Mary pulled out her cell phone again. "I don't know why he hasn't texted me. His phone keeps going to voicemail."

A midnight-black ladybug crawled across the windshield. Ryan activated the wipers, slaying the tiny insect through dismemberment. "Maybe because his phone is dead?" Dead like the bug on his windshield.

The two returned to The Hood Pack Mansion. When Ryan walked in the front door, he was perplexed by a toxic odor that lingered like cat piss puddled inside gym shoes in a locker-room for eons. Mary ran up the stairs to check if Trevor was up there nodding out like usual.

Ryan leaned up against an oak table that held nothing but an empty 40-ounce bottle of cheap malt liquor. The bottom of the bottle was layered with an ocean of wet cigarette butts. *Damn, Trev, you really did hit rock bottom*, he thought.

"He's not here. Let's go try somewhere else," Mary said, marching down the steps in wide strides.

"Where to?"

"Your guess is as good as mine, sunshine." She lifted her arms up in defeat.

So the abandoned hideaway happened to be just that: abandoned. They aimlessly drove around a few blocks, trying to brainstorm where

Trevor could be hiding. Ryan was worried that he'd wound up like that corpse they'd seen getting carried off via ambulance. Mary dreaded the idea that he could have gotten into trouble, maybe with the police or even worse, Anton. But both Mary and Ryan knew that no questions would be answered that night.

"Well, I guess you can just drop me back off at home." Mary was exhausted and the heroin was wearing off.

Ryan looked at Mary. He saw the shame and compulsion in her eyes. He knew it all too well, but his vice was alcohol. "No, I can't send you back there. Let's go get a room at a hotel, and we can search again in the morning." Although she bothered him to pieces, his conscience couldn't allow her to go back there. That place was a nightmare.

"Oh, thanks for the offer, but if he comes back, I can let him know you're looking for him. Jake could return at any time too." Mary was swaying her legs back and forth. She was growing antsy and needed another taste.

Ryan tilted his head and sighed. "If you go in the bathroom, I won't look twice or ask questions. I just need someone with me who knows Detroit and can help me find Trevor tomorrow."

Mary nodded. "Okay, but double beds."

"Of course." She was his brother's girl, and the thought had never crossed his mind. But she did look like a young Farrah Fawcett, only on crack. The rough edges just made her that much more attractive. *Character defects, Ryan. Character defects*, he thought, like his sponsor always reminded him.

"Can I stop back home and grab some clothes first?" she asked.

The search for a decent hotel kept hitting dead ends. Holiday Inn, Baymont, Radisson, and even Motel 6 were booked out. Mary was hesitant to mention it, but with all other options depleted, the Motown Inn always had a room she could call her own. She finally suggested it, and Ryan checked in for the both of them with his credit card. Mary was gun-shy of running into her old friend Ravinder.

She waited inside the car while Ryan went inside to pay for the room. Through the crooked white blinds that looked like they'd been mangled by paranoid tweakers coming in and out of the lobby, she saw the top of the clerk's balding head. The giveaway was his cell phone propped up on a stand, most likely displaying random ice bucket challenges or Tide Pod eating contests on YouTube. This wouldn't be the first time she'd returned since the Gary Nichols incident, but each time took a toll on her broken spirit.

Ryan returned to the car, fetched Mary, and headed up to the room.

Mary noticed the owners of the seedy motel were making some minor repairs, fixing the broken elevator and installing new, sturdy guardrails on the stairs. One too many drunks must have slipped, tasted concrete, and sued the motel. Despite the improvements, the Motown Inn still held the title of Detroit's finest run-down and dilapidated motel. Room 112 was at the end of the corridor. Mary entered the room first.

Ryan almost forgot about the dog. He ran back to car, grabbed his favorite Michigan State blanket from his trunk, and hid Jake's dog, Bulko, in it. He'd happened to catch a glimpse of the white sign with red letters that read No Pets Allowed! Once inside the room, the mutt ran in maniacal circles. He was happy to be finally free from the constraints of the Charger's back seat.

Mary picked out the bed closest to the bathroom. Ryan plopped down on the window-side bed. His only view was of an underwhelming brick building attached to a slightly nicer hotel next door.

"I guess I'll jump in the shower first." Mary started stripping off her scuffed white sneakers, tainted-ivory socks, and faded, low-cut shirt. Ryan turned his back. He had struggled with his own personal issues with lust. Those demons had cheated on his wife, Jessica, only once, with an annoying eighteen-year-old waitress in the walk-in freezer of the restaurant he owned. She'd had jet-black hair, was obsessed with Kat Von D, and always played Candy Crush on her phone.

While Mary freshened up, Ryan made himself comfortable on the bed closest to the window, powered on his phone, and opened up his social media. He hadn't been logged on in days but landed only a handful of notifications. He saw his messenger light up a bright beam of blue through the cracked veins of his screen. The broken screen and all the drywall holes punched in his bedroom were more evidence of his character defects.

There was a text from his wife, Jessica: *Where are you? The kids and I are home now. We hope you have cleaned up. I talked to Jim and he said you seem to be doing well. But if you are out getting plastered I swear we are gone again. Also I heard about your dad and I'm sorry honey. Let me know if there is anything I can do to help.*

Ryan wasn't a good liar, so he didn't want to reply. But he knew she would see that he'd read the message. Throughout his four years of marriage, he'd learned that keeping the peace sometimes meant making a sacrifice. He didn't have to necessarily lie, but he could omit the truth. For Jessica's sake, he would never tell her about the Candy Crush waitress, so why tell her that he was penned up in a hotel with his brother's junkie girlfriend? Of course, his intention was to find his brother, and he couldn't let Mary sleep in that disgusting crack house. But Jessica wouldn't understand that, so there was no valid reason why she needed to be informed.

He texted back: *I am ok and yes I am sober. I wanted to give you space so I didn't message you. Anyway, I am in Detroit looking for Trevor. I know he is in a bad place but Grace wants him home for the funeral and I made a promise to her.*

Jessica replied, *Ok I think that is stupid but be careful. I love you.*

Ryan texted back, *I love you too.*

He decided to distract himself by scrolling through all the mindless political rants, inappropriately hilarious memes, and ads for denim jeans he kept getting after he'd bought his last pair on Amazon. Then he came across a link to an article titled, "23-year-old Detroit man found dead on Gratiot."

The article read: "Detroit police said a 23-year-old man was killed after a shooting outside Fairbound Liquor Store on the corner of Gratiot Ave. and Racine St. According to police, the shooting occurred around 8 p.m. on Tuesday night in an alley behind the store."

Ryan tried to home in on the next sentence, but his eyes got blurry. He was too nervous but had to finish reading the article.

"The victim was transported to the nearest hospital, but the 23-year-old man, who has been identified as Jacob Johnson, died from his injuries. Police are still investigating the shooting and ask anyone with information to call Crime Stoppers."

Ryan's jaw sank and his heart dropped. His intuition was correct like usual, but he'd hoped that this time it was wrong. He'd come here to find

Trevor, help him get clean. But instead, he'd recruited his brother's best friend, who was now dead.

Mary stepped out of the bathroom, wearing only a fawn-colored towel and wet, shaggy hair. Ryan politely turned away but not before catching a glimpse of her coral-pink areola slipping out the side of the towel. For a moment, he again almost forgot about those vows to his wife and his newfound promise to help his brother. *Character defects,* he reminded himself.

"I got some bad news." Ryan repositioned himself on the bed to face the view of the brick wall out the window. He wanted to be a gentleman and not see her in the buff, out of respect for his brother and all.

"Oh yeah? What's that?" Mary tightened the towel around her chest and backside.

"I'll let you see for yourself." He hesitated before turning around and tossing the phone onto her bed.

Mary scanned the article not even a second before the tears arrived. "Oh my God, Jake! This is bad, Ryan. This is bad. Why did you let him leave?" Her voice heightened with rage-induced sadness after each sentence.

"This isn't my fault. He ran out of the car. There was nothing I could do to stop him." Ryan jumped up from his bed and advanced toward the window.

Mary hyperventilated between the fountains of tears streaming down her face. Ryan walked over and offered the grieving woman a hug. Reluctant at first, she accepted the comfort of his arms around her. The scent of Armani cologne and his warm embrace gave her a sense of security.

Pressing against her cotton-and-polyester bath sheet, he absorbed a taste of her pain, just enough to remind him of his own.

The tears slowed down and Mary caught her breath in a single gasp. "It wasn't your fault. I shouldn't have said that. Jake loved that dog. He went plumb crazy and sold him for dope, felt guilty, and went back and stole him from Anton's brother Andre. I'm sure they had something to do with his murder."

Bulko whimpered and lowered his head as he walked underneath the TV table to claim his resting spot. He sulked like the poor guy blamed himself. Then he let out a mournful woof.

"It isn't your fault either, Bulko," Ryan said. "Blame it on addiction, the disease, the beast, the collector of souls."

Those words resonated with Mary. She knew them all too well. "I'm sorry about your dad too. I don't know if I told you that yet. But I am."

"He wasn't your typical dad, let's just say that. He had a lot of demons." Ryan shrugged and looked down at the burgundy motel carpet. "I knew it was only a matter of time."

"I heard that he left to keep your family safe from the FBI and the Department of Homeland Security or something or other. Trevor told me he'd discovered some deep government cover-up shit." Mary had listened to Trevor's endless rants about conspiracy, kidnapped children, and the Pizza-gate hoax cover-up.

Ryan lifted his head back up. "Dad was an alcoholic and womanizer who left us to be with another woman half our mother's age. Yes, he worked for the government, but he made up all that bullshit so it wouldn't crush Trevor."

"That's pretty sad. How long did you know the truth for? That conspiracy theory hogwash made him bonkers."

Ryan sighed. "Too long."

"I think you should have been honest with him. It might have saved him from his obsession with YouTube and conspiracy." Mary stepped back into the bathroom. Seconds later, she returned wearing a different pair of black leggings and a gray University of Michigan sweatshirt.

Ryan glared at her choice of apparel and decided to change the subject. "I didn't know you were a redneck Wolverine." He shot a snarky smile in her direction.

"Oh, I didn't know you were a spoiled couch-burner." Mary said, referencing his Spartans t-shirt and all the MSU college kids who rioted and burned couches every time their home team won. "But yeah, I went to the University of Michigan before I met your brother." She leaned down and weightlessly fell on top of the soft bed, which was void of any dirt on the spread and metal springs clawing through the fabric. The Motown Inn was a dive, but it felt like a five-star hotel compared to her current living arrangement.

"Let me guess: you met my brother and he led you astray?"

Mary perked up, exhaling a slight laugh of embarrassment. "Yeah. Well, I moved up to Michigan from Arkansas to become a Wolverine after my dad died. I got my bachelor's in psychology and was planning to go back for my master's when I met Trevor. But I knew what I was getting myself into, and your brother was just so darn attractive. It was hard to resist."

Ryan clenched his jaw and snickered. "Yeah, my brother is hot."

"Oh shut up." She let out a giggle, followed by that ear-shattering snort.

Ryan cringed and gripped his sobriety medallion in his front pocket for serenity. Face contorted, he restrained himself from taking off or cramming his phone into her mouth. His misophonia was worsening. But the coin always soothed the rage just a little, and his heart rate de-escalated. He closed his eyes and said, "I'm sorry about what happened to your dad too."

"Like you said, it is what it is." She yawned and scooted backward on the bed, settling up against the headboard. "After he passed, I took an oath to never end up like him. Well, look at me now."

"Don't be so hard on yourself. Addiction runs through genetics. Just look at my family." Ryan particularly thought of his dad and brother. "My mom was the only one who didn't get beaten down by substance abuse. Her drug of choice was codependency."

Mary's eyes lowered. "That was my family too before the actual drugs took over. I just wanted to help my pa, ya' know? I was his only child, his baby girl. I tried taking care of him. Ma refused to sit by and let him kill himself, so she swore off him at the end. But not me. I would fetch him Suboxone off the street when he would withdraw. One day I came home and he just wasn't breathing." Her expression shifted, her lower lip quivering.

Ryan leaned closer to her from the edge of his bed. "So, is that why you wanted to become a psychologist?" His eyes bored into her.

A flush crept up her face. "And now I need a fucking shrink and a sponsor." She giggled between nervous hiccups.

A painful thought resurfaced with the discussion of death. She had a friend who just got murdered. How could she forget? Mary had learned the art of disassociation from previous trauma, like coming home after waiting too long in line at Gil's Market for some fresh deer jerky to find her father sprawled out on the floor with a needle in his arm. "I still can't believe it about Jake. He was such a good friend. I mean he was a dope fiend and hustler, but he was a loyal man. He was trying to turn his life around to God, had started reading his Bible, and wanted to get clean."

"Yeah, he talked about his new relationship with God and told me he was going into treatment on Wednesday. That's fucked-up. He was like one day away. I should have never let him leave the damn car." Ryan balled his fist and wanted to plant it right in his own forehead. "I just wanted to help him too, not just my brother. I want to help you, Mary, get off this shit."

"I'm sure you do, Mr. Ryan, and you sound like a good man and all. But you got your own figuring out to do."

"One of the best ways to get through our pain is to help others overcome theirs."

"Wow, you sound like a therapist yourself. Speaking of psychology, whatever happened between you and your brother? I've heard his side of the story, but ..."

Ryan scratched an itch behind his right ear, taking a moment to ponder the question. He wasn't really sure if he had the answer either. "We were real close until Dad left us. Then Trevor pushed everyone away until he lost himself. I had a role to play. I could have stepped up more as a brother, I suppose."

"So that's why you're here now?"

"And that's exactly why I'm here now!"

"So now what?" Mary asked.

Ryan turned off the light and tucked himself under the covers. "We get rest and wake up to find my brother."

The two of them fell fast asleep, each in their own bed. The events of the day had worn on their physical, mental, and spiritual well-being.

Mary woke up at four o'clock in the morning with that overbearing ick in her stomach. At first she figured it was the usual dope-sick hangover. But there were no cold sweats, goosebumps, or heightened senses. No, this brand of nausea resembled a never-ending car ride in grandmother's station wagon—the kind that made your stomach turn and your head spin. She sprung from bed and scurried to the toilet. As the bile exited her weak stomach and entered the white porcelain bowl, she tried to remember the last time she'd had her period. She figured it had been at least six weeks. *Should I get a pregnancy test?* she thought. *No, the less I know, the better.*

"Are you okay?" Ryan asked. He uncovered his head from the sheets and looked around. Bulko was still sound asleep, untouched by the noise that had woken Ryan up at this ungodly hour.

"Yeah, just dope sick," she lied.

Ryan discerned her fabrication but decided not to dig any further. The end of the race to find his brother was closing in. The funeral was planned for tomorrow, Thursday, and the way recent events had unfolded, who knew when Trevor might turn up.

Mary tottered out of the bathroom and held her stomach.

"Are you sure you're okay?" Ryan furrowed his eyebrows, knowing she probably wouldn't answer that question honestly.

"Yes. I just have a stomachache. Let me see if there's any word from Trevor while we slept." Mary unplugged her smartphone from an Android charger she'd pocketed from the Marathon gas station two blocks away. "Okay, I got enough juice in my battery. I don't see any texts or missed calls from anyone." Mary's enthusiasm slipped into disappointment. She dialed Trevor's number only to have her anticipation struck down by an instant voicemail greeting. "His phone is still dead." Her face grew pale and she began biting her thumbnail, pacing the motel room. These were the little tics, much like the loud chewing and slightly annoying laugh, that increased Ryan's agitation. *Character defects … or maybe it's a mental health condition*, he considered.

Ryan got out of bed, stretched his tired bones, and let loose an exaggerated yawn. "You know it's like four in the morning. He may not even be up yet or fully charged his phone. Do you have a phone app that could trace his last location?"

Her eyes went round with disbelief. "Yeah, right. Trevor has a prepaid cell phone. That kind of luxurious app doesn't come with the package."

"Sure it does. You just have to download the app." He shrugged and sauntered into the bathroom. "You know, once we find Trevor … I didn't tell you, but I was going to help him detox. My wife and kids are gone, so it would be the perfect opportunity." He grabbed a complimentary toothbrush off the sink.

Whoosh! Spit! Ptooey! He opened the pint-size travel bottle of generic Listerine. *Gurgle! Spit! Yuck.* "This mouthwash tastes like broken liquid dreams," he said.

Mary was leaning over the side of her bed and sliding her shoes on. "Wait, what did you just say?" Her eyes gleamed.

"This mouthwash tastes like broken liquid dreams." He spat out the last bit of Listerine.

"No, before that."

"I was going to let Trevor come to my house and detox."

Mary's brain lit up like an electrical current conjuring hope. "Yes. I remember now." The events of the other day came flooding back to her. Blind Bobby, white eyes, gross laughter. Premonition. "So, I know this guy. He's homeless and blind. Raging alcoholic and a crack-smoker."

"Sounds like my kind of guy." Ryan reappeared from the bathroom and threw back on his same white-and-green Michigan State t-shirt. He hadn't packed for this impromptu trip to rescue his brother.

"Seriously, he rambled something about how Trevor found his new forever home at The Detox Hotel. He said his own dad had been there in the seventies. I thought he sounded delusional as all get out, but maybe Trevor did check into some rehab and it's nicknamed The Detox Hotel."

"Sounds like a bad Elvis song and a long, desperate shot, but we've exhausted almost all options I can think of." Ryan remained standing, still wiping sleep boogers from his eyes.

"I don't have any data on my phone or know the Wi-Fi password here. If this shithole even has a Wi-Fi password."

"Don't worry, sweetheart. We can use my Google and see if The Detox Hotel leads us anywhere."

The initial search resulted in several ads for spas and luxurious rehabs out west that were well beyond Trevor's Medicaid price range. But hiding at the bottom of the second page was a conspicuous link titled "Recovery Inn, also known as Detox Hotel, outside of Detroit closes its doors after the owner commits suicide following brutal allegations."

"Wow, this is interesting." Ryan clicked on the link to see what other tabloid news debauchery he would find.

Mary bolted over next to Ryan, crowding over his phone. "I can't believe that blind old geezer may have been telling the truth."

"Well, let's not get ahead of ourselves." Ryan held up his hand, palm forward. "Let's read the article first." The original newspaper passage had been converted over to an online article.

> *Lance Burrows, 75, of Detroit, MI, has committed suicide by gunshot wound to the head in an addiction treatment center that was also known as The Detox Hotel. He purchased the abandoned Hawthorne State Psychiatric Hospital in 1971. The hospital closed down in 1918 after several staff were under investigation for unethical methods of treatment, including starving patients, physical beatings, and psychological abuse. Allegations of rape had also surfaced. A psychiatrist was found guilty of brutally stabbing a patient for refusing to take her medications. In tragic irony, it seems history has repeated itself. The deceased Lance Burrows told his patients that he came to Detroit searching for a miracle cure for addiction and had found it when he opened The Recovery Inn's doors to patients nationwide. Some of the guests who left the facility said Lance was a very passionate man but took recovery from addiction to great heights. Sometimes the methods were similar to Hawthorne Hospital's. Patients started coming up missing, employees were walking off the job. There were reports that the CEO Lance Burrows had taken things too far and it didn't feel like recovery anymore. These anonymous sources stated to the Free Press, "It was like demonic sorcery going on there." These allegations prompted more media, auditors, and the federal government to open an investigation into the claims of malpractice. The day before federal agents were scheduled to inspect the facility, Lance Burrows was found dead in a guest room at the hotel from a shotgun blast to the head. Consequently, the facility*

> *was closed and condemned, but several of the patients remain missing. Family members ask anyone with any information to come forward.*

Next to the article was a cropped black-and-white photo of the psychotic megalomaniac Lance boldly standing in front of the hotel. The article was from 1973.

"Wow, that's pretty fucked," Mary gasped, taken aback.

"Do you think that's really where he is?"

"I don't know. Is there an address?"

Ryan skimmed through more of the article and found in tiny font below the hotel's photo: "720 Spiritual Blvd."

"Of course it would be on a road called Spiritual Boulevard," he said.

"Try Google Maps," Mary suggested.

He activated the navigator on his phone but couldn't pinpoint a road with that name.

"This road doesn't exist anymore, according to Google Maps."

Mary scratched her chin, deep in thought. "Well, is anything showing up? A location at least?"

Ryan's iPhone pinged a latitude and longitude. The nearest landmark was outside Detroit: Walled Lake-Novi Wastewater.

"That's right outside Novi. The map is pinpointing the old location of Spiritual Boulevard in the middle of a five-mile radius of nothing." Her expression dulled.

"How many miles?" Ryan asked.

"About thirty."

Bulko's ears perked up, and he wagged his tail like a helicopter propeller on meth.

"Well, let's get some gas and go find my brother."

"I want another burger after we find him."

Chapter 16
Anonymous Demons

5:00 a.m., Wednesday, September 23, 2020

When Trevor woke up, he felt like his temple had been bludgeoned with a hammer. He was bound by rope to his little friend, the wooden chair. Blood was seeping from his wrists, trickling down his palms into a small puddle beneath him. His vision was blurry, but he could see enough to know he was no longer in the time-travel room, room 106. Instead, he was sitting front and center of the main lobby in the grand hotel.

The lobby was almost bare. Two embroidered sofas layered in dust surrounded a gray stone end table stacked with torn magazines and newspapers. A broken chandelier hung above shattered glass on the floor, shards that at one time contained the light's beauty. The floor was coated with cracked marble and crumbled tiles. Trevor imagined his captor leaping like a knight across a chessboard of cracked floor squares to confront him once again.

Visions of the previous night's dream were surfacing. He remembered being in prison with a schizophrenic cellmate named Sherman. Trevor himself had had a lot of tattoos and no longer believed in conspiracy. The parole board had offered him a chance to save his brother, Ryan, and change the course of history. He recalled that the crazed scientists on the parole board were time travelers too. They'd told him they were going to send him back in time to a deserted hotel to kidnap his younger self. They'd advised him to wear a burlap sack over his face to prevent scarring from time travel and to hide his true identify from himself.

The dream was more than just a dream. It was his future. And now, Trevor realized that his captor, the villain in this story, may not have been a complete bad guy. No, the bad guy was himself trying to save Ryan's life.

Mr. X was studying Trevor, glaring down a younger version of himself. Trevor felt like he was swallowing melted copper as he watched his older version size him up. He was clueless about what his older self's next move would be, what would occur next. But it didn't stop him from staring at the older version of himself. Older Trevor gawked right back at him. Two pairs of interlocked eyes were stuck in a long, awkward moment of disbelief and curiosity. Young Trevor felt a sense of internal shock. He never would have imagined himself being that muscular and knew damn well he would never allow such tacky, cheap tattoos anywhere near his body. But there he was, with reading glasses, prison-style ink, balding head, and toned forearms, standing before him. It was like looking into a mirror, only twenty-five years into the future.

"This isn't right. I came back to save you, save us." Mr. X, or Trevor X as Trevor decided he would now call him, knelt and faced himself on the chair. He assumed, based on the timing, that Ryan was still alive and his job was technically finished. But Trevor X had discovered a catastrophic ripple effect of the parole amends mission while his younger version slept.

"I have something I need to show you." Trevor X grabbed the back of the young man's chair and scooted him over to the reception desk. He reached under the counter and pulled out a manila file folder stamped *CLASSIFIED* in faded red ink. Certified documents and confidential mug shot photos tumbled out of loose paper clips onto the ground. Trevor X bent down and grabbed two of the photos. The first one that he showed young Trevor was of a middle-aged white woman with blonde disheveled hair, blue eyes, and a blank face.

A blurb under her mug shot read:

Megan McDaniel, 32, of Grand Rapids, MI, was found guilty of 12 counts of criminal sexual conduct with minors under the age of 12. She was the owner of McDaniel's Day Care and has been working with children under 12 since she was 16 years old. Ms. McDaniel was the third candidate of Parole Mission Amends after the successful trial run of Trevor Dugan in 2045. McDaniel was offered the parole mission at the age of 62. Her mission failed, the prisoner absconded, and three new sexual allegations were filed, with her as the number-one suspect. Consequently, Department of Homeland Security Agent William Dugan was assigned to execute the 16-year-old McDaniel right before the first known occurrence of her sexual abuse.

"Our hot babysitter who tried to see our little dick. Remember the one Dad killed? Well, here she is, and this file reveals who she will become. Dad didn't kill her just to protect us. He killed her to protect all the other boys and girls the sick bitch would fondle over the next twenty years."

Trevor scrunched his nose and forehead like crumpled paper. "And this is a good thing, right?"

"Yes, that was the one good deed from Dad and the government, but it gets better." Trevor X handed over the next black-and-white photo of a younger man with slimy hair and blackheads that trailed across his brow. Trevor immediately knew that face belonged to Gary Nichols. He was afraid to read the details of his file.

"I know who that is and I don't want to see it. This is enough," Trevor said.

Trevor X pressed the silver revolver against his younger head, forcing Trevor's adherence.

The manilla folder was stamped: *File missing.*

"I'm confused. It just says, 'File missing.'"

"I was confused too, little man. But then I found a newspaper-wrapped present waiting for us on a rack in the janitor's closet. A yellow sticky note that read *from dad to his sons* was left on the gift. And the present contained this."

Trevor X reached back under the counter and pulled out a black tablet. He turned it on, and their father's face popped up on the screen. He wore his black rain jacket, hood up, and appeared to be running while addressing the camera. The video quality was choppy and made Trevor queasy trying to focus on his dad's image.

Bill talked quickly into the camera. "Hey, Trevor. By the time you see this, you'll most likely be in the middle of your amends mission saving your brother's life and I'll be dead. You've probably gone through the classified documents and found your old babysitter's mug shot next to a list of gut-wrenching allegations that would make any parent or child cringe. The biggest mistake Clint and Marble made was allowing her to make amends. Some people are too sick, and like her file said, she ran away and committed more horrific acts on children. This is when your trusted pals Clint and Marble, or whatever the hell their names were, brought the Department of Homeland Security in on the deal. They probably told you that you could prevent the torture of children by signing up for parole mission amends and saving Ryan. The bastards probably told you that your grandfather, Randolph, was to blame for those experiments on the children. Well, that's the half-truth. They left out the part where the success of your mission gave other killers a chance for redemption and it went horribly wrong. As a result, more children were harmed. I was assigned to hire Megan as a sitter and kill her before she ever got a chance to touch you. She fell right into the trap. Good job done, right?"

Bill's face was getting drenched, and he kept looking over his shoulder as if someone or something was following him. "Listen, I don't have a lot of time, but the reason Gary Nichols's file is missing is that there's no good news behind his mission. After the success of your mission, more parole amends missions were greenlighted by the parole board under supervision of the military. The military picked and chose which inmates would be eligible for the amends mission. However, under instruction of the government, the parole board never gave Gary a chance to redeem himself after they accused him of murdering his mom and almost killing his father. They sent me to the Motown Inn the night you all checked in to get Gary loaded. The FBI was tracking Mary's and Gary's social media messages and pinged his location. I went out there disguised and gave Jake lethal heroin that I prayed you wouldn't touch. It was only meant for Gary. Right after I completed my mission, Marble and Rollins sent me a fax from 2045. Gary's father had come forward and confessed to killing his wife and framing his son. Gary took the fall for his own father. I killed an innocent young man. And I also put you and your friends at risk of overdosing. But it was a risk the agency forced me to take."

Bill positioned the camera at an awkward angle, right up a dripping tunnel of nose hair and snot. "I know Ryan told you I made up all the government conspiracy about being an open target to cover my affair with Lady Phantom. The truth is that he was right and you were right.

I fell in love with a woman named Rebecca when I was reassigned from the DEA to the Department of Homeland Security. But I also left behind those bread crumbs for you to find. The agency knew I opposed what happened to Gary Nichols, but they continued with their missions, and it didn't stop there. They started building camps, kidnapping children who were on the prison parole board in the future, brainwashing them into obedience, training them to work for the government. If you can't beat them, make them join you. If that didn't work, the cases were point-blank execution. Rebecca and I were going to come forth with the information, but I couldn't put my own family at risk. So we left and moved off the grid. But I had to come back when I knew you both would be here so I could deliver you this message. This is my last message, son." Bill repositioned the camera away from his nose and revealed an empty prescription bottle of Seroquel and a Buck 110 automatic switchblade. "I love you forever and I'm sorry for failing you. But this all didn't just start with you and the success of your mission. It goes back decades ago to my father, your grandfather, Randolph Grey. He gave that little boy the Rubik's Cube in the science lab from a different dimension, but if you can end him there, Clint and Marble never find their vessel for time travel. Find him and destroy him, and everything will be restored."

The screen went static. Trevor didn't know how to respond. He was preoccupied with untangling the chaos of what was the truth and what was the lie. Everything leading up to this moment was in unison with the parole amends mission, but his father sounded more disturbed than Marble or Rollins. "I'm a murderer? Am I a cause of all of this? How do we find Randolph Grey?" he asked his captor.

Trevor X yawned as his patience with himself was waning. "Yes, we're murderers and I traveled back in time to change our fate. There were subtle clues planted in this hotel about how to carry out my mission. Everything was calculated thoroughly and mapped out. The shadow planted them all. Remember the dream, when he visited us in our closet? Randolph is the shadow and we're his host. The only way to kill a shadow is to kill its host." Trevor X extended his gun up to his own temple and fake-pulled the trigger.

He turned his back to Trevor. His young counterpart tried to wriggle his hands free from the binding rope. He was so close to freedom, but his captor turned around in hyper speed, releasing a warning shot from his pistol's chamber. The slug flew directly over Trevor's shoulder, cutting through two interwoven green vines on the perishing wallpaper.

Trevor gasped and his heart sank. He had never met a man willing to murder himself to save the world from himself until now.

"Don't think I don't know your moves. I am you. Don't insult our intelligence." The old man progressed to him and double-knotted the rope even tighter, drawing more blood from Trevor's wrists.

"I don't understand. I thought you came back from prison to save me, to save us. Now you're going to kill us."

Trevor X knew his younger self wouldn't understand the principle of selflessness for the greater good of mankind, but he was surprised he would denounce all the evidence validating the conspiracies he'd been chasing down the last seven years. "Anonymity. You can't see past yourself, Trevor. It's not about us anymore. I thought it was when I agreed to this mission, but the more time I spent in this godforsaken hotel and after finding Bill's message, I realized it's our destiny to burn this hotel down and ourselves with it, as Randolph Grey's shadow has attached itself to us." His voice transformed, becoming dark and coarse.

Trevor pursed his lips. "This is bullshit. Dad lied to us so many times in the past. How can our grandfather be our shadow? He's probably just a figment of our imagination, and there's no proof he gave those scientists the Rubik's Cube. I see now that Dad is just batshit crazy and killed Gary and Megan. Now he's trying to blame his sins on something else. We can't believe a word he says."

"Wrong. I can't believe anything you just said." The old man repositioned the scope of his pistol, perfectly aligned with his younger, stupid little head. He could skip the speech and kill him right now, end both of them once and for all. "You're probably right about Dad being a liar. And I tried to convince myself that the shadow wasn't real. But it's beyond just the shadow. It's this hotel. The voices in the corridor. The digital memories are fabrications through time. They're symptoms of the demon, and the demon is this hotel."

Trevor X started pacing like a lunatic cycling through his mania. His eyes were narrow and rigid. He truly believed sacrificing himself and the hotel could undo all the past, present, and future wrongs. Indeed, trying life again and repeating the same mistakes in a different environment and nature would be the ultimate sin. He just kept walking around Trevor, rambling curses and negative talk to himself like, "We need to die. Fuck, we're the problem. Fuck the shadow too. The only way to succeed is to end ourselves." The side effects of time travel had really distorted his clarity.

A new thought occurred to Trevor. "Can't we burn this place down and the shadow with it? Maybe this hotel kept the shadow alive, and once it's burned down, he'll be gone with it."

Trevor X smiled at the young man's optimism and longing for hope. It was honorable but disillusioned. He grabbed the back of the wooden chair and pushed young Trevor through the lobby. The screeching of the chair legs against the cracked tile floor echoed like the violent screams of whatever lost souls lay beneath. He dragged his younger self down the first hallway to the former assembly hall. Once a space where recovering addicts and alcoholics had congregated, it was now nothing more than a gym tucked under collapsed, rotten beams and the broken bones of tired pews that stabbed open cracks in the hardwood floors.

"Just look at this place. It's dead inside, but it still breathes." The old man pointed at jagged pieces of stained glass covering a demolished podium on the auditorium stage. "Just like us: dead inside. And you can't see past yourself, Trevor. It's not about us anymore. I thought it was when I agreed to this mission, but the more time I spent in this demon-cursed hotel, reliving our past trauma, the more I realized we're an unremarkable, impersonal creature that has served no real purpose other than to leech off society and murder our brother."

Trevor X grabbed the back of the chair once again and thrust the young man forward like a doctor pushing a wheelchair patient back to his deathbed. This deathbed happened to be the hallway in the main corridor. Blood from an unknown source oozed through the maroon carpet, creating massive waves. Young Trevor was being tossed and turned every which way, and he felt that "carousel at the state fair" motion sickness creeping up in his stomach. He tasted stale elephant ears floating around like loose change in his abdomen. A tang of bile almost crept up but was shoved back into his organs.

Trevor X dragged the sick boy to a broken elevator shaft. He kicked the laminated stainless steel elevator doors, bending, striking, kicking until the panels burst open and plummeted into the unknown.

"Thank God," Trevor whispered. But he didn't know why he was thanking God. There wasn't anything about these current events that gave him any reason to be thankful. The image of the river of blood was rapidly rising, closing in on their kneecaps. He knew the blood was just another hallucination, but that didn't make it any less terrifying.

"Don't thank God just yet, young man." Trevor X grimaced, almost amused by the volume of hell that he was about to reveal—a showcase of horror to prove why the two of them as one could not live another day.

On the other side of the trampled door there was no elevator car awaiting their entry—only barren blackness, filled with the screams and whispers of fallen demons. Down below in the dry, dead air rose a catacomb's worth of tormented spirits. Trevor X wanted the boy to see it for himself. The old man pushed him close to the edge. Trevor would have fallen into the abyss if his captor hadn't snatched his collar. Shadows flickered into sight through brief flashes of electric sparks. Inside, Trevor detected crawling, hissing, the gnashing of teeth.

"'The land of deepest night and utter darkness and disorder,' Trevor. That's Job 10:21-22." The old man's eyes leered down at the boy and his mouth twitched.

The color drained out of Trevor's face. He had no words. His expression was one of fear and confusion.

"Don't worry. We've come to save you. This will all go away soon," the old man called down into the darkness. He turned back to Trevor. "The road to recovery is paved with corpses. We have to finish this and set these lost souls free. As long as we're standing, they'll be damned here forever."

"There has to be another way."

Trevor X shook his head. "I almost thought showing you Dad's death wish—the evidence of the truth we've been seeking, the demons of our past and future—would be enough to scare you straight and make all of this right. This was all before I discovered the success of my mission would cost all these lost lives. Dad's right. We have to let go and say goodbye." He almost released Trevor's collar right then and there, sending him into the gaping passageway to hell. That wouldn't kill the demons and burn the hotel, though. Everything needed to be destroyed first.

The shadows crawled up the walls on the side of the shaft, inching their way into the light. Once visible, moth-like wings expanded from their scorched backs. Burning flesh dripped off their skeletal remains. The whispers, screams of torture, and dreadful moans orchestrated a demonic symphony that echoed through the entire hotel. These were Satan's minions, crossed over from the gates of hell through a Rubik's Cube wormhole. The demons outstretched their bony arms and jagged claws, desperately reaching for Trevor, beckoning him to join them in the black abyss.

"The wormhole opened more than just a passageway through time, didn't it?" Trevor asked, already knowing the answer to this question.

Trevor X grabbed Trevor and flung him backward. The chair and Trevor slid back forcefully but halted right before collapsing into the wall. Young Trevor sat upright, intact and unscathed. The blood was now gone and the illusion had faded.

"Bingo! You're smarter than you look! There are all the anonymous demons that have been trapped here since this hotel's very beginning." A wicked smile was drawn on Trevor X's pale face.

"I'll be right back," the old man said before he vanished for a moment.

Trevor strained his muscles, applying pressure on the braided fibers of the rope. Nervous sweat slid down his forehead and cheeks, splattering onto the floor like idle faucet drips. The furious motivation wasn't enough to set him free. He mentally checked out. He remembered that in the prison dream that exposed his future, Marble and Rollins mentioned that he had a son. If this was true, then Mary must have been pregnant around this time. He assumed in the first trimester. She hadn't even been showing yet. He knew he couldn't give up this easy. Out there he had a boy to raise.

Trevor flashed back to reality, and the old man reappeared, toting a rusted galvanized steel canister. The pungent odor of benzene rose from the can's cylinder and wafted into the dead air. The old man whistled and pranced, dousing the decaying walls and blood-stained carpet with the gasoline like an artist dumping paint on a masterpiece canvas.

"What about our son?" Trevor screamed over Trevor X's thoughtless hums and deranged dancing.

The old man ceased his twirling and ran his fingers through his hair. He'd wondered when the poor boy would mention their son. "You mean the crack baby currently cooking inside our lovely and sweet Mary? He'll be born addicted. Mary will die, which is her fate. We can't change that. Now, quit getting sidetracked and embrace these last few moments of our life." He returned to his sickening dance.

Trevor desperately tried to hold on to every precious memory he was about to surrender into the unknown. Meanwhile, the madman continued to prance and flood gasoline over the staircase; the corridors; the dusty, ancient lobby upholstery; and all the security monitors stacked upon each other in columns and rows like static blue *Jeopardy* squares.

From between the cracks in the lobby wall, a small pinewood derby car zipped out and flew underneath Trevor's chair. He knew that car from when he was building pinewood derby cars at age twelve with his older brother in Boy Scouts. Trevor hadn't been able to get his axles to work, and the plastic wheels kept tumbling off. Ryan had designed a pristine car he called "The–Viper" and painted navy blue with red, glaring eyes plastered on the hood. By the time of the derby race, Trevor's car was inoperative. So Ryan selflessly gave his younger brother The Viper, and Trevor took home first place. He'd promised himself to never forget what his brother had done for him, but he'd never remembered until now. Not until The Viper sped past him and crashed into the wall.

The old man was spiraling out of control, moonwalking across the slick, oil-soaked floors. Pausing his Michael Jackson tribute, he pivoted his body in slow, isolated movements. *This crazy motherfucker is doing the robot,* Trevor thought.

Then, while robo-walking toward the gas canister, Trevor X noticed that Trevor's rope had been loosened slightly. Behind the fuel can rested a plastic grocery bag containing some emergency items. Trevor X rifled through the bag then walked over to Trevor's chair. The old man cut the rope ties, liberating Trevor's hands, only to strap them again to the chair with zip ties. He covered his junior version's eyes with a black piece of cloth, making sure his head was facing down, arms strapped firmly to his sides, and legs fastened together. Then Trevor X poured more gasoline around the chair and all over Trevor's body.

In a gravelly voice, the old man sung a tune he'd made upon in prison. "We checked into our new forever home."

Trevor X cried out, "You don't want to see this, young man. Go to sleep. It'll all be over soon. Let's go visit Father in hell. We can be abracadabra gone."

Since Trevor was little, he'd been fascinated with fire. He both feared and embraced its warmth. Trevor X was now harnessing its power for his demise. His young counterpart was bound in darkness but could hear his maniacal laughter. Fwoosh! His ears perked up at the sound of a match striking against an abrasive surface. He felt the heat trail up window curtains and slide down the baseboards of the hallways. As the flames intensified, the smoke thickened and deepened, slithering down his throat, planting embers in his lungs. The heat radiated through almost every part of the hotel. A crimson blaze smoldered, sweeping the main lobby. Showers of sparks and flaring waves licked the walls and ceiling like a witch violently tongue-kissing the hotel's insides. The red flames transformed into a florescent green light that pulsated dark rhythmic beats throughout the hotel.

The emerald glow of the inferno was seen and heard from the distance. Trevor's brother and girlfriend drove up the old dirt road formerly known as Spiritual Boulevard. After slamming the car to a stop, Ryan grabbed his pistol from the glove box and sprinted out from the car. Mary followed. Ryan knew his brother had to be in there. Who else would burn an abandoned hotel to the ground? But he had no idea who was with him in that green inferno.

Mary and Ryan were greeted by pitch-black smoke. Falling debris caved in around them. They both got on their knees, crawling through the wreckage. Enormous sparks flickered a trail to where they hoped to discover Trevor. The heat was relentless. The inhalation of fumes and ash made breathing near impossible. In between the smoke and conflagration, Ryan caught a glimpse of a man who wasn't his brother—a robust and hulking statue. Behind the brute, strapped to a chair, sat a scared young man, screaming. His skin was tinged charcoal from the black smoke. Ryan almost didn't recognize his brother through his new, charred tan.

In a precious moment, time stood still. Ryan had missed many opportunities to help his brother when he was drowning in hurt. For example, when their father caught Trevor eavesdropping on one of his secret telephone conversations and shoved his head into a pillow until he almost stopped breathing, all Ryan could do was hold vantage by the wall. He didn't dare move or speak up. And the time Ryan's high school friend Chad Murphy bragged to their other friends about bullying Trevor, Ryan pretended to not hear, turning a blind eye. He'd failed Trevor then, but right now, in this holy moment, he saw the perfect chance to make his overdue amends. Straight away, he reached for his .38-caliber pistol and put a bullet in the back of the old man's head.

Young Trevor looked up at his captor and felt relief, shock, and sorrow. Relief because it was all over. He was sad because he knew Trevor X had had good intentions. His body was in shock after witnessing his forty-eight-year-old self's head get blown off while in the middle of a burning fire. This was an experience he wouldn't be able to ever explain to anyone, ever. They wouldn't understand. Trevor didn't even really understand. He knew that he'd just watched Trevor X die with an expression of fatal shock on what was left of his face. But his mind couldn't comprehend how or why, even though the time travel, prison story, murder, conspiracy, and parole amends mission all had been explained to him, he failed to register it as a truth.

Mary Hopkins raced over to her tied-up boyfriend and released him from the blistering ropes. Freedom at last! The three huddled together and crawled through a maze of ruin to the liberating fresh air outside.

In her haste to run to the burning hotel, Mary had forgotten to shut the passenger door to Ryan's Charger. So when the three of them approached the car, Bulko got out and jumped up in excitement to see his owner's best friend alive and free. He playfully pulled Trevor down and spoiled him with thick, wet dog kisses. But Trevor had to push back on the dog. He was still spitting up toxic debris. Mary rushed over and tapped his back until his lungs cleared.

Praise God for a second chance, Trevor thought. Back in the hotel, Trevor had accepted his fate, but now he was saved. Now, he saw his brother's rescue as an omen, a signature of hope, and a sign of new purpose. But back in the distance, he could still hear the faint cries of the anonymous demons wailing from the ashes of good intent.

Suddenly, he heard an inner voice that sounded much like Trevor X. *The path to hell is paved with good intentions. But the road to recovery is paved with dead corpses.* Somewhere in that chamber of tortured souls, his grandfather, Randolph Grey, sang a dying song of freedom. The hour was ungodly, but soon sunshine would rise above the house of flames and the demons would be gone. Right now they were just passing back through time, alternate realities, hell, or wherever their fiendish souls had originally arrived from. Trevor's alleged forever home was no more, but on the bright side, he had completed the initial stage of detox. However, the journey of recovery had just begun.

Chapter 17

Epilogue for an Addict (The Last Day of Your First Life)

Bill's funeral was on a Thursday, and it rained. The mood was somber, yet Trevor felt at peace. It was another chapter in his life he could close. The conspiracy was over. He realized his dad had been a pawn of the government but also a murderer and a liar. Although his father did have some good intentions, Trevor knew that the path to hell was paved with the corpses of those intentions. But Bill's stamp on Trevor's life stretched beyond the conspiracy. He was also a representation of Trevor's obsession to fill that void of abandonment—a part of Trevor that needed to be buried along with his father.

Everyone gathered outside in the graveyard behind Marlin's First Congregational Church. There was no military or police presence. No honorable procession to send Bill off to the grave. The city did not sit still when the hearse, followed by black Range Rovers and sport utility vehicles, drove slowly downtown. The traffic only paused briefly for Bill's final ride.

At the funeral, hardly any words were spoken. Grace's longtime friend Pastor Brown spoke a few words, a minimal eulogy at best. Ryan stepped up to the podium and gave a small speech about his dad's obsession with football and cracked a few lighthearted jokes about him being a spy. Each punchline received cricket sounds. Ryan hurried off stage. Grace couldn't get up to speak. Her knees were too weak and her face was flooded with tears.

Mary, cloaked in an elegant black sundress, accompanied Trevor. He was robed in a black Armani blazer that draped over a clean, white dress shirt. Ryan had made a stop at Macy's on the way back from Detroit to make sure the two heathens were presentable. But Trevor kept adjusting his cuffs. He felt uncomfortable in such nice attire.

After the funeral, Trevor made his round of fake hugs and exchanged condolences with the few family members left in the crowd. Family members he hadn't seen in ages and those he knew had judged his life choices approached and patted him on the head like a dog. Trevor cringed at their words.

"I'm sorry for your loss."

"He was such a good man."

"He's in a better place now."

No, I'm pretty sure he's in a place of hell … Trevor thought. He remembered the look on Gary Nichols's face after Bill had poisoned him. But he also couldn't forget Megan McDaniel chasing him behind the furnace with a chef's knife and his dad taking her out with one solid thud. His emotions were mixed at best.

Ryan opened up his home to Trevor and Mary. His wife, Jessica, objected in the beginning, but he'd explained to her that his brother was clean. Ryan made up an elaborate story of how Trevor had completed a treatment program. Although The Detox Hotel wasn't technically rehab, Trevor had come out a changed man. Ultimately, Jessica agreed but made sure to let it be known that the arrangement was only temporary.

Trevor found new solace in his brother and girlfriend. But as close as Trevor grew to Mary and his brother, he never dared speak the truth about that demonic hotel. They never knew the true identity of his kidnapper. Besides, most of it was all a blur anyway. No one remembered the green glow that hovered over them that night. Trevor convinced himself that the shadow that had burned in the fire was only a metaphor. The real demon was his addiction to heroin and conspiracy. He unsubscribed to all his YouTube conspiracy channels and Jungian podcasts, and he vowed to never pick up heroin again in his life.

"So what happened that night, Trevor? Who was the crazy man who kidnapped you?" Ryan asked after a few days had passed.

"Some fucking lunatic. It's all just static and noise. All I know is I got sober there. But never ..." Trevor locked dead eyes with his brother. "Never mention that place again."

No one ever asked the question again. If it somehow accidentally got brought up, Trevor quickly dismissed it by saying, "Whatever happened there made me never want to pick up another drug in my life."

September 30, 2020

The three of them decided to head back to Detroit one last time to pay homage to a fallen comrade. Ryan lied to his wife and told her they were heading to an out-of-town NA meeting. Although, it didn't have to be a complete lie, as they could easily stop at one on the way back.

It was one final trip to The Hood Pack Mansion. The only one missing was Jake. Well, and of course Bulko. Ryan's wife barely allowed Trevor and Mary to stay. She was rigid about not letting a pit bull around her two children. But Grace had her own small home and big backyard. She had lived alone for years, so she gladly took the big mutt in as her own.

The crew arrived at that wreckage of a former address then gathered rocks and sticks in the backyard to build a blazing bonfire in honor of Jake's spirit. Trevor hadn't spoken at his father's funeral, but he had some farewells he'd written down for his lost friend Jake Johnson. He read the letter aloud:

Dear Jake the Snake,

I miss you, brother. I'm sorry I couldn't be there in the end, as I was sort of "tied" up. We found out Mary's pregnant. Ten weeks along. If it's a boy, I'm going to name him Jake. It's so messed up that I even have to write this letter. Addiction took everything from us, man. But there is a way out, and I believe I found it. And I wish you were here to experience it with us. I only have a little less than two weeks sober, but I don't think I want to ever touch that shit again. We're here at The Hood Pack Mansion to say our goodbyes to you. My father passed away, but you were more family to me than he ever was. I know we did a lot of crazy illegal shit, but you always had my back. I'm forever grateful for that. Bulko is in a safe place now. He lives with my mom, and she'll take care of him. I have a lot of amends to make in my newfound sobriety. But one

day at a time. I will make these things right, and I will never forget you, my brother.
Love, Trevor

The letter was gracefully pitched in the fire. Ashes rose up to the clear sky like torn flower petals floating heavenward. All the letters, words, spilled ink were now just a scatter-burned message.

But Trevor believed his lost friend would someday read it. "Until we meet again," he whispered into the sky. Sobbing, he hugged his biological brother who, after years of resentment, had stepped up and saved his little brother's life in more ways than one.

Afterward, Ryan insisted they attend a midnight NA meeting outside Detroit in a little town called Flint, which wasn't exactly on their way back. Trevor picked up a white "surrender" key tag and introduced himself as a newcomer. The meeting was small, with a few old bikers and a short, chubby, balding man named Dave C. who wore a pink-flamingo shirt. The dude looked like he'd just stepped off a jet from Florida. But he wasn't from Florida—he was from Boston. He was in Flint visiting some of his sponsee brothers. They were part of a sponsorship circle of men who traveled all over the country to attend different NA meetings. Dave C. shared with the group members that he was grateful to be "wicked sobah" and told his story.

The Boston native used to live on the streets, eating out of dumpsters and snorting coke off the backs of prostitutes. But he'd been clean for over a decade, and Trevor took a liking to him. He could relate, minus the mainlining of coke off hookers' back regions. Although, that did sound like one shenanigan he wished he could have scratched off his dope-fiend bucket list. It was too bad Dave C. was heading back to Boston. Trevor would have loved to have heard more of his crazy stories at future NA meetings.

Seven months later, little Jake Dugan was born. Mary and Trevor moved out of Ryan's basement and got a cozy little apartment in one of the several hometowns Trevor had lived in as a kid in the Battle Creek area. Two years after the move, Mary Hopkins planned to go down South to visit her mom and stepdad in Arkansas. She never made it out of Michigan. The facts surrounding her death were bleak. Whispers on the street implied foul play, suggesting she'd relapsed on heroin and the dealer had stabbed her seventeen times in cold blood over a measly twenty dollars.

Trevor was left to raise little Jake all on his own in a small two-bedroom apartment on the east side of Battle Creek. He held several odd jobs and minimum-wage gigs, from washing dishes at a local diner to cleaning toilets at Walmart, to support his little guy. Raising a three-year-old bundle of hyper-destruction was hard work, as he discovered. All the responsibility as a young, single dad made him a sorrowful, grumpy asshole.

One afternoon, as the little guy threw a raging fit in his car seat, Trevor fantasized about leaving him in the back seat of someone's car in a grocery store parking lot. But the fantasy never came true. He loved the damn booger too much.

Between the post-traumatic stress from his detox at the hotel and the murders of his best friend and girlfriend, Trevor's fragile mind came tumbling down like a ton of shit bricks. When he slept at night, he dreamed of gasoline showers; demon time travelers; wicked Rubik's Cubes; a penny with Lincoln's head scratched off; and the creepy, brown X-marked burlap sack that the older version of himself toted around on his ugly, fat face. The only thing missing was the shadow. He remembered the shadow clearly but couldn't recall the name of the person the shadow belonged to. His subconscious buried the name of Randolph Grey. The identity of Lance Burrows was a blur floating deep in suppressed memories as well.

Although Trevor was working a program of recovery, he thought he would try seeing one of those social workers who tried to shrink heads. Her name was Sally Long. She had fading red hair with striking gray stripes immaculately woven into her tresses. She was a nice lady, but he could never honestly open up to her. She diagnosed him with post-traumatic stress disorder and major depressive disorder. He liked the fact that she provided him with happy pills. Trevor swallowed them down like candy, but his sponsor told him not to worry—taking medications as prescribed was not a relapse.

The fragments of Trevor's soul were fractured mirrors. He was dying inside to show someone the other side of the mirror. Although much of the thirty-five or so hours he'd spent in that hotel had gone up in smoke like the building itself, there were some details he could never forget. The truth of those details needed to come out, but he didn't trust Sally "Gray

Stripes" with that classified information. *No, she would rat us out, put us in the nuthouse*, a little gnawing voice inside his head told him. He loved his brother, but Ryan was too close to the horrific events of what happened at The Detox Hotel to ever know the truth about it.

One day while rummaging through all of Mary's belongings, Trevor found one of her University of Michigan sweatshirts. A sudden sting of sadness reminded him that he would never get see the beautiful Mary strut around their apartment wearing that old wrinkled sweatshirt. But this article of Mary's clothing gave him one of those so-called "ah-ha" moments of enlightenment. The truth was, Michigan had nothing more left for him. He could find a new job somewhere else.

He packed up all his own belongings and a framed picture of Mary, and grabbed his five-year-old son in the middle of the night. The damn kid was still up playing Fortnite at one o'clock after promising to go to bed. Trevor hadn't a clue where he was heading and had barely any money in his wallet. But a subtle inner voice told him to drive to Boston and find Dave C. with the pink-flamingo shirt.

Trevor and little Jake headed to the East Coast. Dragging his son around, Trevor searched over fifty NA meetings in over three weeks until he finally found Dave C. He was wearing the same exact pink-flamingo shirt with a white bucket hat. He had a cheap little Cheyenne cigar sticking out of the corner of his mouth. The guy looked like a sober Hunter S. Thompson, and his wide gut suggested he took the phrase "Put down the spoon and pick up the fork" as a top priority for recovery.

"Is that Trevor D. from Flint?" The pudgy man jumped up and down. He always got excited to see people he'd met while traveling around the country and visiting different meetings.

"I lived all over Michigan, Dave," Trevor replied, "but I'm gone for good. Leaving my past in my past." He didn't really want to identify Flint, Michigan, as his hometown.

Trevor extended his hand for a polite shake but was welcomed with an overwhelmingly tight hug. He could feel Dave's body sweat seeping through the lightweight fabric of his shirt as the big man squeezed his torso. Although he was uncomfortable, Trevor felt a sense of belonging. He accepted this crazy circle of coffee-bingeing, chain-smoking, and foul-mouthed recovering addicts, where everyone was "wicked sobah," as his new home.

Sweaty Dave became Trevor's new sponsor. They took weeks off in the summer, while Jake wasn't in school, to travel the country and hit various twelve-step meetings. Dave C. explained to Trevor that going to different meetings and expanding his network of fellowship would increase his recovery. Trevor even landed the perfect gig as a recovery coach for a detox/residential treatment center called New Horizons in Boston. He inspired hopeless addicts with his powerful message of recovery—minus the torture, demonic exposure, and kidnapping. And when the time came for Trevor to finally work his fearless moral inventory again since The Detox Hotel, he chose to finally get butt-naked honest with Dave. Like Jung or someone else of psychological significance said, "The only way out is through, the only way through is honest."

The truth was that almost every night, Trevor considered picking up the needle or the pipe just one more time. He thought it could be the only way to block out the noise: those violent screams of death, the treacherous laughter of the madman who had come to save him but ultimately betrayed him. Every night, Trevor had to remind himself that he'd made a promise to never pick up a drug again, and he kept that promise. But he never committed against blowing his own skull out. One night, he went out to purchase a .38 Special, but when he pulled his debit card from his wallet, he saw a picture of his son. He left the gun on the counter and went back home.

Trevor confessed all of it to Dave and even included the horrors he experienced at The Detox Hotel. He held back nothing. Of course, Dave didn't believe a word of it. But that didn't matter.

"I believe you believe that's your truth, and that's all that matters," Dave told him after his confession.

Dave's belief in Trevor's truth didn't matter because Trevor felt free. He'd held that weight on his back like a heavy boulder of concrete excrement.

In 2033, Ryan stepped up on a ladder with a noose around his neck and tied it to the rafters in his garage. Jessica and the kids had moved out after his last relapse. So Ryan called it quits. He was only thirty-nine years old when he passed. Trevor took his death like a boulder punch in the gut from God himself. This death hit worse than Mary's because, for fuck's sake, Ryan chose it.

Trevor had remained in contact with his brother for the first few years after moving to Boston, but over time they just drifted apart. At least, Trevor told himself that lie. Ryan needed Trevor more than ever in his final hour of darkness, but Trevor was eight hundred miles away.

Life got weird after Ryan died. But Trevor never picked up another drug, even after all that hurt. He'd made a promise to himself—the only promise he ever kept. Even though he stayed clean, he grew bitter and isolated himself for years. Thank God little Jake was old enough to tend to most of his own needs because his daddy wasn't exactly father of the year. It seemed like no one could pull him out of his funk of isolation and self-loathing. Dave C. would come by his apartment and knock on his door, trying to get him out of the fetal position and back to a meeting.

"I know you're in there, Trevor, with fingernails as long as snakes. Come the fuck out. An addict alone is in bad company, and you, sir, have the most fucked-up company right now." Dave C. didn't give up on him, but over time the random door-banging fizzled out until Trevor never heard another knock again.

After a few years of feeling sorry for himself and hiding from reality, Trevor started journaling to pass the time and ended up taking a hard look at himself in the mirror. He didn't like who he had become. So, he reached out to Dave C. once again for help. He got offered back his old job as a recovery coach and was determined to succeed. And that's exactly what he did. At the age of forty-five, Trevor became the CEO of New Horizons treatment program. He bought a stupid-expensive home for himself. The day he moved in he said, "If only Ryan and Dad could see me now."

Trevor grew old and never married or fell in love with another woman after Mary. He preferred his own company. This was perfectly fine in his eyes. What mattered most was that he was happy. After all, his son, Jake, turned out to be a productive member of society. Unlike his father, Jake had no past demons to overcome. He had a wife and kids of his own.

But past regret always lingered, and in the year 2070, at the age of seventy-three, Trevor didn't want to be Trevor Dugan anymore. During a late-life crisis, Trevor decided to legally change his name. However, he couldn't think of any other name that he wanted until a little voice whispered the name: *Lance Burrows*. It sounded so familiar. He couldn't recall where he'd heard it before, but his gut told him that would be his new identity.

After his mother passed, all of the living Dugan family, with the exception of his son and grandchildren, didn't exist. It was time to erase that godforsaken name and start over near the end of his natural life.

There was one final chapter in his story that he needed to close, and it happened to be eight hundred miles away on top of a deserted hill near Walled Lake in Novi, Michigan. The land was barren and lonely, with charred timbers standing like monuments of past pain. The broken glass and discarded needles served as reminders of the truth. Those anonymous demons were still clinging to their only living sanctuary. The Detox Hotel, whether standing or burned to ash, couldn't bring Mary and Ryan back from their tombs.

Rotten mattresses and rusted bed frames left behind by derelicts and squatters who'd found temporary refuge after the hotel's demise were overturned in piles. Lance dug through the wreckage, searching for something solid left behind from The Detox Hotel. He needed to see tangible evidence that the hotel had been real and not just a suppressed delusion that invaded his dreams.

The vacant lot remained on the crest of the hill, a looming eyesore against the vibrant blue sky above and a field of dormant grass. There were no remnants left behind of the hotel that had given birth to his demons and his recovery, only the scrapped possessions of the new residents: the addicted and homeless. The hypodermic needles, soiled sleeping bags, empty malt liquor bottles, and brown paper bags that preserved them all reminded Lance of Trevor Dugan.

Trevor as a young man had been a junkie living on the streets, eating out of dumpsters. But Trevor was no more. He was now Lance, and he'd changed for the better long before he'd changed his name. Although Lance thought he would be happy with his new identity, there was this gaping void that he'd been searching to fill for years. He didn't know exactly what it was, but that little voice told him that if he came back to The Detox Hotel, he may discover it. He thought after he buried his father that the void would go away, but it didn't. Another voice told him that if he couldn't find something to fill that emptiness, then his purpose in life was over and he should join Mary, Ryan, and his father in hell.

The location was ideal for a proper send-off to the afterlife. "Everything began here, and now it will end here," he said. His hands shaking, Lance loosely gripped a new .38-caliber pistol he'd purchased at a local pawnshop on his way to The Detox Hotel. "God grant me the serenity to end it all."

In the shadows of towering dead grass nearby, a pale creature lurked. Cold, thick eyes studied the lost human, confused and trampled by time. The creature flipped a defaced penny while humming a tune over a hundred years old that told a story of heartbreak in a hotel.

Lance sensed that he wasn't alone, and he turned in all directions, almost stumbling over scorched cinder blocks and fallen debris. As he tripped, he dropped the pistol, which tumbled out of his sight.

The pale thing watching didn't dare step into the light. Instead, he tossed his lucky penny to his dear friend. When Lance bent over to pick up the copper coin that emerged from beyond the scope of his vision, he discovered a familiar bright shade of blue and white hiding discreetly in the dirt. He brushed off the soil and twigs, unmasking the magic cube underneath.

Lance's mission toward a cowardly death transformed into a symbol of hope that presented itself in the form of a child's toy. He was only a few twists of the wrist away from the almighty algorithm's passage through time. The cube beckoned and taunted him to experience its splendor.

Above all, he was searching for a clue. Maybe he could make it right this time. Instead of being destroyed, maybe the cube was designed to be embraced. He thought of all the hurt he'd witnessed in the past seventy-three years. The pain endured by everyone he loved. He had to try it for himself. It was one last chance to make everything right. He knew it was true when the little voice returned. *End the cycle, save your family, live eternal. Time was never meant to be linear.*

Whispers from a dark place amplified into loud echoes inside Lance's brain. *I promise to be good, Lance. Please let us go. Set us free and come back home.*

From the field emerged the creature, but he was a man—but one not like any man Lance had ever seen except for a nightmare he recalled from decades before. It was all coming back to him now. The man was naked with a bleached flesh tone. His hair ragged, and eyes cold and black. As the abomination shuffled forward on worn legs, Lance recoiled like he'd seen a ghost or a dead relative.

"Don't look so surprised, grandson. I'm here to welcome you to eternity. Today is the last day of your first life."

Although intrigued by his own fear, Lance didn't wait around to see how this introduction concluded. He opened the cube, revealing the wormhole, and dove into the unknown.

Lance was abracadabra! Gone!

"See you in The Detox Hotel." The old pale thing crawled back into the shadowy grove humming a cryptic tune. After a century of wandering aimlessly through time, he had finally found his new forever home.

The End

***

Check out my website www.jonahfrickauthor.com for more information about current works and more.

Made in the USA
Middletown, DE
30 May 2023